Sacred Stories

SACRED STORIES

A Celebration of the Power of Story to Transform and Heal

Charles and Anne Simpkinson, Editors

HarperSanFrancisco
A Division of HarperCollinsPublishers

HarperSanFrancisco and the authors, in association with the Rainforest Action Network, will facilitate the planting of two trees for every one tree used in the manufacture of this book.

Text design by Eric Holub

Library of Congress Cataloging-in-Publication Data
Sacred stories / Charles and Anne Simpkinson, editors. — lst ed.
p.   cm.
ISBN 0—06—250852—0 (pbk. : alk. paper)
1. Storytelling—Religious aspects.   2. Spiritual life.
I. Simpkinson, Charles H.   II. Simpkinson, Anne Adamcewicz.
BL304.S194   1993
291.4'3—dc20   92—56135
                                           CIP

94 95 96 97 ❖HAD 10 9 8 7 6 5 4 3 2

This edition is printed on acid-free paper that meets the American National Standards Institute Z39.48 Standard.

Contents

▼▼▼

Acknowledgments

Because this book is based on presentations given at "Sacred Stories: Healing in the Imaginative Realm," the eleventh annual Common Boundary conference, we want to acknowledge James Carse of New York University for originally suggesting a conference on sacred narratives and psychotherapist Celia Coates for convincing Common Boundary to devote a whole conference to the sacred stories theme. We are also indebted to Edith Sullwold, our conference advisor, for her seasoned guidance and supportive presence, and to Robert Bly, who made suggestions for presenters and helped edit the conference statement of purpose.

We also want to thank Tami Simon and her team at Sounds True for sensitively and expertly recording the workshop sessions that provided the basis for most of the book's chapters. We are grateful to Ned Leavitt, our agent, for his enthusiasm, persistence, and ongoing conviction that the spirit of the conference would continue to flourish in the form of a book.

We are also deeply indebted to the twenty-three conference presenters whose work appears in this book; their generosity, patience, and wisdom were invaluable. We are also grateful to the more than twenty-five hundred people who attended the conference and whose spirited participation inspired many of the presenters to new heights.

Many thanks to Michael Toms of Harper San Francisco, who discussed our progress through the initial editing process, and Amy Hertz and Rachel Lehmann-Haupt, who guided us through the editing and production stages. We are grateful to Random House for allowing us to reprint Maya Angelou's poem "Human Family," which originally appeared in 1990 in her collection, *I Shall Not Be Moved.* We also want to thank Ballantine Books for allowing us to include, in Clarissa Pinkola Estés's chapter, material that originally appeared, in a slightly different form, in her book *Women Who Run with the Wolves* (1992), and Ally Press, which published *Walking Swiftly: Writings and Images on the Occasion of Robert Bly's 65th Birthday* (1992), in which Gioia Timpanelli's story, "The Old Couple," appeared.

We feel a salute to Carl Jung is in order as he and his work were the most frequently mentioned by the majority of the presenters. We also thank the staff at Common Boundary for their ideas, enthusiasm, and willingness to do whatever was needed to see this project through to completion.

Last, our greatest thanks is reserved for Rose Solari, the project's coordinator. Not only did her organizational skills help shepherd errant contracts, permission letters, and manuscripts to the appropriate people at the appropriate times, but her poet's eye, ear, and soul shaped transcripts into polished essays. Rose's love of the material was abundant and constant. We were blessed to have her work with us on this project.

▼▼

Introduction

We live our lives immersed in stories. Newspaper, radio, and television feed us a daily diet of news; friends and co-workers tell us how their weekends were spent; parents punctuate their children's days with bedtime stories; grandparents fondly recall family history over holiday meals; ministers weave parables into their Sunday sermons; and many spend leisurely hours indulging in murder mysteries, romance novels, sitcoms, or Hollywood's latest film offerings.

Stories seem to be everywhere. But while some stories entertain, inform, or teach us, others move us deeply. They change us and bring us closer together. These are sacred stories.

Children's book author Jane Yolen describes sacred stories as stories that tell us "who we are and how we relate to the world and our gods." In her book *Touch Magic*, she writes that in stories, "images from the ancients speak to us in modern tongue though we may not always grasp the 'meanings' consciously. Like dreams, the meanings slip away, leaving us shaken into new awareness."

Yolen's comments highlight two essential elements of sacred stories: that these powerful imaginative vehicles tell us about ourselves and in that way transform us, while simultaneously connecting us to our fellow human beings—be they our contemporaries or our ancestors. But Yolen is quick to point out that not all stories are sacred. "Some are bawdy, some are silly, some can even be immoral."

The critical difference, it seems, has to do not so much with the content of the story but with the process the story ignites. Sacred stories move us; they get us thinking about what is important; they communicate through symbol and metaphor deep truths about the mysteries of life. Upon hearing a sacred story, even if we don't understand the message intellectually, we are aware that some profound lesson has been imparted.

Stephen Happel, associate professor of religion and culture at The Catholic University of America, puts it this way: "A story doesn't have to have religious content to make it holy." Happel points out that in the Christian tradition, Jesus' parables were intended to show how God is present in everyday life. He used images like a woman kneading dough or searching for a lost coin to remind us that the divine appears in the most ordinary realities: bread, money, a tree, a mustard seed. Too often, Happel says, we attribute preternatural and supernatural characteristics to God; we make Him "a bigger and better version of ourselves." Happel sees God in the details of life. In this view, telling one's personal or community story authentically is a religious event. Of course, he cautions, "not every story I tell about myself evokes a divine presence." Some stories are neither self transforming nor community transforming. "But," he concludes, "wherever there *is* that transforming power, God is present."

Happel's perspective is remarkably similar to that of indigenous peoples. In African, Native American, and other indigenous cultures, a story is seen as being alive, as having a life of its own.

"It's a living presence, a spiritual presence," says publisher, storyteller, and writer Joe Bruchac. He describes storytelling as "almost like calling the gods. A powerful spiritual presence makes itself felt, and one can be quite literally swept away by it." Bruchac, an enrolled member of the Abenaki Nation in Vermont, believes that a story can literally tell itself and has at times felt that he was simply following the direction in which a story led him.

Thus, sacred stories should not be seen as mere collections of words; they are not rote, memorized, dead narratives. They carry an energy—a truth, a lesson, an insight, an emotion—that can enter our being and connect us to a distant past and to powerful primal forces.

Sir Laurens van der Post, a writer, biographer of C. G. Jung and a native of South Africa, had, throughout his life, contact with

African tribesmen. In a 1956 lecture delivered in Ascona, Switzerland, to a Jungian audience, he described an experience he had with the Bushmen of the Kalahari Desert that underscored the fact that story—along with dance and music—can be an instrument by which we contact the divine in and around us. The Bushmen attribute great spiritual significance to stories and are known for their storytelling capabilities. Thus, when he was living among the Bushmen, van der Post was eager to have them share their tales. However, he found them quite reticent. Although they would freely share information about how to survive in the harsh desert environment—where to find water, game, and roots—they erected an immovable wall of excuses and digressions when asked about their stories.

Undeterred, van der Post decided that the way to scale their wall of silence was to identify as fully as possible with their daily life, so he went hunting with them. One day, he and some Bushmen participated in a hunt that began at dawn and ended at sundown in the killing of an eland. Bushmen never kill an eland—an animal that figures prominently in their tales—without thanking it with a dance. Such a dance was organized for the next evening, and van der Post was invited.

As the preparations for the dance got under way, clouds began forming and thunder began rumbling in the distance. Van der Post noted that the electricity of the approaching storm mirrored—indeed, added to—the air of excitement surrounding the preparations. "It appeared as if the elements had decided that they, too, would take part in the ceremony of thanksgiving," said van der Post, "and I am sure that is what the Bushmen felt in their hearts."

Just before sundown, the Bushmen began to dance the Eland Dance. When they finished they began another, their Fire Dance—"the greatest dance of them all"—which went on for seven hours. The music increased in intensity and the atmosphere grew more charged. Finally, the lead dancer acquired the power of healing; he approached the sick and worked with them, making strange movements around them and crying out like different animals.

At the climax of the ceremony, the storm came nearer. Van der Post described it in this way: "The deep booming of desert thunder joined with the singing, and in the surrounding veld, the lions feeling the excitement of the dance and the coming rain began to roar, the hyenas to wail, the jackals to bark and owls to screech as never before. I felt as if the whole of the universe had come to a point in that moment. Never had I heard human voices go so far back in time, so deeply down in the pit of being. This I thought was the cry of longing, anguish, and desire of the first man on earth." Then the rain began to fall.

"I can only say that I myself have never felt more dedicated and nearer God than at that moment and stood there almost in tears as one with revelation in a temple," recalled van der Post.

The next day, the wall crumbled and the Bushmen's stories poured out. To gain access to those stories, van der Post had to first experience the world as the Bushmen experienced it, to understand that the outer world in which they lived—the desert sands, hot sun, stars, and animals—also lived within them.

He could then appreciate why the Bushmen respected, honored, and protected their stories. Stories, along with dance and music, kept them intimately in touch with creative forces in the universe. They were potent reminders of the way in which inner and outer, individual and community, human community and natural world were inextricably linked into one pulsating, dynamic rhythmic play of life forces.

In our contemporary world surrounded by faxes and phones, personal computers, television sets, air conditioners, automobiles, and high-rise buildings, it is difficult to recapture the potency of rituals like those of the Bushmen. In the words of storyteller Laura Simms, it is difficult to hear "the words of the ancestors." Simms, who lives in New York City, knows what she's talking about. For her, sacred stories "rise out of silence, out of a deep inner source, but modern life with all its noise and distractions makes these stories difficult to hear."

Nonetheless, Simms persists in finding and telling these stories. Perhaps her tenacity is due in small part to gems of wisdom two mentors imparted to her. Simms tells of the time she attended the very first workshop mythology scholar Joseph Campbell gave after leaving Sarah Lawrence College. Participants were asked to say who they were and what they did. When it was Simms's turn, she said, "I want to be a storyteller." Campbell laughed and said, "Then you'll come to know that all of life is a story." She also relates a similar anecdote involving the late Chogyam Trungpa Rinpoche, a colorful and controversial Buddhist teacher who was based in Boulder, Colorado. When Simms explained to him that she was a storyteller, he replied, "Don't collect any more stories! Open to your gentleness and remember, stories are the ceaseless unfolding of the endless manifestations of the delightful play of the world."

These anecdotes remind us that sacred stories are omnipresent; wherever humans exist, you will find stories. Sacred stories arise as naturally as the sun in the morning. They reflect not only who we are as individuals but also who we are as members of a collective.

In his classic book on fairy tales, *The Uses of Enchantment*, Bruno Bettelheim stated this point in psychological terms. "If we hope to live not just from moment to moment but in true consciousness of our existence," he wrote, "then our greatest need and most difficult achievement is to find meaning in our lives." Bettelheim studied one particular genre of sacred stories—the fairy tale—which he said offered such meaning. He likened fairy tales to great art and explained that "a fairy tale's deepest meaning will be different for each person and different for the same person at different moments in his life."

Bettelheim described a practice used in traditional Hindu medicine that offers a fascinating example of how stories could provide meaning and thus healing. A "psychically disoriented" patient would be given a fairy tale on which to meditate. It was thought that through the story, the patient would not only come to understand the nature of his or her problem but also its resolution. "From what a particular tale implied about man's despair, hopes and methods of overcoming tribulations," Bettelheim wrote, "the patient could discover not only a way out of his distress but also a way to find himself, as the hero of the story did." "The fairy tale is therapeutic," Bettelheim continued, "because the patient finds his *own* solutions, through contemplating what the story seems to imply about him and his inner conflicts at this moment in his life."

Clarissa Pinkola Estés, author of the best-selling book *Women Who Run with the Wolves*, a collection of fairy tales and traditional stories about women's psychological and spiritual nature, also recognizes the healing power inherent in stories. In an interview conducted by Tami Simon of Sounds True, a Boulder-based taping company, Estés pointed out that "the flow of images in stories is medicine—similar medicine to listening to the ocean or gazing at sunrises." Estés says that stories flow where needed, acting "like an antibiotic that finds the source of the infection and concentrates there. The story helps make that part of the psyche clear and strong again."

Joe Bruchac has firsthand experience in seeing that occur. For eight years, he ran a college program in a prison, teaching both adolescents and adults who were incarcerated for a wide range of offenses, including drug dealing and murder. Bruchac—who has mainly Slovak but also English and Native American ancestors—has extensive experience with Native American culture, which holds stories at its heart. He was, therefore, struck by the fact that the prisoners he taught said they had never been told stories. In his English classes, Bruchac introduced them to poetry and storytelling and watched them go through remarkable personal changes. "In tying themselves to the creative impulse," he says, "they became aware of themselves and their place in the world."

Bruchac believes that these boys and men suffered not only from the absence of stories but also from the effect of negative ones. "People often are powerless, alone, afraid," he says. "This is because someone else is telling their story for them: 'You are stupid. You are ugly. You are undesirable. You are useless.' Through storytelling, you can recognize your real story." By embracing and respecting our real stories, says Bruchac, we develop a sense of identity, self-worth, and empowerment.

Laura Simms had similar experiences working in the Bronx with adolescents with special needs. Make no mistake, these kids are difficult, she says. And because they are so difficult, no one wants to deal with them. Yet her contact with them, telling them stories, has been inspiring.

"I love going into the schools now," she says. "It's like I've discovered a secret." That secret has to do with a story's ability to open up lines of communication. On one level, says Simms, "the students think they are being entertained," but there are numerous indications that students are "listening deeply." She points to the "story police," students who post themselves at the classroom door to make sure no one enters the room before the story is finished. These students, she says, are "protecting the space in which something is happening." They are the gatekeepers, keeping the ritual space safe from intrusions. Simms is equally aware that after she tells, say, a South African women's myth, the students "just float out of their seats to tell me their dreams."

Simms also relates the time a 6'2" thirteen-year-old, who was both beautiful and tough, managed to get passes so she could sit in on all three of Simms's classes. At the end of the third period, she told Simms that she too wrote stories and read her a simple story about color. Then she began talking about her life. She explained that every night, she babysat until 11 p.m. She would take her eleven-year-old handicapped sister with her to sit for neighborhood kids. "I'm always tired," she complained, but said that these jobs made her realize she had patience. "I like to help people," she told Simms. "I'd like to be a doctor or a nurse." Up until that moment, no one in the school had known of her long hours, her babysitting jobs, or her career aspirations. "I told my story and she told me hers," Simms explains.

She pauses, then says, "It's really quite simple; it's just being human together. Maybe that's what 'sacred' is."

LIKE THE HUMAN lives that they grow out of, sacred stories vary tremendously. In this book, you will find that the contributors—storytellers, authors, teachers, and psychologists—each have their own ideas about and a variety of approaches to the subject of sacred stories. Yet certain commonalities emerge. There is, for example, an emphasis on the oral tradition of storytelling—some of these essays, in fact, might best be read aloud to "hear" the voice behind the page. Most authors also agree on the healing role of stories and the therapeutic uses of uncovering, telling, and even revising our stories. Additionally, the essays explore the benefits and limitations of living by myths, whether secular or religious. They reveal the lessons that many of our long-cherished tales offer us about socialization and selfhood, and the ways in which cultural assumptions are defined and inculcated by the stories we tell. They emphasize the need to construct healthy stories to replace those that have harmed us and our planet. Each of these themes surfaces and resurfaces throughout the book, linking authors of different generations, backgrounds, and spiritual paths, reminding us of the precious gifts that the imaginative realm of storytelling provides: transformation and connection.

Truly, the subject of sacred stories is one that can never be exhausted. As we continue to search for ways to heal ourselves, each other, and the Earth, stories and storytelling will continue to flourish. We hope that the chapters that follow will encourage readers to seek out the stories that enrich their lives with delight, inspiration, and hope. For stories will be our companions as long as there is life on the planet. As Oren Lyons said in an interview with Bill Moyers:

> Life will go on
> as long as there is someone
> to sing, to dance, to tell stories and to listen.

▼▼

Chapter 1

Sacred Stories and Our Relationship to the Divine

James R. Price iii *and* Charles H. Simpkinson

Every day, all over the country, millions of people go to psychotherapy sessions essentially to tell their stories. Usually, the psychotherapist listens primarily from a psychological perspective. To be heard from a spiritual perspective, one generally goes to a spiritual teacher or minister. However, this dichotomy between the spiritual and the psychological uses of storytelling deprives those on either side of the broader, more inclusive view of human thought and experience that a synthesis of these approaches might give.

In this chapter, James R. Price, Ph.D., an adjunct professor at the Institute of Conflict Analysis and Resolution, George Mason University, provides such a synthesis. Having listened carefully to the personal stories of psychologist Charles H. Simpkinson, he describes how these seemingly secular stories reveal a relationship with the divine. In doing so, he offers a way to join spiritual and psychological understanding, which then deepens and enriches both perspectives, while providing the reader with a more inclusive, holistic view of what it means to be human.

Charles Simpkinson, Ph.D., publisher of Common Boundary *magazine and director of the Common Boundary Sacred Stories Conference, has collaborated before with Dr. Price, including the teaching of a seven-part series on psychology and religion at the Smithsonian Institution in Washington, D.C. Dr. Price has taught at the university level for thirteen years and writes in the area of values and social change.*

W hat is a sacred story? The answer, of course, turns on our understanding of the word *sacred*. If we associate the sacred with the domain of the religious traditions of the world, then by sacred stories we mean the images, characters, and events in the stories those traditions tell: Moses and the escape from Egypt, Krishna and Arjuna on the battlefield, Jesus feeding the five thousand, First Woman and Coyote. These are traditional sacred stories and they have deep roots in the history of the human spirit.

But we should not limit the range of sacred stories exclusively to those told by the world's religions. In contemporary Western culture, for instance, a growing number of people find themselves unable to connect or identify with traditional sacred stories. There is no reason to assume that these people live without a sacred story or have no relationship to what we are calling the divine; rather, the sacred dimension of their lives is not named and revealed by the traditional sacred stories. Thus, we need a way of understanding the sacred that will both illumine divine experiences and enable us to identify sacred stories that do not originate in the great religions of the world. Paul Tillich's perspective on the sacred is a helpful starting place. He suggests that there is a sacred dimension to everyone's life, and that that dimension is associated with our inner experience of "ultimate concern."

What is ultimate concern? To begin with negation, it is not an object of concern. That is to say, it is not a concern about something—such as death, taxes, or the status of gun control legislation. Nor is it "concern" in the sense of anxiety or worry. Ultimate concern is the movement of our spirit within us, the movement of desire from the center of our being. It is the axis of feelings, values, and intentions that directs and motivates what we think and do.

Such concern is "ultimate" because it is rooted in and expresses our felt sense of security, identity, meaning, and purpose. It is the interior movement of our "self" in the unfolding of our lives. Of course, this is not to deny that the movement of our desire is often conflicted and sometimes contradictory. The philosopher Søren Kierkegaard's yearning to "will one thing" is as elusive for most of us as it was for him.

Ultimate concern, then, is not an abstract concept. It names a reality operating within the inner life of every human being. Indeed, basic spiritual awareness requires that we attend to the often conflicted axis of feelings and values that expresses who we are and directs what we think and do; it requires that we try to discern the movement of the spirit in us. That movement is driven by images. Often these images are linked to characters and events in our lives and are therefore narrated as stories. These stories, then, are tales of ultimate concern. Whether or not they draw upon the images and insights of the great religious traditions, they are sacred stories.

It is important to recognize the mutual influence in the relationship of ultimate concern and sacred story. Sacred stories are not simply the outer expression of the inner dynamic of our spirit. Rather, the movement of ultimate concern is itself conditioned by the images, characters, and events of our sacred stories. As we shall see, sacred stories can variously restrict or release the movement of ultimate concern within us; they can either promote or ease the tensions within our desires. Sacred stories reveal our relationship with the divine. The divine cannot in itself be named; its reality transcends all words and concepts. Just as ultimate concern is a movement not an object, so the divine is not an object. It is, rather, the ground of our ultimate concern, the transcendent context for the movement of desire at the center of our being.

In other words, to become aware of our relationship with the divine, we need to ask, "What is the transcendent context of the movement of my ultimate concern?" The words "transcendent context" may be abstract, but the experience is concrete. In the movement of my deepest desires, do I experience myself as abandoned or welcomed? judged or forgiven? threatened or loved? What images of the divine express this relationship?

The movement of our ultimate concern, then, is not the divine. It is, however, the reference point within consciousness that enables us to discern our relationship with the divine. Furthermore, since ultimate concern operates in the context of sacred story, it is through these stories that we discern the nature of this relationship and the images that express it.

This means that the development of spiritual awareness requires three distinct but related tasks. One is to discern the movement of ultimate concern within us. The second is to discern the way this movement is shaped by the images and events of our sacred stories. The third is to discern the transcendent context, the relationship with the divine implied by and revealed through the story.

In what follows, we will clarify these tasks by presenting three sacred stories. In each we will seek to discern the movement of ultimate concern, how it is shaped by the sacred story that carries it, and what the attendant relationship with the divine might be. The first story is an autobiographical sketch that reveals the sacred in nontraditional images and events.

Where the Woodbine Twineth

My mother's side of the family comes from the country. Her father was the smallest and youngest of fourteen children. The family story was that he was so studious he kept a law book in the crook of the plow while he was working in the fields. That's all I heard about him except that his son, Harlan Henry Hoffman, died of blood poisoning at the age of seven after his mother accidentally ran over him in her carriage in front of their home. Young Harlan Henry's death marked the point when stories about the family that stirred up deep feelings stopped being told. After that, whenever somebody or something disappeared, the adults in the family would only say that they had gone where the woodbine twineth.

I had no idea what they meant, but the phrase was used as if it explained everything. It didn't; I could only imagine what they meant. I envisioned an important and mysterious place somewhere out in the country woods.

I tell about this now because I recently realized that when I start feeling close to someone or some project, I begin to fear that I will be abandoned again. I say "again," because as a child each nanny I had disappeared, and the adults always said that she went where the woodbine twineth.

Kelso was my first nanny. She was a marvelously round woman whose face had big, red, soft cheeks. Her large roly-poly arms jiggled as she moved. I felt she must have held me in them a lot because I still feel caressed today when I say her name softly under my breath. She told my brother, sister, and me stories about life in her native Poland when she was working. She did an amazing amount of scrubbing and always had the clean smell of soap about her. I don't remember when it was that I realized she had disappeared. I don't remember any good-byes. Of course, all that I was told was that she had gone to that mysterious place out in the country woods.

Then there was Maude, who was our nanny when we stayed at my grandfather's house. She, too, was a large woman who had wonderfully big arms for holding. I remember her laughing all the time; I could feel her whole body shaking when she laughed while I was in her arms. Her hands smelled like the cleaning powder that had a little chicken on the box; they had the slightly gritty feel of flour from slapping dough around on the kitchen counter.

One night, when I was frightened and crying, she lifted me out of my crib, cradled me in her luscious lap and bosom, and rocked me to sleep with stories. The warm feeling of comfort in that moment still lingers in my body today. Then one day she, too, was gone without a trace. She had, of course, gone to that gentle place in the country woods that all the adults seemed to know so well.

Later, when I was eight or nine years old, a woman of color came to take care of our house and cook. Her name was Tillie. She was skinny and wore a blue and white uniform that was always highly starched. We took a liking to each other. Once, as a punishment, I was relegated for several months to eating dinner in the darkened chambers of our basement. There, under the glare of the bare light bulb hanging from the cobwebby rafters, Tillie and I ate until my exile from the family dining room was over.

While we ate dinner together, Tillie regaled me with frightening stories about African "haints" and other mysteries of the night. When it was just the two of us together in the basement, Tillie wore half of a silk stocking on her head. As she got older, the little hair she did have started turning white at the edges of the stocking. Then it happened: Tillie disappeared. She went where the woodbine twineth, too, and so did my heart.

Since then, I have been waiting for my nannies to return. Sometimes I imagine that somewhere out there in the country woods the seven-year-old Harlan Henry Hoffman, who died so suddenly, is listening to their stories, entwined in their arms as I once was.

In this story, the narrator makes no mention of God, religion, or the sacred. Yet this is a sacred story because it is a tale of ultimate concern. As such, it provides an opportunity for discerning the narrator's relationship with the divine. The first task is to find the movement of ultimate concern in the story, and so we begin with the question, "What is the axis of feeling, the movement of desire revealed in the tale?"

What emerges is a tension of fear and longing. On the one hand, there is a fear of endings and a fear of abandonment. As the narrator puts it, "anytime I start feeling close to someone or some project, I begin to fear that I will be abandoned again." This fear is re-inforced by bewilderment about these losses. They are inexplicable and untraceable, disappearing into that mysterious place in the woods "where the woodbine twineth." Furthermore, the losses have cut deeply. In their course, the narrator reports that he also lost his heart.

On the other hand, a powerful longing operates as a counterva-lence to the fear. It is a longing for healing, a yearning to be held and loved and welcomed as a confidant and friend. Symbolized by the nannies, the yearning for acceptance coexists with the fear of loss. As the narrator puts it, "Since then [since the disappearance of both Tillie and my heart] I have been waiting for my nannies to return."

How, then, does the story direct and shape this movement of ul-timate concern? What possibility of healing or fulfillment is promised? What is the likelihood that the fear will be confirmed?

The longing expressed by the narrator is tender, yet anguished, for the images in the story offer no promise of relief from the long-ing or remedy for the fear. Kelso, Maude, and Tillie evoke won-derful, warm, tactile memories and feelings, but their departures confirm that these feelings are transitory, evanescent. Abandon-ment is the deeper truth of this story, the area of ultimate concern. The final image is especially telling: "I have been waiting for my nannies to return. Sometimes I imagine that somewhere out there in the country woods the seven-year-old Harlan Henry Hoffman, who died so suddenly, is listening to their stories, entwined in their arms as I once was."

Notice that it is not the narrator, but little Harlan who is held by the nannies, listening to their stories. Moreover, he is with them in that inaccessible, inexplicable place in the country woods where the woodbine twineth. Little Harlan is dead. The imagery makes it clear: On this side of the grave, there will be no release for the narrator's longing and no remedy for his fear of abandonment. So it is that the story shapes, confirms, and perpetuates the movement of ultimate concern in the narrator.

What is the transcendent context of desire implied in the story just recounted? The narrator is alone. He operates in a world where he expects his fears of loss to be confirmed and his longing for healing to remain unfulfilled. The relationship with the divine revealed in this story is largely negative. The narrator neither experiences nor anticipates any transcendence of his pain, any answer to his desire. Images of this relationship appear in the cold, aloof adults who mystify the narrator's loss, and in the initially warm, welcoming nannies, who then become absent and unavailable.

Note, however, that in telling the story, the narrator raises a question about the adequacy of this imagery. The very telling of the story is part of the movement of ultimate concern, and in doing so the narrator implicitly anticipates a hearing and an acceptance unaccounted for by the story alone. In the next story, the adequacy of a sacred story to the movement of ultimate concern is explicitly addressed.

The Confessions of an Altar Boy

Our church services were held on the second floor of a big old house. It was there during the early Sunday morning hours that I donned the little black robe that altar boys wore during the communion service. One of the things I looked forward to most was solemnly bowing before I lit the candles on the altar before the service began, and then, after the service, snuffing them out with another, slightly quicker bow. The next best thing was having the minister, a shaggy, soft-hearted, white-haired man, ask me how I was doing while he marked down in his little record book the points I got for serving that morning. Originally, I thought it was the points that mattered, but now I know that it was his looking over the edges of his wire-rimmed spectacles and noticing me that mattered most. I guess the way I showed how much I loved him was the careful manner in which I helped him slip on the white cotton tunic over his black robe before the service. Often it was just the two of us in the quiet of the vesting room next to the altar. It was clear we both felt we had an important job to do.

This ritual went on uninterrupted for four or five years, until I hit puberty. At age thirteen, the serenity of this quiet ceremony came to a halt because of the hormones raging in my body that always seemed to want release from the smoldering cauldron they had created in my crotch. One unforgettable Sunday morning, they escaped from their captivity. There in the vesting room—sacrilege of all sacrileges—next to God's altar and beneath my holy black robe, my hands, despite the desperate cries of my formerly mighty conscience, found the source of the throbbing and aching, and quickly (so as to not offend God too much) ejected the source of my misery. Although no one noticed, I was sure God had witnessed this betrayal of his sacred space. There was nothing I could do but passively allow the full weight of the mighty sin I had just committed to descend on me. God, who clearly resembled my distant and aloof grandfather, a juvenile court judge, was, I was sure, about to strike me with his proverbial bolt of lightning. So it was with great reluctance that I went out to bow and light the candles on God's altar and to hand the communion vessels to the minister so he could offer Christ's body and blood to my fellow parishioners. Handling these vessels after having handled the vessel of my own passion was too great a disparity for my skinny little body to contain. So there, in front of God's altar, I solemnly promised that if he would not let my sexual member fall off (or turn black as my mother had warned), I would someday become a minister and never get married or use my penis again for any purpose other than going to the bathroom.

This ironclad resolution proved to be only temporary; it soon disintegrated under the pressure of a determined biological force far superior to my fear of God. As a result, I had no choice but to cling to my promise to become a minister. Sadly, I could not bring myself to confess this to my minister, even though he asked me every week how I was doing. How could I tell this man of God about the messy pressure between my legs? I didn't, and he eventually retired.

The new minister was younger and brought in many other altar boys; I became one in a crowd. In his sermons, he was always telling everyone in the congregation that we weren't nice enough to each other, that we should go to the hospital, like he did, to visit people who were dying of cancer. I never visited any of those people, but I did feel bad about not going.

Years later, I kept my promise to God and enrolled at Yale Divinity School. I didn't put the real circumstances behind my decision to become a minister on the application form; instead, I wrote something about wanting the training to visit people in hospitals who were dying of cancer.

One of the seminary courses I took was taught by a psychologist who specialized in finding out the real reasons people wanted to become ministers. In one of my early term papers, I told the story of the hormonally swollen altar boy's promise to God. Not unexpectedly, he called me in after class and suggested that I visit a psychiatrist at the Yale Student Health Service.

The psychiatrist seemed to think that religion itself was a disease, but he did help me find a way not to have to stay at school. In our sessions, I was able to release some of the anger I felt at God for having made me come to seminary. The full volume of this release culminated several days before my departure. I visited the chapel while everyone else was at lunch. I walked right up to the altar. The beautiful blue and yellow stained-glass window of Christ was alive with light, and the large silver cross on the altar gleamed in the midday sun. I roared at my fullest capacity, "Fuck you God!" Then I fell down on the soft maroon carpet and cried until I was weak and hoarse. To my surprise, I felt strangely relieved that I was still alive, that I had not been struck by lightning. As I picked myself up, the little altar boy inside me thought of the gentle shaggy minister looking over his wire-rimmed spectacles assigning me points and asking about how I was doing. If he had been there, I might have told him how much he had meant to me and how many important things had happened to me since the last time we were at the altar together.

LIKE A SNAKE shedding its worn-out skin, the narrator describes the painful process of shedding a sacred story that is too restricting to support and affirm the emerging dynamism of his ultimate concern. The story highlights episodes from three periods in the narrator's life—childhood, adolescence, and young adulthood—and captures the developing dynamism of ultimate concern, sacred story, and relationship with the divine in each.

In his youth, the narrator found the liturgical ritual of Sunday morning services—vesting, lighting candles, and bowing—to be a meaningful, supportive vehicle of his ultimate concern. He experienced approval in receiving "points"; acceptance in the clergyman's kindly inquiry, "How are you doing?" and a sense of meaning and purpose in the service itself—"It was clear we both felt we had an important job to do." The relationship of ultimate concern and sacred story here was one of mutual harmony and reinforcement.

Difficulties emerged later when the biological imperative of adolescence fractured the harmonious connection between sacred story and ultimate concern. Succumbing to the fevered release of his "misery," the narrator opened in himself a seemingly unresolvable contradiction between his desire to be approved for doing the right thing, and his desire to be accepted for who he was and "how he was doing" at the moment.

Notice that this sense of self-alienation was driven and shaped by his sacred story. That story led him to interpret his act as the "sacrilege of all sacrileges," a "mighty sin" carrying the penalty of death by lightning. The contradiction between the narrator's desire for approval and the chaos of his desires was "too great a disparity for [his] skinny body to contain." The only available means for resolving the tension was to renounce his desires and surrender himself in an act of penance to a life of ministry and chastity. Alienated from himself, he became alienated from the gentle clergyman he loved.

The narrator's relationship with the divine is easy to discern. God is a judge, vengeful and implacable, righteously demanding great sacrifice to atone for great wrong: in this case, a life committed to God's ministry in return for a life spared from the lightning bolt.

The tyranny of the narrator's sacred story and the untenability of his vow became evident after the narrator enrolled at divinity school. The steadfast denial of his ultimate concern could no longer be sustained and justified by his sacred story. In a dramatic return to the altar, the sacred space of his original vow, the narrator renounced his vow and his God. The adolescent discharge is reclaimed by the "release of anger . . . roared at [his] fullest capacity, 'Fuck you, God!'"

In accepting and reclaiming the legitimacy of his ultimate concern, the narrator rejected an inadequate sacred story and an oppressive image of God. But he did not reject a relationship with the divine itself. In fact, the narrator cast himself, prostrate and tearful, into a new relationship with the divine, a relationship that trusts—even if in anger, desperation, and fear—in the possibility of acceptance. Who this accepting God might be is as yet unknown, but the appearance of the "gentle shaggy minister" is a sign of healing and hope, and the tale itself is a new sacred story.

For our final example, we shift to a traditional sacred story drawn from the Gospel of Luke. Like the personal narratives that preceded it, this story also tells us something about the movement of ultimate concern and its divine context.

The Traveler

A man was going down from Jerusalem to Jericho, and he fell among robbers, who stripped him and beat him, and departed, leaving him half dead. Now by chance a priest was going down that road; when he saw the man, he passed by on the other side. So likewise a Levite, when he came to the place and saw him, passed by on the other side. But a Samaritan, as he journeyed, crossed over and came upon him.

And when he saw him, he had compassion and went to him and bound up his wounds, pouring on oil and wine; then he set him on his own beast and brought him to an inn and took care of him. And the next day he took out two denarii and gave them to the innkeeper, saying, "Take care of him; and whatever more you spend, I will repay you when I come back."

To BRIDGE THE distance we might feel between the stories of our own lives and traditional sacred narratives, let us position ourselves as a first-century Jew might have done in hearing this parable and enter the story by identifying with the traveler. The road to Jericho is notoriously dangerous—we have heard many reports of muggings and assaults—and we move apprehensively down the road with him. Our fears are confirmed when he is attacked, robbed, beaten, and left helpless and "half dead" on the side of the road. Imaginatively, it is we who are in the ditch, half dead. The experience is agonizing, terrifying; at such times our sacred stories are tested and we become intensely aware of our relationship with the divine.

A priest comes along, sees us, and passes by without stopping to help. A Levite ignores us and just walks on. The experience of having our hopes for rescue dashed twice is devastating. How could the keepers of the temple pass by without a word? Our doubts about Yahweh are strong and desperate.

And then the worst happens. A third man comes along and sees us. But he is not a Jew, he is a Samaritan. Jews and Samaritans are traditional enemies. We know it is all over. The Samaritan then "crosses over and comes upon [us]." We are helpless and about to die. God has forsaken us.

The sacred story and the relationship with the divine that we see here are familiar: The world is dangerous and we have to take care of ourselves. Despite the talk and the temples, God does not save us in a crisis. Our deepest fears will be realized.

But amazingly, we are wrong. Our worst enemy picks us up, binds our wounds, takes us to the inn, and provides for our needs. This is a reversal of our expectations and a challenge to the sacred story described above. The parable suggests that sometimes, what seems to be the confirmation of our deepest fears is, in fact, an opportunity for healing and recovery.

In the story, the Samaritan is Yahweh in disguise, God revealed as compassionate, caring, and involved. What this sacred story suggests is that at those times when all we can imagine is disaster and death, it is possible to trust that a larger story is at work—a story that will support the movement of our ultimate concern and lead us in the direction we need to go.

THREE BASIC POINTS draw together the threads of this essay. The first is that everyone has a relationship with the divine. Denying the existence of God or rejecting institutional religion does not alter this fact. All of us are constituted by a movement of ultimate concern, a movement that we experience variously as threatened, abandoned, welcomed, or judged. It is in discerning this movement and its context, illumined and revealed by our sacred stories, that we discern our relationship with the divine.

Second, relationships with the divine can take various forms. The sacred stories considered in this essay illustrate three different types. The first type amounts to a denying of the existence of a relationship. It is rooted in the experience of feeling vulnerable, abandoned, and alone. In "Where the Woodbine Twineth" the imagery of the aloof, dismissive adults and the warm but unavailable nannies expresses this relationship. In "The Traveler" it is captured by the priest and the Levite who abandon the wounded and helpless traveler to his fate.

The second type of relationship is marked by the sense of being accountable to a set of divine laws. The experience is one of being bound by expectations and standards that originate outside oneself in the realm of the divine. In "Confessions of an Altar Boy" the image of God as the demanding, punishing judge is one expression of this relationship.

The third type of relationship is characterized by a sense of acceptance and support for the movement of one's desire. In "Confessions of an Altar Boy," the narrator implicitly embraces this in renouncing a relationship with the divine rooted in an experience of guilt and judgment. In "The Traveler," this relationship is expressed in the image of a wounded and helpless man being healed and cared for by his worst enemy. In both cases fear of annihilation is superseded by an experience of gift and acceptance.

Our relationship with the divine can take a number of forms; some relationships (and hence some sacred stories) are healthier and more life-giving than others. In the "Confessions of an Altar Boy," the narrator rejects an oppressive sacred story and a fear-driven relationship with the divine to risk the possibility of a new sacred story. In "The Traveler," the narrative challenges and undermines relationships with the divine based on the fear of abandonment. Implicit in these stories is the assertion that certain movements of ultimate concern are healthier and more life-giving than others: Self-acceptance is preferable to self-denying guilt, and openness in the face of fear brings better results than yielding to the need to control.

We can critique our own sacred stories based on our discernment of whether they promote or inhibit the emergence of an authentic movement of ultimate concern. Whatever the difficulties and pitfalls of this task, it can also bring enlightenment and joy. In examining the nature of our sacred stories, we cultivate our spiritual awareness and remind ourselves of the importance of discerning our relationship with the divine.

▼▼

Chapter 2

Our Mythic Stories

SAM KEEN

Combining a background in theology with an acute sense of the psychological and spiritual problems of contemporary life, author Sam Keen is an astute social critic. From Your Mythic Journey *(coauthored with Anne Valley Fox), in which he examines the kinds of decisive events and decisions that shape a meaningful life, to the best-selling* Fire in the Belly: On Being a Man, *Keen's books are united by his attention to the myths and stories that shape our lives, whether healthy and nurturing or outmoded and harmful.*

Sam Keen holds advanced degrees from Princeton University and Harvard Divinity School. He has lectured and conducted workshops at more than two hundred universities and institutes in the United States and abroad. His essays on contemporary social and spiritual problems appear regularly in a variety of magazines and journals, and he is one of the leading spokesmen for the men's movement in this country.

P eanut butter is, for me, a philosophical principle having to
do with storytelling. We all ate peanut butter early in our
lives, but some people have abandoned that, thinking that
once they grew up, they didn't need peanut butter. But I have always loved peanut butter and I always will. Peanut butter, like the
stories of my life, represents continuity.

One of the problems in the modern world is that everything is
discontinuous. It used to be that we believed in an essence, a soul, a
story, a myth that we lived by; we came from small communities
with shared guiding principles based on a shared point of view.
Now we live in what people increasingly call a postmodern environment. What postmodernism means at its best or worst is that
we don't have links of continuity in our lives. We have given up
the quest for deep, internal continuity; instead, we are filled with
information that comes to us from outside.

We are the first generation bombarded with so many stories
from so many "authorities," none of which are our own. The parable of the postmodern mind is the person surrounded by a media
center: three television screens in front of them giving three sets of
stories; fax machines bringing in other stories; newspapers providing still more stories. In a sense, we are saturated with stories; we're
saturated with points of view. But the effect of being bombarded
with all of these points of view is that we don't have a point of
view and we don't have a story. We lose the continuity of our experiences; we become people who are written on from the outside.

If we are always being inhabited by other lives and other
dreams—if they are being pumped into us by television and other
media that tell us who we are and what our story is—there cannot
be any continuity in our lives. This leads to very serious questions:
Without continuity, how can we form any real relationships?
How can we make vows? How can we establish depth over time?
Will the effect of this saturation with stories that do not belong to

us be that modern life is just a series of one-night stands, sexual and/or philosophical?

Now, peanut butter was something I loved as a youth. It is something I know speaks deeply to my essence. Gradually, by looking at my experience and weaving it together, I have come to know that in this lifetime there will never be a time when I do not love peanut butter. I have, in other words, learned enough about myself to know there is a story that binds my life together and peanut butter is part of that story.

One reason the work of Joseph Campbell, the great mythologist, has become so popular in recent years is that there are so many of us who have realized that the great stories by which we used to live no longer infuse our lives with meaning. The old stories, the great stories, are gone. Nietzsche said in the beginning of our century, "God is dead." What this means is that the idea of God no longer governs the way we organize our lives.

If we look at medieval villages, we see they were organized around cathedrals; belief in God shaped the city's organization. The story the medieval city tells us is this: God is in his world and all is right in our world. Here are the pictures of who we should be like: the saints. Here is the picture of womanhood: the Madonna. Life was organized around those principles.

However, if we fly over modern cities, we see they are organized around financial centers. Perhaps they were once organized around manufacturing centers, but now only parts of Third World countries are arranged in that way. Our cities are organized around banking and money centers because, with the Industrial Revolution of the nineteenth century, we substituted the idea of progress for the idea of God. Man became the instrument, through technology, to create a brave new world. The great story all of us have been living much more than any Christian story is the myth of progress.

That myth was lived out in our culture as every immigrant group said, "Our children will have a better life here than we had." *That* was progress. But near the end of the 1980s, we found that the myth of progress was false. We began to realize that the technological story of triumph is a story we can't continue to live out because of the effect it has on our environment. If there isn't anywhere we can put our garbage, then our children are not going to have a better life than we had. Progress, in fact, will have to come to an end.

Therefore, in our lifetime, we have seen something that perhaps no generation in human history has seen before: the death of many organizing myths that generations before us lived by. For example, just a generation ago, about one-fifth of the world's population lived with the organizing myth of communism. It had all the essential mythic elements: heroes, heroines, enemy systems. With the collapse of the Berlin Wall, the organizing myth of communism died right in front of our eyes. Think of those films of a flower, maybe a rose, opening up in time-lapse photography. What we have seen is a speeded-up film of a myth dying before our eyes.

So here we are in a world where the organizing myths—what I think of as the great peanut butter principles—are gone. Underlying that is a great anxiety; we are all asking, "What stories can we live by?" One way to begin to answer that question is to start telling our own stories.

We need to ask our parents for their stories; we need to share stories with our friends. The real stories that will sustain us will only come out of a community where we tell and listen to other stories. The act of telling a story creates community and, at the same time, elicits more stories.

Instead of telling and listening to stories, we often seek the meaning of our lives in others' stories. We let the church, the state, the university, our professions, and even current social trends tell us who we are. We do everything but look under our own hearths for the stories of who we are.

Recently, we have even begun to look at other people's mythology, thinking we will find the stories of who we are in exotic stories of long ago and faraway peoples. While there is a tremendous value in studying another culture's mythology, if we are not, for instance, Native Americans, we will not find our animating stories in Native American myths. The animating myths we live must be found in the details of our own lives.

The story of Rabbi Ben Isaac of Krakow illustrates this idea. The Rabbi was a very poor but very pious and wise man. One night he had a dream in which a figure said to him, "If you go to Prague and dig beneath a certain tree behind the emperor's castle, you will find a great treasure."

The Rabbi, being a man who trusted dreams, went to Prague, but the castle was guarded. He couldn't get across the bridge. So he lived under the bridge for a while and became friends with the captain of the guard, such close friends that one day he shared his story. He said, "You know, I had a dream that if I got into the castle grounds and went to a certain tree and dug there, there would be a treasure."

"Ah," the captain of the guard said, "you're a very foolish man. You really can't trust stuff like that. You know, dreams are just throw-away items, the trash of the mind. I have dreams myself." Then he added, "For instance, I had a dream that over in Krakow there lived a poor but wise and kindly man, probably not unlike yourself. His name, as a matter of fact, was Rabbi Isaac. I dreamt that if I just went to his very poor house, and dug behind his stove, I would find a treasure that somebody long ago had buried there. Now, that's foolish, isn't it?" And so Rabbi Ben Isaac thanked him, went home, dug behind his own hearth, and found the treasure.

If we are going to uncover our own mythologies—separating what we want to keep from the mythological systems we were raised in and what we want to discard—we have to uncover our own stories.

The fundamental stories—those we have to tell about ourselves and each other in order to be whole—are creative, constructive stories that reflect great truths. But the myths we encounter from sources outside of ourselves may or may not reflect great truths. They may or may not be creative myths. Hitler's Nazi Germany was informed by a myth that did bind the nation together, but it was a false and destructive myth. There are other, more creative national mythologies that provide more life space. The same is true of family myths: Some families tell stories that are very nourishing and capacious, while others tell stories that are very constricting.

Social trends can also offer either limiting or constructive myths. One of the problems of our particular time is that people have discovered the power of being a victim, and there is a great social rush to see who can claim exclusive rights to the story of victimhood. I believe it is right that we should want to discover the degree to which we have been wounded by others. Even if we had the best of parents, parents are fallible people, and we were all loved either too much or too little or in the wrong ways. The world, it seems, is not calculated to fulfill all the desires of the human heart, particularly the infantile human heart. We have to inhabit the story of our pain and struggle; we have to tell the story of our personal warfare, which is what tragedy is—the story of "me against it."

But we need to be careful not to let the social trend of victimhood get us stuck there. If you came from a dysfunctional family, or if you're an adult child of an alcoholic, you are, in some sense, always going to be that until you stop telling that story. I approve of all the Twelve-Step groups, but I also approve of graduation. If a man who hasn't had a drink in fourteen years says, "I'm an alcoholic," I say, "No, you're not. You're stuck on an old story." We have to be aware when a certain myth is no longer useful, is no longer animating our lives.

Mythology is, in fact, one of the most confusing and important words of our time. Myth's archaic function was to tell us the deepest truths of the world in story form. For example, in the beginning the world was without form and void, and the spirit of God breathed upon the waters. And God said, "Let there be light," and there was light.

No one—except perhaps a fundamentalist Christian—believes that this is a literal account of the creation. But it was and is a very deep way to say, "We live in a created world that has been given to us. There is a kindly intelligence that we call God behind this order in which we live." Whether you believe that or not is beside the point. The point is that there isn't a better way of expressing that idea than through that story. That's what myth means.

What we too frequently ignore is the negative aspect of mythology, which is that myths often govern us unconsciously. The philosopher George Santayana said that those who do not remember history are condemned to repeat it. Another way of saying that is if we don't remember the myths that are living us—if we don't know which scripts, which metastories we are living out—all we can do is repeat other people's lives. The great discovery of Twelve-Step programs and other forms of addiction treatment is that if I don't remember the story of an alcoholic family, I'm going to repeat that story. But there is a distinction between remembering a myth in order not to repeat it, and getting stuck in that memory so that in fact you do continue to live out the pattern you are trying to learn to let go of.

Families have myths. Ethnic groups have myths. Even nations have their own myths. Søren Kierkegaard, the great Danish philosopher, said that every culture plays its own music; that music enchants and encapsulates us and takes away our freedom.

The only way to free ourselves is to examine those myths, disenchant ourselves, and then discover which of those songs we want to keep. There is a vast difference between a song you can't get out of your mind and a song you have decided you want to hear again and again.

I believe that to free ourselves of the destructive myth of progress we need to discover our personal mythologies, our personal stories. I am not so foolish as to think that I or anyone else will create a new mythology. However, we are living in a time when there is a clash between an old, dominant mythology and an emerging mythology. The old mythology, as I've said, is the mythology of progress. The alternate myth—which is beginning to emerge through ecology, feminism, the new physics, the men's movement, and other sources—is the myth of interconnection.

We are living in the mythic battleground between those two systems: one dying, the other trying to be born. By becoming conscious of the myths we're living, we can make a conscious choice about which side we want to be on in that battle, which myth we want to live out.

Becoming conscious of the myths we are living means really examining our own lives and asking the deepest questions. I don't pretend to know all the questions that we must ask ourselves in this process, but I do want to make three suggestions.

A good place to start is with the question, "What are my gifts?" This is related to a second question, "What is it that gives me joy?" Joy is very different from pleasure or happiness because joy involves struggle and pain as well as triumph. And the third question—one that is particularly important to me—is, "At what point is there an intersection between my gifts and the needs of the world?"

I use the word *vocation* instead of *destiny* because it implies "calling," an appeal to us from the outside. There is an appeal going on now, for instance, that says half of the world's population doesn't eat regularly. We hear that; some people's vocation is to answer that. Other people's vocation might come from hearing the appeal, "We have too many people; we must reduce the population." At some point there will be an intersection between the gifts that we have and the needs of the world. When we follow that, we experience joy, because there is no greater joy than that of giving what we have to give and finding it gratefully received. The great model of that is sexual intercourse between people who love each other, where there is no difference between giving and receiving.

This definition of vocation has a political component; I always use the word myth in a political sense. Myth is political because it always tells you about power: who's up, who's down, who is to be killed. This emphasis on the political and incarnate component of mythology is something I find Jungian approaches to this subject lack.

The Jungian approach is, to my mind, Gnostic in that it wants to rise above the earth, above wrestling with evil; it turns evil into the concept of "shadow," which can be dealt with psychologically. It does not grapple with political realities. I rigorously avoid using the word *archetype* because I have never seen one; it seems to me to be a very vague concept masquerading as semigenetic or semibiological truth, or as a kind of required pit stop on the path of life. What Jungians call archetypes, I call metaphors, and that is a much more negotiable word.

I also believe the notion of archetypes lends itself to a very conservative political philosophy, because if there are only six archetypes, it means that the models have already been invented. In other words, as you analyze your life, all you have to do is follow the models; the characters are already given. But we are currently facing problems in our society for which there are no historical precedents, and so those models—those archetypes—cannot be very useful.

What we have to discover now is how to husband the Earth and reconnect ourselves to the commonwealth of all sentient beings. This is our ecological imperative: If we don't do this, we are going to die. But we cannot do it through archetypes just as we cannot do it through the mythologies of other cultures. We definitely cannot do it through the mythologies of a pretechnological people because we are not going into the future except as technology users. Our problem is, how can we form an appropriate technology that will allow us to survive and honor the Earth? There is no archetype for that; it has never been done.

Ultimately, we have to learn to reinhabit a world where everything around us speaks to us. We have created a world that surrounds us but does not enrich us with stories; we live in anonymous ways, not knowing the source of the water that comes from our taps, not knowing the animals around us except through Walt Disney movies. Our environment is made for us by other people; stories come at us from television and from so many other sources that have nothing to do with us. We have to learn to live again in a place that speaks to us.

Somewhat recently, for the first time in my life, I realized that I wanted to live in a place where everything I do is connected to stories. So three years ago, when I bought a piece of land and needed water and didn't know where to get it, I walked until I found a place where ferns grew, high up on a bank, beside a little trickle of water. I began to cultivate that trickle of water, digging under a rock half as big as a house. After a month I had several trickles of water coming together into a stream. I put a concrete block there, and built a redwood box to tap the water. When I finally had the water tested, it was good and it was sweet.

When friends visit and drink that water, I tell them the story of how I worked to get to it. I'll also be able to say, "See that tree? My son and I planted that tree. And my son helped me build that house." And I'll tell the story of planting the tree and of building the house.

I want to live that way; I want to live so that the stories that en-rich my life come from the people and the land around me, and so that my friends are people with whom I share stories. We will weave together a community in that way. And so, when we come to die, we will look around us at the world, and everywhere we look, we'll see only stories.

▼▼▼

Chapter 3

Composing a Life

Mary Catherine Bateson

Mary Catherine Bateson, Ph.D., is the author of the best-selling book Composing a Life, as well as a memoir of her parents, Gregory Bateson and Margaret Mead, With a Daughter's Eye. Bateson has written widely on a variety of linguistic and anthropological topics and has done research and taught in the United States, the Philippines, and the Middle East. Currently, she is Clarence Robinson professor of anthropology and English at George Mason University in Fairfax, Virginia.

Here, Bateson explores the benefits of composing a personal narrative of one's life history that can accommodate disparate, even conflicting commitments while providing threads of continuity. She believes that the ability to create and re-create our life stories in this manner enables us to think and act with more clarity and creativity, particularly when adapting to unforeseen changes. Throughout, she emphasizes the value of being able to interpret our personal histories with flexibility and enthusiasm for the creative process that living a life can be.

There are three meanings that "composing a life," as a phrase, has to me. Two of those meanings apply to different arts, in that I see the way people live their lives as, in itself, an artistic process. An artist takes ingredients that may seem incompatible, and organizes them into a whole that is not only workable, but finally pleasing and true, even beautiful. As you get up in the morning, as you make decisions, as you spend money, make friends, make commitments, you are creating a piece of art called your life. The word *compose* helps me look at two aspects of that process.

Very often in the visual arts, you put together components to find a way that they fit together and balance each other in space. You make a visual composition of form and color. One thing that you do in composing a life is to put together disparate elements that need to be in some kind of balance, like a still life with tools, fruit, and musical instruments. This sense of balance is something that women have been especially aware of in recent years because they can't solve the problem of composing the different elements of their lives simply by making them separate, as men have.

Of course, less and less are men able to do so. But for a long time it was possible for men to think in terms of a line between the public and the private. A man would go to the workplace and then, at a certain point, he would switch that off and go home to a different world where the atmosphere was different. He could switch gears from one aspect of his life to the other.

But it hasn't been possible for women to separate their commitments in quite the same way. It is one thing in the traditional nuclear family for the husband to go to the office and stop thinking about his family during the day because he has left his wife in charge. It is quite a different thing for both parents to go off and feel that they can completely forget what is happening with the family. Many women have the sense that the combining of different areas in their lives is a problem that is with them all the time.

What this has meant is that women have lived their lives experiencing multiple simultaneous demands from multiple directions. Increasingly men are also living that way. So thinking about how people manage this is becoming more and more important. One way to approach the situation is to think of how a painter composes a painting: by synchronously putting together things that occur in the same period, and finding a pattern in the way they fit together.

But of course "compose" has another meaning in music. Music is an art in which you create something that happens over *time*, that goes through various transitions over time. Looking at your life in this way, you have to look at the change that occurs within a lifetime—discontinuities, transitions, and growth of various sorts—and the artistic unity, like that of a symphony with very different movements, that can characterize a life.

Those two meanings of composing a life—one that relates to visual art and the other that relates to music—will crop up again in this essay. But what I want to emphasize is a third meaning, one that has to do with the ways in which you compose your own *versions* of your life. I'm referring to the stories you make about your life, the stories you tell first to yourself and then to other people, the stories you use as a lens for interpreting experience as it comes along. What I want to say is that you can play with, compose, multiple versions of a life history.

There are advantages in having access to multiple versions of your life story. I am not referring to a true version versus a false version, or to one that works in a given therapeutic context as opposed to others, or to one that will sell to *People Magazine* as opposed to ones that won't. I am referring to the freedom that comes not only from owning your memory and your life story but also from knowing that you make creative choices in how you look at your life.

In the postmodern environment in which we live, it is easy to say that no version is fixed, no version is true. I want to push beyond that and encourage you to think about the creative responsibility involved in the fact that there are different ways to tell your stories. It's not that one is true and another is not true. It's a matter of emphasis and of context. For example, one of the things that people do at meetings is to introduce themselves. I was at a conference recently where, in the course of two days, I introduced myself three times. One person who had been there all three times came up to me and said, "You know, you said something completely different every time." Of course I did. The context was different.

Imagine the choices you have in saying things about yourself and about other people. These are real choices, but they are made in the presence of a set of conventions. Think of an introduction as a literary genre. There are things you include and things you don't. Those decisions are related to who you're talking to and where you are, as well as who you're talking about.

You can do the same with versions of your life history. For instance, most people can tell a version that emphasizes the continuities in their lives, to make a single story that goes in a clear direction. But the same people can also tell their life stories as if they were following on this statement: "After lots of surprises and choices, or interruptions and disappointments, I have arrived some place I could never have anticipated." Every one of us has a preference for one of these versions, but if we try, we can produce both. My guess is that there are a lot of people reading this who think of themselves as growing and developing and moving to new things. That's part of the intellectual context many of us are in. But some of us, by preference, experience our lives as a discontinuous process.

For example, one version of my life story goes like this: I already thought of myself as a writer when I was in high school, and there hasn't been a year since college that I haven't published something.

Now I spend half the year writing full-time and half the year writing and teaching. Many of my students are future writers.

That's one version of me. The other version goes like this: I planned in high school to be a poet. But I gave up writing poetry in college. The only writing I did for years was academic publish-or-perish writing. When I became unemployed because of the Iranian revolution, shortly after my mother died, I dealt with unemployment by starting to write a memoir. I suddenly found that I could write nonfiction. Now I'm considering switching again and writing a novel.

Both of these are true stories. But they are very different stories.

One person told me that there had been so much discontinuity in her life that it wasn't hard to think of a discontinuous version, but it was painful to tell it. I think that is a problem many people have. Because our society has preferred continuous versions of stories, discontinuities seem to indicate that something is wrong with you. A discontinuous story becomes a very difficult story to claim.

I would say that the most important effect of my book, *Composing a Life*, has been to give people who feel that they've been bumped from one thing to another, with no thread of continuity, a way of positively interpreting their experience. You might be uncomfortable with your life if it has been like the *Perils of Pauline*, yet many of us have lives like that. One strategy for working with that is to make a story that interprets change as continuity. One of my favorites was someone who said, "My life is like surfing, with one wave coming after another." He unified his whole life with that single simile.

The choice you make affects what you can do next. Often people use the choice of emphasizing either continuity or discontinuity as a way of preparing for the next step. They interpret the present in a way that helps them construct a particular future.

One of the most striking examples of this is the way people talk about divorce. Some people approach a divorce by emphasizing what was wrong with the marriage all along: "Finally we got a divorce. But it's been awful for twenty years." I think some of the anger that develops in divorce situations comes from a need to re-create a continuity. But then there are some who don't need to create continuity by tracing the problem back. They emphasize the discontinuity and view the problem as absolutely new. Perhaps they will tend to emphasize loss in that situation, rather than anger.

When I started writing *Composing a Life*, the issue that I wanted to write about was the issue of discontinuity. Part of my interest in this was based on two events in my own life. One was that I had just gone through the experience of losing, in a rather painful way, a job that I cared about. I had been forced to change jobs before, because of my husband changing jobs, and I had had to adapt to that situation. So what I set out to do was to look at a group of women who had been through a lot of transitions and who were able to cope with the changes. I was asking the question, "How on earth does one survive this kind of interruption?"

The other circumstance that made me focus on the issue of discontinuity had to do with my experiences in Iran. At the time of the Iranian revolution, my husband and I had been living and working there for seven years. We, and a great many of our friends, had to make fresh starts; many people became refugees. The way they interpreted their situation was absolutely critical to their adjustment. I could see very clearly, among them, that there were those who came into the refugee situation with a sense that they had skills, that they had adaptive patterns that they could transfer to the new situation. They were emphasizing continuity. Other people came into the refugee situation feeling that their lives had ended and they had to start from zero. You could see that the choices people made about how to interpret the continuities and discontinuities in their lives had great implications for the way they approached the future.

Much of coping with discontinuity has to do with discovering threads of continuity. You cannot adjust to change unless you can recognize some analogy between your old situation and your new situation. Without that analogy you cannot transfer learning. You cannot apply skills. If you can recognize a problem that you've solved before, in however different a guise, you have a much greater chance of solving that problem in a new situation. That recognition is critical to the transfer of learning.

It can be very difficult to recognize the ways in which one situation or event in your life is linked to others. When I was working on my memoir of my parents, *With a Daughter's Eye*, I found an example of this in my father's life. Some of you may know my father, Gregory Bateson, as a great anthropologist, a great thinker. But in the middle of his life, he went through a difficult period that went on for some time. From year to year he didn't know whether he would have a salary, whether there would be anything to live on.

His career at that time must have seemed totally discontinuous. First he was a biologist. Then he got interested in anthropology and went to New Guinea. He did a couple of field trips that he never wrote up. During the war he wrote an analysis of propaganda films and worked in psychological warfare. Then he did a study of communication in psychotherapy. Then he worked on alcoholism and schizophrenia, and then on dolphins and octopuses. Somehow he turned into a philosopher.

One of the things that I realized while I was putting together the memoir is that only when he drew together a group of his articles—all written in very different contexts for very different audiences, with apparently different subject matter—and put them into the book called *Steps to an Ecology of Mind*, did it become clear to him that he had been working on the same kind of question all his life: The continuous thread through all of his work was an interest in the relationships between ideas.

The interruptions that forced him to change his research focus were absolutely critical to pushing him up the ladder of logical types, so that ultimately he could see continuity at a very abstract level. His insight, his understanding of what he had been working on all his life, was a result of a sometimes desperate search for a continuity beyond the discontinuities. So even when I was working on the memoir, I was picking at this question of continuity and discontinuity, and examining the incredible gains that can come from reconstruing a life history by combining both interpretations.

Of course, in composing any life story, there is a considerable weight of cultural pressure. Narratives have canonical forms. One of the stories that we, as a culture, respond to is the story in which the hero or heroine's end is contained in the beginning. For example, there is a film about Henry Ford that I happened to see recently on television. In one scene, he sees his first horseless carriage as a little boy and falls in love with it. In other words, you have an episode in childhood that prefigures all that is to come. Think about how many biographies you have read in which the baby who grew up to be a great violinist loved lullabies, or loved listening to the radio: stories about talent that was visible from the very beginning.

One of my favorite examples of this is a story from the life of St. Teresa of Avila, a counter-Reformation saint. When she was a child, part of Spain was still controlled by the Moors, part of the country was Catholic, and part was Muslim. When she was ten or so, she set out, with her younger brother, for the territory controlled by the Moors in order to be martyred and go to heaven. This becomes an appropriate story to prefigure a life of self-sacrifice and dedication to God. There are many biographies and autobiographies that have this pattern.

Another popular plot is one that we can think of as the conversion narrative. It's a simple plot. Lives that in reality have a lot of zigzags in them get reconstrued into before-and-after narratives with one major discontinuity. One very interesting example of this is the *Confessions of St. Augustine,* which tells the story of his life before and after his conversion to Christianity. The narrative structure requires that he depict himself before conversion as a terrible sinner, that he devalue all that he did before he was converted, and that he dredge up sins to talk about so that he can describe a total turnaround.

Reading this book today, what strikes me is that St. Augustine after his conversion to Christianity was not that different from St. Augustine before his conversion to Christianity. He pursued a reasonable intellectual life. He was a seeker. He experimented with different things. After his conversion, it is true, he disowned his mistress, who had borne him a son, which is construed, in this story, as a sign of virtue. But he continued to be, as he is throughout the narrative, profoundly self-centered. The universe was apparently organized around bringing him to God, and other people were very peripheral. In that sense, you can follow the same story throughout the book.

A more complicated example of a conversion story is *The Autobiography of Malcolm X.* Much of the book tells the story of how Malcolm X, who had been a thief and a pimp, was converted to the Nation of Islam, Elijah Muhammad's American Black Muslim movement. About two-thirds of the book is written as a conventional conversion narrative: "I was deep in sin and then I was saved by Elijah Muhammad."

But then another big discontinuity occurs. Malcolm X becomes disillusioned with the corruption within the Nation of Islam and with Elijah Muhammad in particular. He breaks with them, makes a pilgrimage to Mecca, converts to orthodox Islam, and starts his own Black Muslim organization in the United States. So inside this book you have the image of somebody who developed an interpretation of his life to support the validity of one particular message of salvation, and then had to flip over into another one. It's an extraordinarily interesting and unusual story because the conversion happens not once but twice. One very common example of the uses of the conversion story shows up in Twelve-Step programs. Many Twelve-Step programs essentially convey the message that if you can construe your life in such a way as to support a turnaround, we will help you construct a new life. But you have to define yourself, as St. Augustine had to define himself, as a sinner, or as Malcolm X had to define himself, as having been duped by Elijah Muhammad. An emphasis on a turnaround becomes the condition for moving on to the next stage.

The conversion narrative can be a very empowering way of telling your story, because it allows you to make a fresh start. The more continuous story, in which the end is prefigured in the beginning, is powerful in different ways. But what I want to emphasize are the advantages of choosing a particular interpretation at a particular point in time, and the even greater advantage of using multiple interpretations.

The availability of multiple interpretations of a life story is particularly important in terms of how different generations communicate with each other. When we, as parents, talk to our children about our lives, there is a great temptation to edit out the discontinuities, to reshape our histories so that they look more coherent than they are. But when we tell stories to our children with the zigzags edited out, it causes problems for many of those children. A lot of young people have great difficulty committing themselves to a relationship or to a career because of the feeling that once they do, they're trapped for a long, long time. On the other hand, they feel they've got to get on the right "track" because, after all, this is a long and terrifying commitment. I think it is very liberating for college students when an older person says to them, "Your first job after college need not be the beginning of an ascending curve that's going to take you through your life. It can be a zigzag. You might be doing something different in five years." That's something that young people need to hear: that the continuous story, where the whole of a person's life is prefigured very early on, is a cultural creation, not a reflection of life as it is really lived.

The ways in which we interpret our life stories have a great effect on how our children come to define their own identities. An example of this occurred in my own life when my daughter was becoming a teenager. She said to me, "Gee Mom, it must be awfully hard on you and Daddy that I'm not interested in any of the things you're interested in." I said, "What do you mean?" She said, "Well, you're professors. You write books about social science. I'm an actress. I care about theater." I said a secret prayer because it was clearly a very tricky moment. Maybe she needed to believe in that discontinuity. Maybe it was worrying her and she needed to get away from that discontinuity.

But what I said to her was, "Well, to be a social scientist, to be an anthropologist, you have to be a good observer of human behavior. You have to try and understand how people think and why they behave as they do. It strikes me that that's pretty important for a good actor." She has been telling that story ever since because it gave her permission, first, to pursue what she deeply wanted to pursue without feeling she was betraying me and her father. But it also gave her permission to use anything she might pick up from us by giving her a way of construing the cross-generational relationship as a continuity.

As parents, we also need to be flexible in how we construe our children's lives. Recently, I was in Israel visiting on several kibbutzim. Many of the older people on the kibbutzim are in distress about the fact that their children do not want to "follow in their footsteps." Their children want to travel. They want to live in the city. They want to go to the university. Some of them even want to leave Israel and emigrate.

I started having a series of conversations with the older people in which I would say, "Tell me about your parents. Were they farmers? Did they live on a kibbutz?" People would say things like, "Oh no. My father was a tailor in Poland. He lived in the city." Then I would ask how their parents felt when they became socialists and Zionists and came to Israel. In many cases the answer was, "They were appalled." Sometimes the answer was, "They were thrilled that I was doing something they never could have done."

What the parents I was talking to did not realize is that their children were indeed following in their footsteps. Their children were doing exactly as they had done: leaving the location, lifestyle, and convictions of their parents and going out to do something new in a new place.

The continuity and the discontinuity are at different logical levels in each of these examples. If you can be aware of those different levels simultaneously, it can give you an advantage in coping with your life. Otherwise, it may happen that when you are trying to achieve continuity, you actually create the opposite effect. You may be looking for continuity in the wrong place.

If you create continuity by freezing some superficial variable, the result, very often, is to create deep change. This is something my father used to talk about in relation to evolutionary theory. He used the example of a tightrope walker. The tightrope walker is walking along a high wire, carrying a very light bamboo rod. To keep his balance, he continually moves the rod. He keeps changing the angle of the rod to maintain a constancy, his balance in space. If you froze the rod, what would happen to him? He would fall off. In other words, the superficial variation has the function of maintaining the deeper continuity. In evolution, the deeper continuity is survival. For the tightrope walker, it's staying on the high wire.

I found an interesting example recently of a group of people who were able to maintain a deep continuity in their lives throughout many superficial changes. They were members of an order of Catholic nuns, between the ages of fifty-five and sixty-five, whom I was invited to address at a convention. They were all women who had joined the order before the reforms. When they joined, nuns lived in convents. They wore black habits and white headdresses. They never had friendships. They were told what to do in every way.

Then came the reform of the religious orders. It is well known that at that time many nuns left their orders. Some of them left because they felt there was too much change; others, because they felt there wasn't enough. But the interesting thing to me was the question of who stayed.

Among the people I talked to, it was clear to me that those who stayed were those who were able to ride the changes and to adapt. At some fundamental level, they were able to bridge all the superficial changes, and to say, "My commitment is the same commitment that brought me here in the first place." They were people with an extraordinary capacity to translate. The people who were fixated on the habit or the details of ritual couldn't stay when they lost those things.

It's worth giving some thought to what kinds of things deserve to be held steady and what kinds of things it's most adaptive to vary. I think you can argue that one way of looking at addiction is that the addict is trying to keep something steady, a certain level of intoxication, that is, in fact, producing profound and worsening change. An addiction is a constancy of the wrong kind.

When you are able to see multiple levels of change and consistency, you are empowered to make your own decisions. I think this is true of diversity in general. I want to offer one final example from my own life. People who have one famous, successful parent are often locked into the problem of whether or not they succeed in living up to the model of that person. One of the things I gained by having two famous and very different parents is the freedom to be myself.

For a long time, I thought that my interests had nothing to do with theirs. When I went to college, I was fascinated with linguistics. I read the work of Edward Sapir and Benjamin Whorf and decided that linguistics was going to be my life's work. Nobody had told me that linguistics as done by Whorf and Sapir is a branch of anthropology. So I walked, as a total innocent, into the family business. But I opened up a branch in a new neighborhood.

▼▼▼

Chapter 4

Science as Story

F. David Peat

Perhaps best known for his writing on chaos theory, physicist F. David Peat approaches the stories that science has to offer us with clarity and passion. The author of numerous books, including Synchronicity: The Bridge Between Matter and Mind *and* Turbulent Mirror: An Illustrated Guide to Chaos Theory and the Science of Wholeness *(the latter coauthored with John Briggs), Peat is one of those rare writers who is able to make complex scientific subject matter intelligible to a general audience. He has also lectured widely on numerous scientific topics.*

Though Peat has been a working physicist for many years, he still manages to communicate, in both lectures and essays, a genuine sense of awe at the way the universe fits together. Currently he is most interested in exploring the bridge between matter and consciousness and in studying Native American stories; both of these interests are reflected in the essay that follows.

My ideas about the importance of stories and storytelling are influenced by my encounters with Native Americans. In them I have found affirmation of my own intuition about science as story: that science is the creation of stories that interpret the interconnectedness of the universe.

A phrase that reflects this interconnectedness that my Native American friends use is "map in the head." Most of us think of a map as a road-map, a representation of territory. But the Native American "map in my head" is a place where people have experiences. It contains time because it holds events that happened in the past. It also contains the stories that people tell about the land.

Late one night I sat around a fire in Alberta, watching the northern lights and hearing people tell stories about that part of the country. Many of the stories that have been passed down about that land have to do with the figure of an old man, Napi, who was the Creator. Various aspects of the land are referred to in terms of their connection to that figure: the old man's elbow, the old man's chin, the place where the old man rested. When I heard the stories being told that night, it was as if the land was being re-created. The next day, when I walked through that landscape, I was living the story of the old man's life. I had acquired a "map in the head."

To me, that map is a metaphor for finding a place that connects chaos and order. It is a way of integrating meaning, of bringing things together. That map teaches us about space and time and sacredness; it tells us how to move through the world. Like a good story, it helps us make connections.

The aspect of science that interests me the most is that place where chaos and order are connected. On the one hand, there are the rigid structures of nineteenth-century physics, which are often limiting and mechanical because they block off certain possibilities. On the other hand, we have chaos, which can be very exciting but perhaps too unwieldy for your life to contain. I am interested in the place in which chaos and change are available but also contained: the place where what is popularly called "chaos theory" comes to life.

Before I get too far into the details of that theory, I would like to make one point. Some contemporary thinkers, such as Carl Sagan, look to science to confirm absolute truths. It is as if they say, "For ten thousand years we have lived by myths, by stories. Now truth can replace those myths."

I do not subscribe to that position. To me, science is story. Perhaps it has more power today than other, older stories in that it affects so much of how we operate in our environment. Those other stories are much more about containing meaning within a group, giving an order to behaving, to celebrating, to acknowledging spirits. But the belief in science as ultimate truth can result in too much confidence in our mental capacity, in our ability to manipulate the environment. I see tremendous danger if science isn't recognized for what it is: a beautiful story of incredible creativity.

Chaos theory began with Henri Poincaré, a French mathematician, physicist, and philosopher who was Einstein's contemporary. His discoveries took place in the field known as the "mechanics of closed systems." Classical scientists believed that in closed systems, such as solar systems, any random event that disturbed the system could only come from outside. Thus, Newtonian equations could accurately predict the patterns of rotation within a solar system. While theoretical physicists knew that slight corrections had to be made to those equations if the system involved more than two bodies, they still believed that those corrections could be made and that correct solutions to the equations could be approximated.

But Poincaré found that the approximations did not always work. While sometimes the addition of a third body to a given system would cause only a slight alteration in the orbits of the other two, there were cases in which one of the bodies would grow unpredictably erratic in its orbit and even escape the solar system altogether. There was nothing in Newtonian physics to account for that.

Imagine how potentially shocking this discovery was at the time. One of the great triumphs of physics up to that point had been the discovery of the beautiful regularity of solar systems. Suddenly Poincaré says, "Yes, but wait a minute. In the very heart of this is chaos. Shift something very slightly and the whole system can become chaotic. It may go on rotating for millennia, and then disrupt."

Historically, the shock of Poincaré's discovery was diluted because the theory of relativity came just a few years later. But in the 1950s, Poincaré's work was rediscovered and physicists again began to think about the forces that either keep a system orderly or contribute to its chaos.

Prior to that rediscovery, physicists had developed several ways of studying the order in any system. One way is through the observation of something called an attractor. The attractor is like a magnet in that it pulls the system toward it. To visualize an attractor, imagine a landscape with a valley surrounded by mountains. For a variety of reasons, objects tend to roll down the mountains and settle in the valley. If the landscape and all that it contains are a system, the valley is an attractor.

Another way to approach this concept is to think of people interacting in a group as an example of a system. If everyone is rather calm except for one man who is agitated and doing a lot of gesturing, the rest of the group will find ways to indicate that this is inappropriate. They will calm this person down and eventually he will begin to behave like the rest of them. The other members of the group are functioning as an attractor: a collection of things that interact to bring about some normalized behavior within the system.

The *limit cycle* is a more complex attractor. A good example can be found in many predator-prey relationships. Take, for instance, a lake that is stocked with trout and has only a few pike. The pike have a plentiful supply of food: lots of trout for them to eat. The pike flourish and breed, eating what seems like an unlimited supply of trout.

But after a while, the trout cannot breed fast enough to keep up with the numbers that are being killed by the pike, and the number of trout starts to decrease. The pike have to compete for food, and they begin to die off. The situation reaches a point where the number of pike is again quite low. Then the trout start to increase. The system oscillates, but it repeats the same pattern. This is called a limit cycle, and it is a kind of attractor.

There are also attractors that function in multidimensional ways. I can, for example, draw a doughnut in one, two, and three dimensions. Despite the changes in dimension, it is still a doughnut: It is still regular in its shape, still attracted to a particular order. I can draw it in four, five, or six dimensions; I can develop vortices within vortices, making the system more and more complex. But it still contains a regular attractor. The system is still being pulled back to a particular shape.

In each of the preceding examples, the systems themselves are fairly orderly. When I locate the attractor, I can predict to a large extent the behavior of the system. But in chaotic or turbulent systems, how do I predict behavior? This is where the discoveries of the last several years come into play.

In the example of the doughnut, I referred to the possibility of going from one to two to three to four dimensions, always maintaining an attractor. Lev Landau, a Russian Nobel laureate, theorized at one point that turbulence could be explained or defined by considering more and more dimensions. But to find the attractor in a turbulent system, those dimensions do not work.

What physicists have found is something called a *strange* attractor, which functions in between the second dimension and the third. That dimension is called the *fractal* dimension.

A fractal is a picture of a strange attractor. But a fractal cannot be understood by breaking it down into smaller parts and analyzing it. I can magnify and magnify a fractal, but at every stage I will see a replication of the whole. It contains, within itself, the shape of the whole system. I can look at an infinitely small section and the fractal will still be unceasing in its complexity and richness.

What the discovery of the fractal dimension entails is a whole new way of looking at turbulent systems. If the fractal is a picture of the strange attractor and the fractal cannot be broken down, then the strange attractor is infinitely complex. All of the other examples of attractors that I have discussed so far have varying degrees of complexity, but they are finite. Even a vortex within a vortex is finite, describable and understandable. But the fractal attractor tells me that the system's behavior is so complex that it can never be completely analyzed.

This contradicts the long-cherished assumption that scientists can arrive at the truth of a thing by analyzing it. Of course, that assumption is responsible for many discoveries. For example, we now know that it is possible to break down matter into molecules, atoms, elementary particles, and beyond. If I were to follow this way of thinking, the most beautiful and revealing mathematics would also be the mathematics of the most elementary level of the universe. It should be possible to discover, through that, how the Big Bang happened. If I could push through to that fundamental level, I could get to creation.

This is a very beautiful and seductive idea. Unfortunately, it does not apply to the fractal. I cannot get to the essence of a fractal by breaking it up. The truth of a fractal lies in how it was generated. The fractal is self-similar and self-generating. The ultimate truth behind it lies not in analysis of its smallest part but in a recognition of how the thing was generated, how it came into being.

That truth lies somewhere between chaos and order as those terms are commonly used. The chaos is, in a sense, contained; the fractal, however revolutionary in its revelations, is an attractor and lends a kind of shape to the system. But the fractal also represents a way in which science itself is admitting that it has a limit. There are places where our desire to manipulate, control, and predict the behavior of the universe cannot take us.

Before the birth of chaos theory, one of the most exceptional scientific minds of the twentieth century struggled with the limitations of physics. The Austrian physicist Wolfgang Pauli helped Werner Karl Heisenberg, German physicist and Nobel Prize winner, develop quantum theory and created the first theoretical interpretation of that theory. Pauli was so uncompromising that his colleagues called him "the whip of God." At twenty-one, he wrote a book-length review of the theory of relativity that inspired the admiration of Einstein.

But for all his intellectual sophistication, Pauli's personal life was a mess. He married a cabaret singer who left him after five weeks. He drank a lot and was physically thrown out of more than one bar. Finally, he went into therapy with C. G. Jung.

Therapy led Pauli to think about the study of physics in Jungian terms. Just as Jung posited a subjective and objective side to the unconscious, so Pauli began to think in terms of a subjective and objective side to matter. He said that while physics emphasized the rational, analytical side of the universe, it refused to recognize the subjective side. This disturbed him very deeply: that physics would not acknowledge the irrational in matter.

Now that there is great interest in chaos theory, Pauli's concerns have a new validity. There is almost an illusion, with this theory, that somehow science has triumphed over matter: We understand chaos. We can simulate it on a computer, we have equations for it, so in a sense there is nothing to be afraid of or mystified by anymore. But to me, what chaos theory can do is help us accept and connect with the undefinable and inexhaustible in the universe.

How can this scientific information—this story about our universe drawn from physicists and philosophers—provide humankind with useful images or metaphors that could lend a sense of cohesion to the direction we are taking? How can these discoveries, like any good story, offer us instruction, insight, and hope?

One message can be drawn from the process of discovering the fractal dimension itself. I referred earlier to Landau's theory that the way to analyze turbulence was to go into more and more dimensions. But the answer was to make a nonlinear jump, to move into the unexpected area in between the second and the third dimension. When we approach problems in our own lives, we often feel that our options for solutions are limited; we are locked into conventional, logical problem-solving. But we can look at the discovery of the fractal dimension as a metaphor for how we might approach problems in our own lives: by making a nonlinear jump.

Another metaphor for that nonlinear jump can be found in the poetry of Gerard Manley Hopkins. Hopkins uses the word *inscape* when referring to the way in which we can merge with the natural world—the way we can absorb and live with it, like a "map in the head." For him, inscape was infinite and unbounded. Hopkins writes: "And for all this, nature is never spent. There lives the dearest precious deep-down things." When I look at the universe in terms of chaos theory, I see an inexhaustibly rich and subtle image. What the discovery of the fractal dimension points to is the idea that nature is never spent, but is infinite.

My act of entering into the natural world exposes my own infinite creativity and subtlety. But I must remember that every atom, tree, and rock is inscape. If I see the landscape as outside myself, something to be controlled and analyzed, I may get a lot of useful technical information. But that kind of information is limited and empty without a sense of inscape.

Of course, many of the greatest physicists have realized this. Consider this quote from Heisenberg, written after the night he discovered quantum theory:

> I had the feeling that through the surface of phenomena, I was looking at a strange, beautiful interior and felt almost giddy at the thought that I now had to probe this wealth of mathematical structures nature had so generously spread out before me. I was far too excited to sleep and so, as the new day dawned, I made for the southern tip of the island, where I had been longing to climb a rock jutting out into the sea. I now did so without too much trouble and waited for the sun to rise.

We see that he had an extraordinary sense of working into the center, and of the mystery of everything he studied.

My perception is that, like the fractal, events, processes, objects, and people are all inexhaustible. A friend of mine, a gallery director, says that every day he is in a new dialogue with the painting that hangs over his desk. He never exhausts the painting; you can never exhaust another human being. Sometimes it is easy to believe that we can exhaust the rock, the tree, and the atom, and we can exhaust the thing called the human brain and the human body. We think we can come to the end of all that and can get the ultimate equation.

My Native American friends would argue against that idea by saying there are spirits in every natural thing, in the trees and in the rocks. I have to respect and acknowledge them as separate from myself; they are not an observer-created reality. All systems arise out of their own being, their own authenticity. The rock and the stone each have a voice, an authentic voice, just like the voice of a person who is an authentic person. That voice comes from their own being. It is not conditioned by or contingent upon everything else around them. The rock, the tree, the atom, the molecule—all have their own inner authenticity. Those of us who have lived lives of intellectual pursuit need to hear this. For all that theory, we need the balance of matter that a "map in the head" can give us. We need the stories of Mother Earth to keep us in balance.

▼▼

Chapter 5

Dream as Story

EDITH SULLWOLD

Edith Sullwold, Ph.D., is a Jungian therapist who teaches and supervises therapists in the United States, Europe, and Africa. Former director of the Children's Center at the C. G. Jung Institute of Los Angeles, and of Turning Point, a group for children with serious illnesses, she is best known for her work with the creative use of the imagination in therapy with children, adolescents, and adults.

Sullwold has also worked both personally and professionally with dreams for nearly thirty years. Whereas some might see dreams as merely chemical and/or electrical brain activity, Sullwold strongly believes that dreams are stories from one's psyche that carry a profound wisdom. Dreams, she explains, are like someone knocking on the door: "They are saying, 'I have something to tell you.'" Because the stories our dreams tell us are not always easily captured in rational thought, Sullwold encourages the use of creative, frequently nonverbal means—such as clay, paint, movement, and music—to explore them. In the following pages, Sullwold elaborates on the concept of dreams as important personal stories and offers specific suggestions for creating a relationship with them that will deepen and enrich the dreamer's life.

My view of dreams as stories comes from my own work with dreams over the last thirty years. During the time of my analysis and training, I spent some time in Zurich, where I heard many stories about Carl Jung. The following is one I particularly like because it confirms that dreams are ultimately a mystery.

It is said that a favorite student of Jung's went to visit him when he was in his eighties and living in a little tower on Lake Zurich. They went for a walk, and Jung began to tell him a dream. Jung would tell anybody his dreams: friends, students, the farmers who lived next door. He said that often their comments would give him some new insight that he couldn't reach himself; sometimes, people would say things that felt so wrong that he got a hint of what might be right. This student, as he was walking, listened to the dream very carefully. In great awe—as the students, of course, would have been of Jung—he said, "Oh, Dr. Jung, it must be so marvelous, having worked on dreams for so long and being the age you are, to be able to understand your own dreams." And Jung said angrily, "No, no! Don't you understand that your dream always remains a mystery, particularly to yourself?"

You see, you never know exactly what your dreams mean. You can't codify them into ordinary knowledge, but they have a kind of energy that brings tremendous vitality and, often, clarifying insight to your life. Our consciousness is limited. One function of a dream is to tell you something that is beyond consciousness. If you try to understand dreams with your ordinary, conscious mind, you'll never get those pieces which lie outside your awareness. This is why it is good to tell someone else your dream and to dance around the dream—that is, to find out something about it from all sides. One way to work with dreams is to work with associations. For example, if you have a dream about someone, does it remind you of somebody else, and what is that person like? Association is one way to dance around so that you get some sense of familiarity.

Another way is to look at what is symbolic in the dream. If you dream of a frog, is it a frog prince or an ordinary frog? A third way is to see the dream as a story, because dreams are inner dramas. I remember working with someone who brought in a stack of typewritten dreams and said, "These are my dreams." I thought, "Those aren't dreams. Those are like synopses of operas written down on a piece of paper; they are not the dreams."

A dream is an event that captures the body, the imagination, and the soul. That is, the senses record the experience in sound and sight, often accompanied by subtle movement of the body; the imagination provides the images, symbols, and story; and the psyche or soul activates the energy to produce the dream. A dream is also a dramatic event. The Greeks understood drama profoundly, so much so that the theater was central in all their major healing temples. They put on plays with exaggerated life situations that could reflect, in a more subtle way, the lives of the spectators. Everything in Greek theater was bigger than life. If you look at many of your dreams, they contain impossible happenings. But if you reflect back on them, perhaps they give you some insight into subtle aspects of your life that you are overlooking. To see them as drama, to see them as story, can be another way to begin to capture more of their significance in your life.

For example, you might look at your dreams in relation to aspects of a story, as you might look at a novel or short story. Where does it take place? Is the place familiar or unfamiliar? What is your feeling about the place? What about the characters? Who are they? They may not all be human; they may be images, animals, or some significant objects. And again, are they familiar or known to you, or are they unknown?

One way of working with the characters in a dream or a sequence of dreams is to think about them as main characters and extras. If you look at your life, you can remember those people who have been absolutely essential. There are those who have passed through—you may remember two or three out of your kinder-garten class—and the rest you wouldn't recognize any more. They're the backdrop. But essential characters have vitality and meaning in your life. If you dropped any of them out, your life would be quite different. So look at your dream and see those char-acters, objects, or images that have the same kind of essential qual-ity in relationship to you.

Some years ago in Switzerland I saw the opera *Aida*. I had seen it once in Italy in a huge outdoor field; to the great enthusiasm of the Italian music lovers, they brought in elephants. In Switzer-land, there were no elephants, just gold. Not only was the stage set gold, but all of the characters wore gold, all of them. And into this dazzling gold setting came Aida, dark and dressed in a bright blue dress. Her character so contrasted with the backdrop of the others that the audience was struck by her image. Very often in a dream, a character, image, or symbol will catch you that way. Those are the ones that you know are essential, are worth working on and per-haps befriending in a very deep way for the rest of your life.

Another thing to ask would be, what is the issue? What is the core of this drama? Is it a question, or perhaps a crisis, or some state of confusion? What is the juice of the drama? What motivates the story?

Then, just as you would look at a story, ask yourself what is hap-pening in the dream? How does the action develop? Look also at the ending, the resolution. Does the dream resolve itself? Is the question that has been asked answered? Or is the question still alive? Is the question one that needs to be asked continually?

If you look at your dreams and get used to living with them, you will see that they have a sequence. We are, after all, continu-ous beings, but sometimes dreams don't feel like that. A dream may have content that seems to have nothing to do with the dreams that preceded or followed it. Very often, however, a dream sequence will state the same issue or the same question in many different ways. The psyche is very kind. If you don't get something one way, it will show it to you another way, then another, and yet another. Very often a question is not answered, but each time it's asked it becomes more vivid and more alive to you, and perhaps more clear.

Most important is to ask about the meaning of a particular dream in your life. Why did you have it? What is it teaching you? Is it bringing new knowledge that expands your awareness of yourself? Something that gives the reason behind the dream? Is there a question it is asking about your life?

In a King Arthur legend there was an old king who was very ill and could only be healed when a knight asked the right question. Asking the right question in that story was essential to the old king's healing. You might look at that mythic story as a metaphor for dream work. The old king who rules the old kingdom would represent your old standpoint, your old way of being in the world. Asking the right question of your dream can wake you up to what you haven't paid attention to, to what is new, what is fresh, and what is being brought into your life that you haven't quite lived before. Asking the right question is essential to understanding your dreams.

Finally, it is important to integrate your dream stories and the information you get from them into your life. Otherwise, the dream is just a disconnected drama, which is not the psyche's intent. The psyche's intention is to heal. It tries to give you information that will allow you to live your life more fully and with more awareness.

For example, my husband had a dream in which an artist friend of ours—whose work has been shown in many galleries—had composed an opera. In the dream, my husband found himself on stage, singing a solo. Shortly after he had this dream, my husband was asked to display and talk about the paintings he had done for the preceding fifty years. Although his paintings, inspired by the inner world of images and dreams, had always been done only for his own reflection, the dream made it clear to him that this work was now to be "on stage," exposing to an audience his part in the opera of life. He accepted this invitation to "sing a solo."

In this example, the integration of the dream into the dreamer's waking life came quickly. Sometimes such integration may not come for years. If you read Jung's autobiography, you will see that some striking dreams he had when he was small—as young as five—were still working in him in his old age. You might have powerful dreams that stay with you, and only later can you say, "Oh, that's what that is about." It doesn't mean the dream hasn't affected you in that period of time, but perhaps the confirmation in your life doesn't come clear until some time later. As you get older and have much more of a story to look back on, more of your life begins to make sense. "Oh, that's why that happened!" "Oh, that's why I made that choice!" There's a weaving together that begins to give your life—both inner and outer—some cohesive meaning.

I'll give you an example from my own dream life. At the time I had this dream, I was working with Mary Whitehouse, who was one of the founders of the dance therapy movement and a close friend. It was a very important time in my life. Until that period, I thought the only reason to have a body was to hold my head up. Working with my body was a very moving and profound experience for me. It brought out creativity that had not been alive before.

IN THE DREAM, I went to my lesson with Mary. There were two other students there. Mary took us all down to an open area at the bottom of a hill to dance. When we got to the bottom, we sat on benches and watched some monkeys that were separated by a fence from people who sat in the seats. We watched them, especially a green one on the left who was wrapping his arms around himself and twirling. My husband was sitting next to me. We began to talk to the monkey and were surprised when he began to talk to us.

Now, LET'S LOOK at the dream aspects I referred to before. The setting consisted of being with a very dear friend of mine who helped to reconnect me to my body and for whose work I had tremendous respect. That was familiar. However, I had always danced alone with her, not publicly. In this setting, there were two other women dancers and we were in a public arena. The unfamiliarity was that there was something of a performance about the work that had not been there before. It might be that some insight I would have in this unfamiliar setting would be applicable not only to me but also to a larger collective.

When we actually got to the arena, it turned out that it wasn't the dancers who performed but the monkeys. We were thus not an active part of the drama but passively watching unfamiliar figures who were perhaps there to teach us something. The monkeys were behind a fence in this dream, a fence that perhaps indicated the barrier between the familiar and the unfamiliar—the consciously known and the new material from the unconscious.

The greatest surprise, of course, came in the character of the monkey who talked. He was clearly the spokesman for the unknown, the one with the new lesson. He was the predominant character in this dream, the "Aida" of the drama. My husband's presence there was very important because he believes that animals know exactly what you say to them and can communicate, so he appeared in the dream as someone who really understood that it was possible.

Beginning with my husband's understanding and led by my own curiosity about what the monkey said, and wondering why a monkey should come into my dream-story, I decided to ask the monkey himself. I began by writing a dialogue between us, a written conversation of the sort that Jung describes as "active imagination."

I: What is it that you have to say?

Monkey: To play, to twirl, to spin, this is the way.

I: But play? Isn't it work that's needed?

Monkey: To really play would be work for you. It is letting go in the head, letting the inside spin you outside, letting the center take over and tumble you. Just let the outer extremities follow. Just do it, let go.

I: But, monkey, I have two other questions. Why do you have no neck? And what are you doing in the tree?

Monkey: No neck. Of course that would interest you. I have none because I am still so much in nature, and there hasn't been a split between my head and my body. You see, I don't need to turn my head around so much to locate myself. Look at me now in the tree holding on with arms and legs and tail. I can see very well from this spot in the tree, of course, and the moon is in my favor tonight.

This kind of communication with the monkey—about how to be in the body; how to play, to move, to be more free—had been very much inspired by my work with Mary Whitehouse. But the monkey reinforced the sense of the absolute animal naturalness of this connection with physical agility and form. He was the exaggeration of this point of view, the kind of exaggeration the Greeks played with in their dramas. And the message was collective, because I was not—am not—alone in disconnecting my natural relationship to the body from my mind and soul. It is still a collective issue. But the monkey also gave me a lesson not only about my physical body but about my spirit, which needed to move more from the inside out, a hint of which was in his statement about the moon. I still had curiosity about that statement, but sometimes it is good to let some aspects of the dream remain a mystery until they want to show themselves.

I wanted to record the visual image of the dream-monkey, so I drew him as he had appeared in my dream, in a tree against the moon. A week later, I made another drawing because I wanted to see him again. In this drawing, the monkey was sitting on a rock near a pond reading a book. This drawing turned into a story that I wrote down. The monkey had gone into the pond and, under some rocks, found a box of old manuscripts. Some of them were very wet and rotten. But he brought the manuscripts back up and began to read to me from them. This is part of what he read:

> Monkey: I'll take up the second sheet now. It's yellow and wrinkled, as though someone wanted to throw it away but changed his mind. It says,
>
> > Beware of the sun, behold the moon.
> > Behold the moon in the darkness.
> > This darkness brings light.
> > Pure light is too bright and flattens the image.
> > The moon gives depth and dimension to life.
>
> I: What meaning does this have?
>
> Monkey: I think you understand most of this, at least on the surface. The dark is the unconscious, the moon is the feminine which lights it. Being incompletely lit, there is something unknown, at least unknowable in terms of mind. The logic of intellect will flatten because it leaves out that which is mysterious. What I think you may not understand is the other quality, the darkness. Besides its soft enfolding, intimate quality, which is so feminine, there's also a quality of danger in the blackness; hidden

things lurk in the corners. This blackness in you, which
needs the illumination of the moon, is something you
have not come to terms with yet.

Here, the monkey was not just teaching me of my body, but
about the feminine aspect of spirit represented by the soft light of
the moon, by the darkness of night, and by the mysteries of the unknown.

As I have grown older—some thirty years have passed since the
dream—remnants of the issues of this dream still remain. For example, sometimes tension appears in my neck, reminding me of a
disconnection with my own natural physicality; then I remember
my friend the monkey, a teacher of "no-neck," comfortable in his
tree with arms, legs, and tail, and I laugh and relax. And often, in
the full moon, I see not the "old man" in the moon but the face of
the monkey, speaking to me as a friendly companion, reminding
me of the softness of the moonlight—not the bright sunlight of intellect—and the subtlety of the imagination that speaks in the
quiet of the night.

IF YOU WANT to work with your own dreams like this,
there are many ways to approach them. You can spend time writing about your dream, or writing dialogue with some of the characters. You can continue the dream in a story. You can draw an
illustration of it, or make something out of clay.

I suggest, however, that you don't try to do it all in one sitting.
If the dream figure is full of energy, it's like having a new friend.
When you have a new friend, you don't just say, "Let's have a cup
of tea. Good-bye." You stay with her or him for a long time, and
you do different things together.

Writing the story of your dream can allow you to have a deep
conversation with something unknown. Write a dialogue, as if
you were writing a play or a novel. When you write in that

way—novelists and playwrights often talk about this—you can develop the characters to a point where they take over. You no longer have control of them. For maybe the first ten minutes, it feels like you're making it up, but all of a sudden something happens and you are much more of a witness to the voices that are speaking.

When you dialogue with figures from the dream, it is important that you and the figures be in equal partnership. In other words, don't just listen passively to the figure. Question it, challenge it, say, "I don't think so." The unconscious and your conscious mind should be in a real relationship. When you do this, a very amazing thing happens. The barrier between the two begins to drop; you begin to have two friends, both aspects of yourself, talking to each other.

In a significant passage on dialogue, Jung says that unless the conscious mind and the unconscious learn to dialogue with equality and respect, we probably will not learn to do that person to person, group to group, or nation to nation. The psyche is your training ground to give an equal voice to both the inner unconscious knowledge and to the knowledge that your consciousness already has.

Another way of working with dream as story is not only to write it but also to illustrate it, on paper or in sculpture. One of the things that's very important, I think, in drawing, painting, or working with clay, is to forget what happened to you in kindergarten. Back then, if your painting went up on the wall, you were described as an artist, and you had to be a good artist. If your painting didn't go up, then you weren't an artist. In this way in our culture, we stop ourselves early on. In artistically rendering the dream, I am not referring to what I call gallery art; I am referring to an expression of yourself.

Drawing or sculpting a dream is a very powerful way to bring solidity to the images. But often, by the time you draw the dream image, it has already moved on. What happens is something like what happened to me. In my second drawing, I drew not the actual image of the monkey in the dream but the monkey doing something else. In that way, I continued the story.

I call this work second-chaptering. The dream is the first chapter, and then you second-chapter it either in drawing, writing, or perhaps even dancing it. Jung said it beautifully: "Often the hands will solve a mystery that the intellect has struggled with in vain."

Whether it uses the hands, body, or poetic voice, the imagination wants to move the story onward, giving us the second or third acts of our personal drama. This desire of the imagination, combined with the creative energy behind it, leads to surprises and new solutions, which we could not have found through rational, intellectual problem-solving.

Practically, you can continue a dream in several ways in a waking state. For example, if in a dream you miss a train, you can second-chapter the dream by imagining what you would do and writing that down in story form. Or, if you were to paint a scene from the dream, you might discover that some new element wants to emerge in the painting that was not in the dream, leading the story onward.

Sometimes you find figures in your dream stories that you don't particularly like. This happens frequently, and it's important to also pay attention to these figures because they can bring something new and essential to your life. However, you may have frightening dreams in which there is a force that feels very powerfully negative. In those cases, it may not be appropriate for the ego to deal with that force or those figures directly.

My metaphor for that is, if you meet a snake on the path, you don't go up and shake hands with it. In dream work, if you encounter a powerful, frightening, and perhaps very negative force, bring in, through your imagination, another equally powerful balancing force. The snake, for example, is often balanced by the eagle in medieval paintings, which display an understanding of the balance of two equally powerful figures. You see other examples of this balance of forces in Buddhist iconography, where you have both wrathful deities and benevolent deities. You have both sides. In certain aspects of Christianity, you have the devil and you have Christ.

In all of these examples, you have a balancing that is not just from the ego. This is very important to pay attention to because it can be very overpowering to deal with negative forces only with the ego.

You also see this in fairy tales and myths. Red Riding Hood could not deal with the wolf by herself. She could have been swallowed by it; she needed the woodsman to rescue her with his axe. In doing this kind of work with dreams, especially in dialoguing, we may need to summon the "woodsman" to deal with the "wolf."

Many people ask how they can develop the capacity to remember their dreams. First, you can set a clear intention when you go to sleep. You can say to yourself, "I really want to catch the dream in the morning." That can be quite effective, as is having paper and pencil near you so you can capture the dream immediately. Again, it is about the amount of attention you give to that realm. If you put a certain amount of energy into your relationship with dreams—working with them, trying to integrate them into your life—the psyche will respond to your friendship. As I have said before, the psyche is there to help you. Once it finds out that you've plugged in the telephone, it'll start calling you up, giving you the latest chapter of your life story.

The whole point of working with dreams is to effect change in our lives in a very real way. Otherwise, it is just an intellectual exercise or fantasy. The point of integrating your dreams into your life is to do some healing, and to expand your awareness of who you are and what your place is in the world. Joseph Campbell had a marvelous word for this work: He called it "shape-shifting." That means that you and your perceptions don't have to stay stuck. That is what the dream wants to do—to move things around in your life, to give you the insight and courage to become more fully humane in the service of the world.

▼▼

Chapter 6

Story as Medicine

CLARISSA PINKOLA ESTÉS

Author of the best-selling Women Who Run with the Wolves: Myths and Stories of the Wild Woman Archetype, *Clarissa Pinkola Estés has traveled the country telling and interpreting stories that celebrate the Feminine. In both her spoken and her written work, Estés's mission is to help contemporary women recover the* Wild Woman *within—a natural creature filled with passion and creativity, whose wisdom instructs, protects, and heals. Her approach combines a knowledge of Jungian psychology and traditional storytelling with an unsentimental view of the predicaments that many women face; her insights into the* Wild Woman *archetype are both beautiful and useful.*

A senior Jungian analyst and former director of the C. G. Jung Institute in Denver, Colorado, Estés is cantadora *(keeper of the stories) for the state of Colorado and has produced numerous audiotapes of her storytelling; a new book,* When This Tree Has Stood Many Winters: Myths and Stories of the Dangerous Woman and the Power of Age, *is due out in* 1994. *A portion of the following essay previously appeared in* Women Who Run with the Wolves.

Whenever a fairy tale is told, it becomes night. No matter where the dwelling, no matter the time, no matter the season, the telling of tales causes a starry sky and a white moon to creep from the eaves and hover over the heads of the listeners. Sometimes, by the end of the tale, the chamber is filled with daybreak, other times a star shard is left behind, sometimes a ragged thread of storm sky. Whatever is left behind is our bounty to work with, to use toward soul-making.

The time for story is most often dictated by inner sensibilities and outer need. Some traditions set aside specific times for telling stories. Among the pueblo tribes, Coyote stories are reserved for winter telling. Certain tales of Eastern Europe are told only in autumn after harvest. In archetypal and healing work, we weigh when to tell stories. We carefully consider the time, the place, the person, the medicine needed. But most often, even these measurements are frail. For the most part, we tell stories when we are summoned by them, and not vice versa.

In my traditions there is a storyteller legacy, wherein one storyteller hands down his or her stories to a group of "seeds." "Seeds" are tellers who the master hopes will carry on the tradition as they learned it. How the "seeds" are chosen is a mysterious process that defies exact definition for it is not based on a set of rules, but rather on relationship. People choose one another, sometimes they come to us unbidden, but more often we stumble over each other, and both recognize the other as though over eons.

In this tradition, the best stories, the deepest medicines, are considered to be written like a light tattoo on the skin of the one who has lived them. The training of *curanderas, cantadoras,* and *cuentistas* is very similar. It comes from the reading of this faint writing upon the soul, from the development of what is found there. Story as medicine is different from story told for amusement only. Story as medicine drums itself up through the teller's bones. It comes fluttering through the dark unbidden. No gold lies above ground. It is all mined in the farther reaches of psyche. It is toiled toward, not picked up. It is lived, not memorized.

Also in the *cantadora/cuentista* tradition, there are parents and grandparents and sometimes godparents of a story. These are the persons who taught the story to you, or gifted you with it (the mother or father of the story), and the person who taught it to the person who taught it to you (the grandparent of the story). The crediting of the tale is very important, for it is the genealogical umbilicus; we are on one end, the placenta of the vast Self is on the other.

The godparents of the tale are usually those who gave a blessing along with the tale. A blessing constitutes a kinship relationship, a kind of lifetime co-consult on story as medicine, as well as ongoing discussions of preparation, placement, and purification of the teller in all conceivable instances.

Because learning to apply story as medicine implies a familial relationship down through a story's ancestral lines, it sometimes takes a long time to tell the genealogy of the story before we come to the story proper. This listing of the mother of the story and grandmother of the story is not a long, boring preamble, but spiced with small stories about the forebears themselves. The longer story that follows is then like a second course.

Storytelling is bringing up, hauling up; it is not an idle practice. Though there are story trades, wherein two people exchange stories as a gift to one another, for the most part they have come to know each other well; they have developed, if they are not born to it, a kinship or devoted relationship. And this is as it should be.

Although some use stories as entertainment only, they are in their oldest sense, a healing art. Some are called to this healing art, and the best, to my lights, are those who have lain with the story and found all its matching parts inside themselves and at depth.

They have innate and uncanny knowing about how to identify the medicine, how to gather the medicine, how to mix it, apply it, replenish it at intervals, and when to cease.

In dealing with stories, we are handling archetypal energy. Archetypes change us; if there is no change, there has been no real contact with the archetype. Archetypal energy conscripts the handler, requires some psychic shielding, and oftentimes dictates rest afterward. Therefore, the handing down of story is a very big responsibility. In the best tellers I know, the stories grow out of their lives like roots grow out of trees.

Sometimes a stranger asks me for one of the stories I've mined and shaped over the years. As the keeper of these stories, I can give them or not. It depends on no five-point plan, but rather on a science of soul, depending on the day and the relationship. The mater-apprentice model is the kind of careful atmosphere in which I have been able to help my learner-apprentices seek and develop the stories that will accept them, that will shine through them, not just lie on the surface of their being like dime-store jewelry.

Stories, particularly healing stories, depend on the amount of self—the gristle, blood, and bone—that the teller is willing to put into them. Not all story is medicine. Generally, a story is not medicine unless it has caused the teller to laugh or weep. It is not medicine unless it causes the teller to feel suddenly stabbed or invigorated with some odd fiery notion, unless it forces from them a spontaneous roar of recognition, or a long cry of angst. It is not medicine unless it causes the teller to feel the familiar thump of a set of words, sounds, or images dropping down into or piercing his or her own psychic trove, and thereby watering or flooding or satiating in a way she or he has been yearning for.

In the *cantadora* tradition of storytelling, as in the *mesemondók* tradition, there is also what is called *La Invitada*, "the guest" or the empty chair, who is present at every telling. Sometimes during a telling, the soul of one or more of the audience comes and sits there, for it has a need. Although I may have planned a whole evening of considered material, I often change it to mend or play with the spirit that comes to the empty chair. "The guest" always speaks for the needs of all.

I encourage people to do their own mining of story, for the scraped knuckles, the sleeping on cold ground, the groping in the dark, and the adventures on the way are worth everything. There must be a little spilled blood on every story if it is to carry the medicine. If *La Destina*, Destiny, smiles upon you and brings you a true teacher who helps you to learn the medicines and telling ways that are unique to you, so much the better.

My own approach to soul-making was shaped by the storytelling traditions with which I grew up. Mexican and Spanish by blood, and later adopted by a fiery family of Hungarian immigrants, I am Latina by nature and Magyar by nurture.

In both my families, the older women are the keepers of the teaching stories. These they relate to the young girls at significant times, as well as during their hours spent together in work. Story is the way in which mature women pass on information abut women's inner and outer lives to their nieces, daughters, and granddaughters.

When I neared twelve years of age, one of my aunts, Kathe, gave me the tale of Bluebeard. In this story, the French and Slavic versions are mingled. As she used to say, "To be on the safe side, a teller must always know four versions of each tale: one for the mind, one for the spirit, one for the soul, and a cleaned-up version for the visiting priest." This is *not* a cleaned-up version.

OFF IN THE White Mountains, not far from here, there is a convent almost no one knows about. In that stone catacomb, the nuns keep a relic, a hank of hair that, when held up to the light in a certain way, reveals a cruel blue cast. No one knows how the nuns came to possess that hank of hair, but it is said it was cut from the dead body of a failed sorcerer. I know someone, an old woman from our village, who has seen it, and so it must be true that a long time ago there was indeed a man named Bluebeard.

Bluebeard courted three sisters. When he first visited, the two older sisters remarked, "He just does not look right, for in certain lights, his beard seems blue." The youngest sister simply said, "I am frightened of him."

But one day Bluebeard came to them leading horses dressed out in bells and long red ribbons, and he took the mother and all three sisters riding in the wood. There is not a woman alive who does not wish to ride upon a horse bedecked with bells and ribbons. The small band stopped under a great spreading tree. There they consumed a beautiful repast Bluebeard had prepared himself. He hand-fed the daintiest of treats to each woman. There is not a woman alive who does not want to be hand-fed treats. They all had a wonderful and tender time.

After Bluebeard rode home again, the two older sisters said, "Well, he is perhaps not as odd as we thought, but still, he does have that bluish beard."

The youngest sister said, "He was very kind to me. It seems to me that his beard is not really all *that* blue."

Shrewdly, the next time Bluebeard called, he asked for the youngest sister's hand in marriage. She consented and when her mother asked, "Are you certain you desire to do this in truth?" and "What about his blue beard?" her daughter replied, "His beard is not really *that* blue."

So the couple was wed, and they journeyed to Bluebeard's castle in the forest. One day he informed her he must go away for a while. "While I'm gone," he said, "you have my permission to bring your sisters here to keep you company. Here are all my keys. You may open any of the doors in the castle, and you may do whatever you like with whatever you find. But see this one tiny key with scrollwork on top? Do not use that one." His wife agreed and sent for her sisters right away.

The next day, she and her sisters began to explore the castle. There were one hundred doors in each wing. They unlocked each door and when they threw them open, behind they found stores of money, food, weapons, and clothing—everything one could imagine. They danced from room to room enjoying themselves very much; unfurling bolts of silk, sifting through handfuls of glass beads, staring in awe at piles of spindles and brooms. They continued until they had used all the keys except for the tiny one with the scrollwork on top.

"Let us find the door for this last key," they agreed. They passed through the entire castle once more, trying the key in each door. At last, they descended into the cellar and saw a small door there that was just closing.

They put the key into the lock and turned it. The door opened into a room too dark to see into. So they lit a candle and held it inside the room. There lay dozens of decapitated women—their blood thick on the floor, their hair thrown into piles in one corner, and their skulls piled like apples in another.

The sisters cried out, slammed the door shut, and leaned against each other, breathing and sobbing. They shook the little key out of the lock. The key was covered in blood. The sisters tried pressing upon the key with their fingers. But it was to no avail, for the little key continued to bleed drop after drop of dark red blood. The youngest sister put the key into her pocket and ran to the castle kitchen—by the time she arrived, her dress was stained with blood from waist to hem. She covered the key with spider web to try to staunch the blood, but the key continued to bleed. She scrubbed it with ashes, but still the key bled. She held it into the fire to sear its wound closed, but still the key wept its bright red blood. The key would not cease its bleeding.

Her thoughts were those of a desperate woman. "I shall hide it in my wardrobe then," she thought. "No one will ever find it and that will be the end of it." She raced to her chamber, threw open her wardrobe, and placed the key far back on the top shelf. She shut the door and leaned against it.

Just then, the sound of Bluebeard's return was heard. He entered into her chamber. "Well, wife, how was it while I was away?" he asked. "All was well," she replied.

"And how are all my storerooms?" Bluebeard peered at her. "They are very fine," she replied. "Then you'd best return my keys," said Bluebeard, looking strangely excited.

And no sooner had the keys passed from her small hand to his great one than he exclaimed, "Something is missing here. Where is the smallest key?"

She made up a story and said that while she and her sisters were riding, the key ring fell from her sash, and that when she picked it up, the littlest key was missing. Though she had searched and searched in the forest, she could not find that key.

Bluebeard reached out to her as though to caress her cheek, and she thought for a moment that she was safe. But instead he seized her hair and dragged her toward the cellar, bellowing, "You have betrayed me, and for that, you die!"

He pulled her down, down, down into the dark and dank basement. The door to the killing room opened at his command. She held onto the door frame, pleading, "Please, let me make my peace with my God. Just a quarter hour before you take my life!" Something in him relented, and he agreed.

She ran upstairs to her chamber, posted her sisters on the ramparts, and knelt to pray. Soon she called out, "Sisters, do you see our brothers coming?" They cried down, "We see nothing." She prayed some more and called up again to her sisters, "Do you see our brothers coming?" They replied, "We see a whirlwind of dust off in the distance." She cried out one last time, "Sisters, my sisters, do you see our brothers coming?" "Yes," they chorused, "they have just entered the castle on horseback."

At that moment Bluebeard thundered into her chamber and took her into his arms, not to love her, but to strangle her. Just then, her brothers burst into the room. They tore her out of his arms, routed Bluebeard onto the ramparts, and there with swords and daggers, they slashed him to pieces and left him for the carrion.

IF WE UNDERSTAND each character in a tale as representing an element within a single woman's psyche, we can learn a good deal about women's lives and women's choices. Like dreams, fairy tales have personal, collective, and archetypal meanings. Interpretation of fairy tales and myths is most closely aligned with analysis of dreams. Interpretation is an artful medicine, a form requiring a touch of the *taltos*, the wandering stranger, and much *curanderisma*, the healer's inner sight.

Bluebeard represents a force that can be called the *natural predator*. When we observe a noticeable depletion within the psyche, it most often emanates from an oppositional force within us that wishes to capture us, force us down, dismantle our drives, our desires, our inner lives, our implementations and follow-throughs. Freud called this psychic urge that is set upon the ruin of oneself or of another, the "death wish." However, he did not concretely expand the principle. In reality, the lack of knowledge about the psyche's natural predator is an enormous stumbling block in many women's lives.

Let us understand this more closely. All humans are born with a potential for a nay-saying function within their psyches. Jung called these *complex nodes* and regarded them as present at birth. When a person's outer life is disturbed in a major way, the potential of the natural predator node increases, fills out, and begins to act as a fragmentary but powerful force of the psyche.

So, if a woman has had a difficult upbringing—if she has had emotional, spiritual, or physical trauma in her life—assaults to inner, creative, or active life—these cause the once-potential-but-now-real predator to manifest itself as a loud and brittle critic, an accuser and ambusher within the psyche. Thereafter, each time a woman attempts to achieve a hope or a dream, each time she strives for something new, the natural predator—now grown large—will attempt to defeat her by both disparaging her and wreaking havoc with her plans.

When women are involved in projects or commitments that are not good for them, they are being lured by their own internal predator, enticed into some sort of mess. The internal predator can attack any area of a woman's life. It might say, "You cannot write a book, create an artwork, begin or complete a dream," causing the writer to stop writing, the artist to never begin. It might say, "You cannot have a lover because there aren't any decent ones," or "You cannot use your money to enrich your environ or mind or body because you have already committed yourself to a house, car, and charge card."

As you can see, the predator is insidious but not very subtle. If your instincts are intact, you can overrule its snicker-snackering in your mind. Women need intuition intact to recognize the predator, the psyche's Bluebeard. In the story, the two older sisters recognize immediately that something is not quite right about that bluish beard. The youngest sister is frightened at first, but she overrides her intuition because of the pleasure she feels in his company. Women tend to overlook their intuition if they believe there is pleasure or some sort of gain on the other side. The youngest sister in this story embodies this tendency.

The youngest sister also represents that part of our psyches that wishes to believe the best of everyone. To do this, she denies the reality of the situation; she denies that his beard is blue. As women, we have spent years resolving difficult situations that came about because, for just a moment, we said something wasn't what it really was. Whether you are a woman-loving woman, a man-loving woman, and/or a God-loving woman, it is almost a chronic and devastating rite of passage in our culture to say "yes" to the wrong man, woman, idea, or direction.

It is significant that it is the youngest sister who overrides her intuition with hopefulness. We all begin life ready to believe the best of everyone. But some of us maintain that quality into adulthood, often because we believe we are somehow made more spiritually pure by cleaving to such an ideal. But there is nothing "pure" about continuing to expect the best from a given situation or person despite massive evidence to the contrary. It is, in fact, very painful to continue to allow the natural predator in the psyche to trample our knowledge. Even if we believe we can stand the pain—that we can, in a sense, afford to keep paying for our mistakes in judgment—we would be well reminded that we may be hurting others as well. Every time we are wounded by continuing to act from the youngest sister's frame of mind, the people who love us are hurt also. After all, they have to take care of us, giving advice that, as long as we stay in the youngest sister's pattern, we will not heed.

The older sisters in this tale represent that part of the psyche that really does know better. This is something that we women need to repeatedly tell ourselves: We *do* know better. The mother in this story is not much help to the youngest daughter, but the older sisters are really quite wise. They do not overlook that blue beard. They are not misled by the natural predator. They do not believe that something is what it is not; they trust their instincts.

The room in the cellar is also representative of an aspect of women's psyches. Behind all other doors in the castle there are great treasures. But behind that small hidden door there is a horrible secret. What lurks behind the door is the woman's dead life; the pieces of her soul that have been cut away, thrown away. The natural predator of the psyche is planning to sever another part of the woman's life through its predation of the youngest sister.

The woman who is not at home in her instinctive nature must discover how to avoid this killing ground. She must stop the internal predator from killing off her ideas, her creativity, her poetry. This tale makes reference to ancient healers' remedies in the use of cobweb, ashes, and fire in efforts to staunch the bleeding of the key. These are all methods once utilized to heal wounds. One might say that for this kind of bleeding, the usual palliatives are not effective.

And this key that should open a woman's life to riches, treasure, to the divine—this key is bleeding to death. It reminds me of all the women I have known whose spirits are truly bleeding to death. No matter what remedies they seek, no matter who their friends are, no matter if they have a new lover, they cannot heal the wound with external palliatives. The solution for the bleeding key is to reduce the natural predator in the psyche to a size one can control at will. This is done by reclaiming intuition and acting upon it.

In our culture, there has been a breakdown in the handing down of knowledge through the matrilineal lines. The important healing stories that should be passed from mother to daughter— stories that teach us how to contain the natural predator, how to keep that cellar free of dead women, how to cause something to grow in the room meant for incubation instead of murder—have been lost. Without the instruction these stories provide, women too often lose touch with their instinctual and intellectual lives; they become buried beneath what we think we should feel and what we think we should want. The calling up and revivifying of cohesive instinct is the first step in our initiation, our soulful education.

Women's instinctive nature is embodied by the Wild Woman archetype. What stands behind this archetype is almost too big to put a name on, but it urges the complete integration of female soul into waking life. I think of wolves as the model for this archetype because they are among the most cohesively integrated creatures on the face of the earth. In the wild, wolves live completely within their own cycles—their sexual, hunting, play, sleep, roving, and nurturing cycles. When captive, wolves, like women, become depressed, their hair falls out, they become wan, they have trouble reproducing. This is the same for women: When the wild nature within is not fed, not allowed to manifest itself, all else loses luster and falls to dust and bones.

I am using the word *wild*, not in its pejorative sense, as in "out of control," but in its original meaning, "to be natural." Women can reclaim their original self-protective instincts by noting how wolves defend themselves in potentially threatening situations. Wolves do not just leap for the kill unless it is clearly and instantly warranted. First, they prick up their ears. They look as if they are asking, "What is this? Is there harm here?" All intuition, memory, and instinct come to bear in that moment. Next they show their incisors to whomever is troubling them.

Then, if the other creature continues to advance, the wolf growls. If the creature continues forward, the wolf may bark, growl some more, show more teeth. Its ears will point downward, its brow will furrow, its tail will be down, as if to convey, "I mean it, you had best back off."

Next, depending on many circumstances, including how big the other creature is, the wolf will either flee—because to flee can be noble, believe me—or fight with the other, not necessarily to kill, but to wound it, weaken it. The all-out last resource is to go for the kill.

Women need to use these increments psychically when dealing with psychological and spiritual threat. We particularly need to remember that first step—to call upon our intuition, to heed what we discover. If we skip this measure, we will be lost and for a long, long time. The resetting of instinct via intuition is one of the most important things women can do in service of a cohesive nature.

The Bluebeard story shows us what can occur when this initiation into the instinctive nature does not take place properly. Once we begin to recognize the internal predator for what it is, we can begin to find ways to contain or control it.

Some people are uncomfortable with the fact that it is the brothers who rout Bluebeard; they feel that once again the masculine is taking care of everything for the feminine, and that perhaps it would be better to have a feminine element that could destroy the predator. Actually, the gender does not matter here. The presence of muscle in the psyche, a force that is willing to defend the harmony of the psyche is what is important. It does not matter to which image it is attached.

One of the most essential facets of fairy tale interpretation is that the feminine and masculine components within the psyche are not the same as "woman" and "man" in the outer culture. Jung proposed that a woman's psyche is at least one-quarter masculine, and a man's psyche is at least one-quarter feminine. I think there are many ways of combining these two hues.

Regardless, for a woman, masculine energy can be understood as a bridge between the inner and outer worlds. It can be understood as the catalyst for work initiated, the cathexis for ideas made manifest. Except for those stories about giantesses and ogresses, almost all fairy tales characterize psychic muscle with male figures. I feel that a woman, to be fully developed in her instinctive nature, has to have the ability to manifest something in the world. Otherwise, she is always on the receptor/receptacle end; she has many ideas that are never born, lots of thoughts and feelings that never find their way out of her skull or her gut.

So we can interpret the brothers in this tale, not as "men," but as the energy in the female psyche that takes action, that can act to contain and dismember the Bluebeardian dissembler. Reducing the predator, the Bluebeard, to something containable and manageable is the second initiation of the wildish woman. The third is to become attuned to the cycles of life and death, to know when things must die and when they must live, to know the difference and to be able to follow through with each.

When I was a little girl, I saw a wolf mother kill one of her pups. The pup had fallen into a fight with a larger animal and was terribly destroyed; nothing could have saved it. The she-wolf picked up the pup by the web of its neck and hit it against the trunk of a tree. As a child I felt deep sorrow but was somehow not irreparably wounded. I knew instinctively that the pup could not survive. There is a time to let go of even the things that are most precious to you—segments of your life, your feelings, affiliations, old and new relationships, ideas and affinities. Sometimes you simply outgrow them. In either case, they no longer serve you. They prevent life from going forward in any bountiful or useful manner. At an entirely different level, in creating art, always some is thrown away to make the image, the piece, the message grow stronger. There is an old Hebrew saying from the great Rebbe Israel: "Any fool can write. It takes a visionary to erase." An integral and cyclical life requires that some aspects always be let to die, some breathed into life.

Rollna, a compañera of mine (between us, we have five daughters), once said that no woman had a right to remain naive past the age of twelve. At first, this idea made me squint and make a mouth. But then, I realized that a woman who maintains a studied naiveté can never have a real life. She can never have depth and breadth. She is a woman who stands without shadow, without color, without light.

I believe that "not knowing" is something we women must learn to relinquish voluntarily, guided by those who have gone before us. Otherwise we remain locked in our youngest sister mindset, vulnerable and ready to be deceived, dismembered in a wholly destructive manner, killed without resurrection following; Osiris scattered without an Isis nearby, or, as I first heard from Jungian analyst and author Jean Shinoda Bolen, "Good Friday without Easter Sunday following."

Although there is much, much more to the exposition of this tale, I leave you with this: One of the most significant elements of the Bluebeard tale is that the youngest sister must be able to remember what she sees in the cellar, to hold it in consciousness. Initially, she tries to remain imperceptive, herself half-dead-while-alive. She hides the key in the closet and says, "I saw nothing." But retrieval of instinct dictates that the sight of the dead in the cellar be held attentively, that the question of what has been intrusively killed off in our own vital lives be asked aloud and answered specifically and deeply, that we intentionally remember the painful things that happen to us so we can do something about them, that remedies be applied and, if necessary, freshly invented. The recovery of these cycles constitutes the wild nature of women and places her in her own strength at its best. The wild nature is alert, insightful, foresightful, hindsightful, and fierce. In its essence it is most definitely friendly, but most decidedly not tame.

▼▼

Chapter 7

The Sacred Does Not Shun
the Ordinary

Gioia Timpanelli

*Gioia Timpanelli is a nationally and internationally acclaimed storyteller
who has been performing for more than thirty years. An early and certainly a
central figure in the storytelling revival, she has authored an Italian traveling
diary,* Traveling Images and Observations, *and a book of Tibetan stories
entitled* Tales from the Roof of the World. *She is currently writing a book
of fiction for William Morrow based on Sicilian tales.*

*Timpanelli displays an innate storytelling ability. Her language is rich and
evocative; her stories, circular. She believes that stories create an opening—"a
verbal ruse"—that leads to a clearer grasp of life and the world around us. In
the essay and story that follow, we see how everyday activities contain hints of
their sacred context.*

If the soul could have known God without the world,
  the world would never have been created.

                                        Meister Eckhart

Careful living in a specific place is the foundation of our old folk tales; this mountain, that tree, this badger, that golden fish, Eagle, the women coming in with the baskets, the North wind, March, the stars, and on and on and wondrously on. One story holds us among the many things of the world. It does this while nurturing the Imagination, which is not a superfluous gift but a necessity for seeing with the material into the structure of our real lives. What seems both outside and inside are experienced in the same place; what seems small and hidden is an entire world.

Unlike secular stories, which happen in the common perception of time passing, sacred stories are consecrated to truth and teaching and are not attached to our usual perception of cause and effect. Rather, they are stories without time—showing us no-time—so we can experience the world from within and without at the same moment. Even if the stories have a beginning, middle, and end, we understand that this form allows the communication of the enduring, the *always is*. Thus, we can perceive that they are stories "from that time"; we can hear the sacred story and experience the eternal. Often, these holy stories are memorized, so that nothing is out of place, for stories and words have a real place in the world. Sacred stories, seen also by their subject matter, explain, point, reveal the truth, inspire, and show reverence for the sacred world.

Profane stories, that live outside the temple, rely on what happens, how and why. They give a vivid sense of our living, our passing, our mortality. Our profane stories speak extemporaneously from the moment, from personal experience and understanding, from error and mistake, from a windfall picked up after a storm. These ordinary stories are good, bad, or indifferent teachers, uncommon treasure boxes of the human mind and mirrors of its soulful life. The old folk tales especially have a sneaky logic found in poetry, metaphor, and dreams. We can be thankful that they are not given to large statements on meaning, for like the heart, to whom they constantly speak, they prefer experience to discussion, unity to separation. Everything in them has weight, even a feather blowing here and there. They live in the particular while trying to talk politely about everybody. Full of lively images, these old tales carry with them the magic of the created world. Although humble, they hold the possibility of experiencing the miracle of an ordinary day.

"The Old Couple" is a short story based on a four-line Sicilian folk tale, first heard in Sicilian.

The Old Couple

For R. B.

She thought she had dreamt angels, not a frightening dream but not quite a comforting one either. For, after all, she and her husband were so old, so very old. "We're at the bottom of the hill," he had said just last evening. "But that's where we've always lived," she laughed, "and besides, there are many things to do at the bottom of the hill, Sweetheart." She smiled when she thought that after all these years, she still called him Sweetheart and he still called her Treasure. "Why do you call me '*Tesoru*'?" she had asked him once, long ago. "Ah," he said, "when I was a young boy wild grape vines grew like treasures in the woods. You are like those vines to me, for I never knew what they would bring, and their value is never what others think." That evening while peeling potatoes she thought of his words and was so moved that tears came to her eyes, so that from then on potatoes, tears, and treasure all shared a common place in her heart.

Now when she thought of this, she laughed and called out to him in a loud voice, "*All'angiuli ci piaciuni li patati?*" ("Do angels like potatoes?")

"What?" he shouted back. "Are my brothers coming? Did you say Angelo is bringing potatoes?" He stepped out the door to search the hillside above for their nephew who did come once in a while to look in on them. "No," she said more quietly, "I was just wondering if angels liked potatoes."

When he saw no one, he shrugged and called back to her, "I think you're mumbling. I can't hear you." Later he would ask her. He touched the handle of his shovel and went back to a worry he'd been having since dawn: How long would he be able to pick up a shovel, or even be able to do the most simple thing? A pain that had been lurking became present; he made a fist against it and waited. But by the time the pain left, the worry was gone as well and he felt able again. The animals are blessed, he thought; in this, the animals are blessed. Again he shrugged, but this time he picked up the shovel at the door and began to walk down the steps.

How funny, she thought, *patati-frati, angiulo-Angelo.* He just didn't hear me. And then she remembered that her dream angel had not said a word; maybe it knew that they were both quite deaf by now. Suddenly it was all too much for her, and she just had to sit down.

At the same moment something made him turn so that he saw her fall back into the chair—as though someone had gently pushed her. He came running in to her. "What is it? *Chi c'è? Chi c'è?* What do you want?" he asked anxiously. She never liked this kind of attention. She waved her hand to put distance between herself and his alarm: "*Nenti, nun vugliu nenti.*" "Do you want a glass of water?" he persisted. "No, please, Sweetheart, I'm all right now; my legs just didn't work for a minute. Thank you." She touched his hand. "Please don't worry, I'm fine. I'm really fine. I'm going out to finish digging the holes for the new little vines. It's the right time, you know." He paid no attention to this and came back carrying a glass of water shaking in his hands.

She took the cold glass from him and sipped a bit of water to please him. He made a satisfied sound, nodded, and then waited while she started looking around for a safe place to settle the glass. She found the spot and put it down. What does this spot mean? she asked herself. He helped her up and then he moved slowly back to the door. She walked over to the stove and picked up a few sticks of wood. "You know," he said, "I was just thinking we might make ourselves a nice plate of potatoes and eggs for dinner." "That's funny," she said, "I was just thinking the same thing."

While this was going on in the little house below, by chance two travelers were about to round a bend in the road, which would give them a view of the little house and the valley beyond. One was a curious fellow who looked around, taking in as much as he could, gesticulating as he walked in his peripatetic way, hitting first one side of the road and then the other. He spoke the whole time in a running commentary about everything he was seeing. The other walked quietly without curiosity, his step deliberate and quite steady, like a native of the place—in this case a Pirzisi— who knew this hillside from birth, walking over the familiar and the unfamiliar with the same solid step. Much escaped the animated walker, and as he talked his sardonic tone could clearly be heard and noted by anyone caring to listen. On the other hand, his companion remained silent, was barely noticeable except for a triangular bit of light that came from the back of his neck, from something that the setting sun caught and reflected. A donkey in the field below turned; the silent man looked up briefly and their eyes met, neither surprised. The donkey looked on, waiting to see if the newcomers were real news for him or not. As the two men came to the top of the hill, they saw at once the little house and the ancient couple working at something in the field below. The talker stopped and watched. Verifying his suspicion, he turned with a sly smile on his lips and in his usual tone said:

"Teacher, look at that old man. What's he doing planting grape vines at his age?" It would take five years at least to get some grapes out of those new little things, and it was plain the couple were too old, too old, to see *that* vine mature. The Teacher looked up; the donkey turned back, shifted his weight, and waited. "*Maiestru*, isn't that truly foolish?"

The old man had just finished digging, and the old woman was gently placing each plant, with its new, delicate, bright green shoots growing at daring angles from the old darkened stem, into the newly dug hole. Everywhere along the branches these new buds had burst or were about to burst into the familiar leaf of the grape vine. Now, this done, the old man quickly finished covering the roots while the old woman expertly patted the earth around each plant.

"Why don't you just ask them what they are doing," said the Teacher, and the student immediately walked down the hill to them. Just as they had finished the row, he came up to them and asked the old man:

"What in the world are you planting grape vines for at your age?" "*Buona sera*," said the old man.

"*Buona sera*," said the old woman.

"*Buona sera*," said the student, looking at them.

He repeated his question: "*Chi stai facinnu chiantannu racina alla vostr'età?*"

A warm spring wind came up suddenly, and the two stood swaying a bit, like two gnarled trees grown together in sympathy and place. "*The good*," began the old man; "*is never lost*," finished the old woman. She walked away repeating the old saying under her breath, getting pleasure from saying it again, "*U bunu nun e mai persu.*" The old man waited a minute, exchanged good evenings again with the traveler, and then went on about his own business, watering the new plants. The old woman came back with more water, and when he finished she slipped her hand under his.

"What do you suppose he thinks 'The Good' is?" she asked.

"Only God knows," he said.

She took the bucket from him and went to water a bit of wild mint that she had seen growing in the field. A bright reflection off the watering can caught her eye, and she looked up in its direction but could not see the other traveler's face, the setting sun behind him was so strong.

The talker ran up the hill to where the Teacher stood waiting.

"*Maiestru,*" said the student, "the old man said, 'the good is never lost.'" "And the old woman, what did she say?"

"Teacher, the old man started the saying and the old woman finished it. I guess we can say they were of one mind," he said, thinking for a minute and then beginning to laugh good-naturedly for the first time.

"For their good words to you, the old couple will drink wine from that place."

"From that vine, Master?"

"Yes, from there."

The travelers walked out of hearing, the donkey turned away and found something delicious to eat, the old man looked at the row, satisfied, and, humming to himself, drained the last bit of water from the can. He looked up in the distance where the new oaks they had planted five years ago played in and out with the old ones. Maybe he would walk to the woods tomorrow. Maybe.

The old woman looked up at the sky. It was so beautiful; so many running sheep clouds. She started for the steps, felt her dream for a second. There was no doubt, she thought, somewhere the angel of chance was present.

▼▼

Chapter 8

Story Food for Women and for Men

Robert Bly

"Sometimes a person needs a story more than food to stay alive." Had not
Badger, a character in the Barry Lopez fable, Crow and Weasel, uttered that
aphorism, translator, poet, author, and men's movement mentor Robert Bly
might have. Much of Bly's work emphasizes the importance of paying attention
to the soul and its needs, particularly the need to feast on the images and symbols
of stories. A consummate storyteller, Bly knows well how to host such a banquet.
He offers us mythological kingdoms where bears are kings, mountains are made
of glass, and magic flasks yield unlimited supplies of every conceivable liquid re-
freshment.

Bly and other storytellers keep the oral tradition alive. Stories were the vehicles by which our ancestors passed on critical knowledge of how to survive in the
world. Therefore, they are most powerful when spoken aloud. For this reason,
you might want to read the following story, "The White Bear King of
Valemon," out loud, and allow the images and cadence of the story to feed your
soul.

Once upon a time, once below a time, or once inside a time there was a king with three daughters. The third daughter was especially feisty and adventurous. One day she was wandering in the woods, and she saw a white bear lying on its back playing with a golden wreath. After a while she said to the bear, "I'd love to have that wreath."

The bear said, "What are you offering?"

She said, "I will give you all of my jewels."

He said, "What good are jewels to a bear?"

She said, "I'll give you my crown. "

He said, "What good is a crown to a bear?"

"Well, what can I give you for the wreath?" she asked.

"For a wreath like this, you have to pay with yourself," the bear said.

She said, "Do you mean..."

"I do," he said, "I'll come next Thursday (Thor's-day) to your father's castle and fetch you."

She walked home. At dinnertime she told her father about the strange event that had happened to her in the woods. "I offered him jewels and a crown, but he wouldn't accept it, so I've agreed to marry the bear."

Her father said, "It's a rash decision. What is the wreath like?"

"Oh," she said, "It's round; with golden leaves, and it's about a foot across."

Her father took careful note. Then he called his goldsmiths and said, "Start now. Melt down gold. Make a wreath of this sort. I want this wreath done by tomorrow evening." So they worked all night and all the next day, and at dinnertime the king brought his youngest daughter the wreath.

She said, "It's not quite right. It's too large." So that night the king forced his goldsmiths to stay up all night again and make a smaller wreath. He brought it to her Wednesday morning.

"The original was a little fatter," she said.

So the King ordered the goldsmiths to go to work all night again. The third wreath had leaves that looked like maple leaves instead of oak, and she rejected it too.

On Thor's-day morning, the king took all three daughters aside and said, "As you know, in our country, the oldest daughter marries first. That means, my dear oldest daughter, that you will have to marry the bear this morning. Get ready." The King then ordered his palace guards into the courtyard and said, "When a white bear comes, shoot him." When the bear arrived, they raised their guns. The bear looked at them, roared, knocked them all down, and walked straight past them into the castle. "I'm ready now to welcome the bride," he proudly announced.

When the oldest daughter came out, the bear said, "Climb on my back." She climbed on and they started for the woods. When they were about a mile away, the bear said, "Have you ever *sat* more softly than you are sitting now?" She said, "Oh yes, on my father's lap I sat more softly than I am sitting now." The bear said, "Have you ever *seen* more clearly than you are seeing now?" She said, "Yes, on top of my father's tower at the castle, I saw more clearly than I am seeing now." He said, "Oh, hell, it's the wrong bride." He threw her off, and she had to walk home.

The next Thor's-day the king told his second daughter, "Today it's your turn. Prepare for marriage." He had meanwhile invited a number of soldiers and musketeers from the neighboring castles, so he had a small army waiting. When the white bear arrived, again he just growled, stood up on his hind legs, knocked them all down, and walked into the castle. He said, "I'm ready to welcome the bride." The second daughter came out and off they went.

About a mile away from the castle, the bear said, "Have you ever *sat* more softly than you are sitting now?" She said, "Yes, I re-member in my father's lap I sat more softly than I am sitting now."

The bear asked, "Have you ever *seen* more clearly than you are seeing now?" She said, "Yes, once looking out from my father's tower, I saw more clearly than I am seeing now." He said, "Oh dear, wrong one!" He threw her off, and she had to walk home, too.

By next Thor's-day, all the available soldiers in that part of Norway had arrived, plus cannons. The king said to the youngest daughter, "I grieve over this situation. I know you don't want to leave." But she was already dressed. When the bear arrived, he saw that the whole castle courtyard was full—soldiers, muskets, swords, and cannons. What did the bear do? He stood on his hind legs, growled, rushed, knocked them all down, and walked in. He said, "I'm ready to welcome the bride." The youngest daughter came out, and the bear said, "Climb on my back."

They were about a mile out of town when he said to her, "Have you ever *sat* more softly than you are sitting now?" She said, "Never." He asked, "Have you ever *seen* more clearly than you are seeing now?" She said, "Never." And the bear said, "Ah, she's the right one."

So they made their way to his castle; it turned out that he was known as the White Bear King Valemon. The odd thing about him was that at nightfall he would turn into a beautiful man and the couple would spend the night together. The princess never actually saw him, but their nights were full of joy and delight. When they would wake up in the morning, he would be a bear again and go out into the forest and do what bears do. That's how it was. Something about this life suited the princess, and three years passed in this way. Each year the princess gave birth to a child, but each time the child disappeared as soon as it was born. The disappearance of the child was only one more strange detail in a strange situation.

Then one day she said, "I want to go back and see my father and mother." The bear agreed that she could go if she wanted to, but warned her, "Listen to what your father says, not to what your mother does."

So she returned home. Her sisters were very curious and asked many pointed questions about her life with the bear. "Does he manicure his claws? Do you eat fresh-killed meat? Do you sleep in a cave all winter?"

She told them, "It's not like that. We live in a castle; it's a calm and peaceful place. At night he becomes a man, and although I've never seen him, we make beautiful love."

"You never see him at night," they replied. "How do you know he's not a monster or a dragon? What if one night he just eats you whole? That could happen. As your older sisters, we're worried about you. We certainly don't carry any grudge, but it seems clear to us that this so-called king might be dangerous."

It turns out the mother and father were listening to their conversation. "I think you should let things be as they are," the father said to his youngest daughter. But the mother said, "Take this candle back with you. One night, after he has fallen asleep, light the candle and hold it up to his body. Then you'll know one way or the other. That's my advice."

The princess brought the candle back to the Bear King's castle. The first night home they made love, and when her lover fell asleep, the princess got up, quietly lit the candle, and held it up to his body. She started with his feet; they were small and shapely and seemed beautiful to her. His shins and knees were elegant. She moved the light up over his thighs; they were strong and well-shaped, and all other things in their vicinity handsome and fine. She found his stomach flat and his chest firm. He was without a doubt a man and now that she had seen his strong body, she was even more curious about his face. But as she lifted the candle higher, one drop of hot wax fell on his shoulder and he awoke.

"Why did you do it?" he cried out. "If only you could have waited another month I could have been a human being both night and day! Now I have to leave." He became a bear and rushed out the door.

She cried out, "I don't want you to go!"

"It's too late. I don't have any choice! I cannot stay," he answered.

He rushed out of the castle, toward the forest, and she ran after him and grabbed onto his fur. He ran on all fours through trees and brush. She held on as hard and as long as she could, but the underbrush and branches tore at her, and she fell off. The bear rushed on ahead and the princess found herself on the forest floor alone.

She wandered in the forest for a long time without shelter or food. If she met anyone in the forest she would always ask them if they knew where the White Bear King Valemon might be. The answer was always the same: "I've never heard of him." One day she came upon a hut. An old woman lived there with a small girl. When the raggedy princess knocked, they took her in and gave her food. The princess spoke sweetly with the old woman. Then she got down on the floor and played with the little girl and asked her many questions about dollhouses and crickets.

When the wandering princess was about to go, the little girl said, "Mother, she's been so good to us. Could we give her the scissors?" The old woman said, "If you want to, we will." The scissors were special. Whenever a hand opened or closed the scissors, cloth appeared on its own. Whatever sort of cloth that was desired— cotton, embroidered linens, satins, lace, flannel, and plaids. The princess was glad to have the scissors. As she thanked them, she asked the old women, "By the way, have you seen the White Bear King Valemon?"

The old woman said, "Yes, I have. He came past here about a month ago. He was traveling very fast, heading west."

The princess was glad to hear that news. She walked on in the forest, toward the west, and soon saw a second hut also inhabited by a small girl and an old woman. After the old woman had served her tea, the princess had her own little tea with the daughter and asked her questions like, "Have you learned the alphabet yet? Do you know any good stories? Do you go to school? Do you have any friends in the woods?" This went on quite a while. When she was about to leave, the daughter said, "Mother, she has been so good to us; could we give her the flask?"

The flask was strange and special—when you lifted and turned it over, any liquid that was desired poured out. If you thought "cognac," cognac came, or cold water, wine, or jasmine tea. "If you want to give her the flask, we will," the mother told the child. The daughter was glad to give it to the kind princess. After the princess thanked her hosts, she turned to the old woman and asked, "By the way, have you seen the White Bear King Valemon?"

The mother answered, "Actually, he rushed by about a week ago. He was going very fast toward the west. I don't know if you can catch him."

So the king's daughter kept wandering. After a while she happened on a third hut in which another old woman lived with a young girl. After tea, again the princess played with the child. She helped her make little dolls out of pine cones and asked her many questions. "What do you want to be when you grow up? Do you think animals are like people?" When the princess was about to leave, the young girl said, "Mother, could we give her the table-cloth?"

This tablecloth had magic in it. When it was spread out on the table, food appeared on its own—cheese, roast duck, salmon, sweet and sour soup, lamb stew, or chocolate mousse. Any dish that was desired. The old woman said, "If you want to give her the table-cloth, we will."

As the visitor was about to go, she turned to the old woman and said, "By the way, have you seen the White Bear King Valemon lately?"

The mother replied, "Yes! He came by here about three days ago, going west. I heard he's on his way to the glass mountain."

The glass mountain! What glass mountain? The glass mountain. So the princess set out for the glass mountain. After hours of walking she saw it looming over the trees. The sides were slippery and steep. As she approached the base she noticed the ground was covered with the bones of all the men and women who had tried to climb it and failed.

She noticed nearby yet another hut. When she knocked at the door and was invited in, she realized that it was different in several ways from the previous huts she had visited. A middle-aged woman, not young, not old, lived there with four young children. There was evidence of a man's tools. The princess saw no food anywhere; the family was obviously starving. Everyone's clothes were tattered. Soon the children confided in her. "Oftentimes we have no food. But sometimes our mother puts stones in the soup and boils them. She tells us that they're apples, and the soup tastes better. That really helps."

It didn't take long for the traveler to open the tablecloth and lay it out. Soon there was lamb, good cheese, and fresh potatoes. The mother and the children ate and ate. And the flask poured orange juice and milk and hot cider. While everyone was eating the scissors made dresses, winter coats, woolen trousers, winter underwear, shawls, and socks. After they had eaten all they could, the tablecloth made salt beef, dried cod, and goat cheese to last the winter. When everyone had been provided for, the princess turned to the mother and asked, "Do you know the White Bear King Valemon?"

The woman said, "Are you the one? Are you the woman who looked at him, and whom he had to leave behind?"

The princess said yes, she was that one and explained how she had been searching for him for a long time.

"Well," the mother said, "the White Bear King is nearby, but he is going to be married in three days."

"He is?" the princess said in a low voice. "To whom?"

"Her," the mother replied.

"What do you mean, Her?"

"Her. The Great One. She lives on top of the glass mountain. No one can compare to her. She has great power and a great appetite. Fat dogs tend to disappear when they get near her. Sometimes she eats a hundred roasted songbirds for lunch. She has skeleton fingers that serve her tea and a small pine tree grows out of her nose. Many animals serve her; they bring her news from distant places. If you want to get the Bear King back, you must get to the top of the mountain soon. The wedding is in three days."

The princess thanked the woman and started out to climb the glass mountain. It was not easy. She could get no hold and slipped to the bottom again and again.

The thin woman watched her and finally came out and said, "This isn't going to work. My husband, who is a blacksmith, will be as grateful as I am for your feeding and clothing the children. Nothing could have been more wonderful. He is coming back tonight. I'll ask him to forge iron claws for your hands and feet. That's what you need. They'll get you up the mountain."

So that's how it went. The husband returned, the children told him the story, and he stayed up all night making the iron claws. Just after dawn, the princess put them on and started her climb.

When she got to the top, she found an elaborate castle, and in front of it a terrace surrounded by low walls. She had brought the flask, tablecloth, and scissors with her, and soon the fragrance of

French cognac, Armagnac, Persian rose-water, dark red wine, and champagne floated over the porch. The princess laid the tablecloth out on a huge table and soon appeared roast beef, squash, and roasted turkey. The wonderful smells drew The Great One on to the terrace. When she got close, she could see oysters on the half shell, smoked salmon, baked halibut, cherry pies, and chocolate mousse. A little yellow bird songbird came flying by; the Great One picked it out of the air and ate it whole. Then she screamed: "Aahii! This sort of food is exactly what I want for my wedding. How did you do all this?"

The princess said, "The tablecloth you see spread here is magic, and it produces any food you would like to have."

"I want it! How much?"

"No amount of money can buy it."

"What do you want then, tell me!" A sparrow flew out of her hair.

"I want one night alone with the Bear King."

"Haaaa!" the Great One screeched. "One night you may have. Come here at ten o'clock tonight and my maid will show you where his room is. Just knock on his door. Have the tablecloth ready to give to my maid."

So that's the way it happened. The deal was made. You should know, however, that the Queen of the Glass Mountain, the Dear One with an Appetite visited the Bear King first. He was in his human form.

"The wedding is coming up, get lots of rest. Here's a little apple wine that I made especially for you. It will help you sleep," she said.

He drank it, and a sleeping potion took effect. When the princess, full of hope, knocked later in the evening, no one answered. She walked in the room and found the Bear King sound asleep. No matter how much she talked in his ear, sang to him, and shook him, he wouldn't wake up. She waited beside him all night, and he never awoke. At dawn she gave up and left.

She knew the Great One would come out for a walk on the terrace in the morning. This time the princess gathered wine glasses from the kitchen, Russian teacups, German tankards, and Czechoslovakian goblets painted with gold. She turned the flask over and filled them with black Turkish coffee, English tea, the finest champagnes, red and white wines, cherry liquers, vodka, and aquavit. When Bride-of-All-Beings came out, she was delighted.

"I want champagne for my wedding. Around here they produce white piss and call it wine. Where did all this come from?"

"The flask you see here is magic; when you turn it over, it pours whatever drink you want."

"All right, what's the deal? Name your price," exclaimed the Great One.

"I want one more night with the White Bear King Valemon."

"That must be because you had so much fun last night." Her tusks gleamed. "Bring the flask here at ten o'clock and give it to my maid."

The princess waited impatiently all day, but that Dear Lady, the One Who Uses Boys' Bones as Toothpicks, visited the bear first. He was in human form. She offered him a goodnight drink, and he took it. When the princess knocked on the door, no one answered. She entered the room and again found him sound asleep. She spoke to him and reminded him of their old love and how dear they had been to each other. Then she told him how long she had been searching for him and how long she had suffered with the cold and the forest, but he never fluttered an eyelid. She started to cry sitting by his bed, and she cried all night until dawn.

In the morning the White Bear King awoke, knowing nothing. He opened the door to his room. As he was leaving, two carpenters who slept in the room next door stopped him and spoke to him.

"Do you know that there was a woman crying in your room last night? We heard it through the walls."

He thought, "How can that be? Is it possible she is here?"

The princess guessed that the Great One would come out for her morning walk. This time the princess began work with her scissors, and soon the tables were covered with Parisian wedding gowns, velvet stoles, lace veils, bridesmaid dresses, traveling frocks, elegant black gloves, Spanish scarves, sashes, and darling jackets. Soon the Queen with Two Sets of Teeth came by carrying a rabbit she had just snatched up and saw it all. "This is perfect! It will all fit me well. I'll try them on today, and wear them tomorrow morning. How much?"

"No amount of money can buy these scissors."

"All right. What is your price?"

"I'd like a last night with the White Bear King Valemon."

"As you wish, honey. I don't know what they taught you in school. I'll take these clothes with me and you bring the scissors here at ten o'clock!"

The Queen of All the People, the One-Who-Is-Always-Hungry, visited the Bear King for a nightcap in the usual way. When she offered him the glass of wine, he turned slightly to the side, and, choosing a time when she wasn't looking, poured the drink down his shirt into a little bag he had tied around his neck. A few minutes later, he said, "Oh, I feel so sleepy!"

Now the Queen of the Glass Mountain, being of great intelligence, became suspicious. He seemed to be asleep, but she said to herself, "Something's not right in this room. I can smell it." She decided to test him, so she took a darning needle and drove it right through his arm. He didn't move. Not even a quiver crossed his face. "Ah, he's got to be asleep," she said. She was satisfied and left the room.

When the princess arrived, the Bear King was awake. How glad they were to see each other again. How they laughed and cried and told each other how terrible the waiting had been. When a time of suffering is over, it seems charming to retell it all, even while you weep. So they talked until dawn, and then they heard the carpenters stirring in the next room. They thanked them for the message they had given, and then the White Bear King asked them to make a little adjustment on the wooden bridge over which the wedding party would walk. The carpenters said, "We think that's possible."

The wedding began early the next morning. The procession started with the bride in front, as in Norwegian weddings. She wore a veil over her tusks, but the winds that rushed past her kept blowing it aside, and the fire coming from her eyes frightened the onlookers. Many people wept. They had become fond of the Bear King and felt so sorry that he had to marry The One. But nothing could be done. The Queen of the Glass Mountain ruled and no one could say no to her.

When the One Who Makes Bones Sing reached the midpoint of the wooden bridge that led over the chasm to the church, the floor gave way, and she fell through and disappeared into the river. They did not know if it was right or wrong, but it made the people of the mountain happy, especially the princess and the Bear King.

The carpenters then nailed firm boards over the bridge and the procession continued. Now the Bear King could marry his true bride. The women in the kitchen were overjoyed, and they kept bringing out food. All the farmers and their wives, and the fishermen and their wives for miles around ate food as they had never tasted before and drank wine that made them dizzy. The dancing went on until all the wine and akvavit was gone; then they danced a couple of hours more just on apple cider.

The next morning the White Bear King and the princess traveled back to her kingdom to have a second wedding at her father's castle. On the way, they picked up the three children, one at each hut. As it turned out, these children were the ones who had disappeared each time the princess gave birth. They were so glad to be united again with their real father and mother. The wedding was the greatest ever held in the people's memory; even the two sisters danced.

ALTHOUGH I'VE AGREED to say a few words about this story as a sacred story, it is presumptuous in a way to say anything, and very easy to make misleading remarks. Everything I say, therefore, is tentative; a great mystery surrounds stories this ancient.

Our story is a sacred story because the images—the white bear, the golden wreath, the lifted candle, the children nourished on stones—resonate in some holy place. The images feel like scenes from some drama long lost, carrying information we are just now remembering.

It is said that that one distinction between the folk tale and the genuine "fairy tale" or "teaching tale" lies in the nature of the main character. Johnny Appleseed is a human being and takes his part in an honorable folk tale. The Great One, The Queen of the Glass Mountain, is clearly immortal. She is closely related to the Hindu goddesses Durga and Kali, or to Rangda in Balinese culture. German, French, and Italian tales tend to overlook her. However, the great Russian, Norwegian, and Indian stories include her under many names. The Indian saint Ramakrishna, who lived in the nineteenth century, once saw a waking vision of Kali. He saw her come out of the Ganges and described her as radiant with light and joy. He watched her give birth to a baby and hold it in her arms with such tenderness and delight that he felt deep peace. Then she began to change, her face became long. In amazement, he watched her eat the child. Then she went back into the the Ganges.

The story emphasizes her tremendous appetite to indicate how close she is to the biological center of life. No judgment is made on her appetite; one does not judge the divine. So this story is sacred because it makes room for two forms of the divine, the Lady of Great Appetite and the God of the Bears.

There is another reason to suspect that our story is a precious survivor from ancient religion. It is a local northern European version of "Amor and Psyche," the tale central to Greek mythology. "Amor and Psyche" survived the destruction of pagan religious material because Apuleius inserted it in the center of his Latin novel, *The Golden Ass*, written in North Africa circa A.D. 155. We know from the context of that book that the tale belonged to the worship of Isis.

In Apuleius's book, the masculine hero, who has strayed too close to sorcery, gets turned into a donkey and remains so for the entire story. Only in the last pages does he become a human being when he eats rose petals that Isis has blessed. As a donkey, he hears the story of the magic castle and lifted lamp. Both Marie-Louise von Franz and Erich Neumann have written extensively on this story—von Franz in her book called *The Golden Ass*, and Erich Neumann in his book, *Amor and Psyche*. The lifting of the lamp, and the distress it causes, is famous in mythological and psychological commentary. Almost all commentators agree that the lifting of the lamp is related to the soul's intention to increase its consciousness; some relationship that has earlier been allowed to remain "in the dark" becomes illuminated. In human life this illumination often causes the relationship to end. A break occurs, which is painful in the extreme. So the story asks what the soul is willing to pay for increased consciousness. That is a proper theme for the sacred story.

We might also say a few words on the difference between the version of "Psyche and Eros" preserved by Apuleius, which has clearly been elaborated or intellectualized in the Alexandrian manner, and the northern European version you have just read. The most noticeable difference is that in the Alexandrian version

the Being Who Changes at Night to a Man is the god Eros. As a
Greek god, he belongs to the heavens. The bear god, by contrast, is
close to earth. There is much wit around the portrayal of Eros that
fits well with the Greek habit of intellectualizing the divine, perhaps so that the mind could play with the Holy. It was fashionable
at that time to make gods charming. The Bear King Valemon, by
contrast, is a bear, and we feel ourselves closer to the belly—to
Ursa Major—and to the old bear religion of the Stone and Bronze
Ages. I think the Norwegian version is closer to the root story.

In the Alexandrian version, the youngest daughter of the king
is Psyche, which is a Greek word for soul. Psyche has imaginative
associations with the butterfly. Souls after death, freed of the mortal cocoon, were traditionally compared to butterflies. But it seems
better storytelling not to label the daughter "the soul." Those two
exceptions granted, we see that the two stories proceed on a parallel path with many minor and local variations. For example, in the
Alexandrian version, the parents fear the daughter is marrying
Death; her parents say a tearful good-bye to her as she leaps from a
cliff. But a kind wind takes her down to the valley where the mysterious castle lies. It is there where strange events occur and she
makes love to the bear king. Both stories involve a divine being
making love to a feminine soul.

In both stories the heroine eventually returns to her parents'
home, and the mother furnishes a lamp or candle and advises her
daughter to use it. The Norwegian tale retains or adds a delicate
grace note, namely, the father's advice, "I think it would be best to
let things remain as they are." That advice turns out to be wrong,
but it catches us for a few moments, and we can all feel our own
ambiguous opinions, as to whether the soul should or should not
risk the candle.

In the Norwegian version, the first strong image is the golden
wreath. The ancient spiritual traditions, to which the neo-Platonists
such as Plotinus returned, declare that it's important that we enter

this life with no memory. Therefore, at the moment of birth all the divine knowledge we possessed before we were born disappears. Sometimes an astonishing event happens to us that helps us recall what we once knew. The gold wreath and the bear shock the "soul" (the youngest daughter) into remembering that lost knowledge.

We note that the bear was playing with the wreath, so there's something playful about the whole process of remembering. The fact that the bear is white helps one understand that the knowledge we have lost is spiritual. We get a flavor here of religious ideas older than the Judeo-Christian understanding, and more wild. The scene in which the bear rolls on its back playing with the wreath seems to me a healing image.

The story is also an initiation story for women. It introduces a woman to something divine that she did not meet in her parental house. We know that in stories, youngest daughters, like Shakespeare's Cordelia, sometimes represent the soul. We can therefore say that it is also an initiation story for the soul, and so applicable to men and women. Lastly, it is an alchemical story. In alchemy, one begins with lead and depression. After a long period of self-development and inner work, something appears in the vessel that could be described as gold. So this wreath is a promise.

It seems so strange that the soul's male lover is a human being at night and a bear in the daytime. We could say that when the human soul approaches the divine, the gap is so enormous that the divine may appear as half animal. There is a chasm between human beings and animals, also. Dionysus expressed this double truth in Greece: he was a bull. Apollo was a python; Aphrodite was a dove; Demeter was a snake. Approaching the divine is a dangerous act. At the start of our story, the bear seems charming and almost ready to adapt to human ways, but as the story continues, it becomes clear that the bear, being half divine, is a little too intense for human beings. Tremendous psychic danger hovers around him.

The toughening that human beings need in order to meet that intensity gives rise in the Alexandrian version to a sequence in which the heroine, in order to fit herself for the relationship, has to go through many difficult and elaborate initiatory tasks, such as separating black and white seeds or getting wool from the golden fleece. After she fulfills those tasks, the Greek heroine comes into her psychic abundance; the Bear's lover achieves her never-empty flask through deprivation, solitude, starvation, and wilderness.

There is also a psychological reading of this story as well as a mythological one. Brooding in that way over the relationship between the Bear King and the princess, we could say that their union resembles a relationship between a contemporary man and woman where neither talks. They only make love. The two are symbiotic, they merge, they don't need words. That is lovely, but the story implies that it isn't entirely right to live in such an unconscious relationship. The candle must be lighted, even if it breaks the relationship.

What the soul needs on this planet is suffering, not success or harmonious relationships New Age seminar leaders try to bludgeon us into. Dostoyevsky says it over and over again: Raskolnikov (which means "schizophrenic") is split—he needs a descent.

Throughout the scenes in which the bear carries each daughter on his back and asks her questions, there is a shrewd humor. The two older daughters answer that they saw the world more clearly from their father's tower, because they feel allegiance to the father's way of seeing. As Jungian analyst and author Marion Woodman would say, if that's the case, they can't be connected to the bear. A daughter like that has no right to waste the bear's time. This test is a very sharp way of intuiting which souls are ready for initiation into the sacred and which are not. The scene is meant to be psychologically disturbing.

We also feel disturbed when the princess falls off the bear's back as they rush through the forest. We gather that it's time for her to come down from her inflation. The divine moves much faster than we do. The Persian poet Hafez wrote: "The light lit in the hermit's cave goes out in the conventional church." Letting go of the bear's fur means returning to the normal, boring, bitter, limited, sad human state. Wandering scratched in the forest suggests a long time of loneliness, which a man or woman may experience for twenty years or so, between ages thirty-five and fifty-five perhaps. Busy in a career or not, one is alone in the forest, and not being fed. The awareness of not being fed is essential. I think the story suggests that we don't find the three huts until we know the desperation that comes with not being fed. It turns out that there is some source of abundance that we knew nothing of when we were eighteen. Once it comes, the soul can satisfy that internal craving, as represented by the starving children.

We can contrast a psychological reading and mythological reading of a sacred story in the following way. Psychologically, each of the characters in the tale are read as energies, all of which exist inside of us. For example, when a woman hears the story, she may notice that the adventuresome daughter energy is inside her, as well as the playful bear energy. She may also recognize herself in the old women, the children, and the carpenters. If she doesn't face her own dark side, she may claim that the Woman of Great Appetite, the tusked one, is a patriarchal invention. This is a fashionable habit these days. We know the patriarchal culture is perfectly capable of projecting the dark side exclusively onto women, and there is massive evidence of that chicanery. But it is a delicate matter when to act on such healthy suspicion. The evidence around this story suggests that it comes straight out of matriarchal culture in its basic outline. The tusked energy is inside a woman, as well as the so-called male bear king, the two stepsisters, the starving children, the blacksmith, and the carpenters. A woman reading the story may be struck by the awesomeness of it all, and the shocks are intentional.

A man reading the story will immediately welcome the idea that the Bear King is inside him, as with the carpenters, but he may be disturbed if he has to agree that the energy of the Queen of the Boar Tusks is a part of his soul. If you ask most men about that energy, they will change the subject. It's easier for him to see it on the outside of the women he is arguing with.

So when we read a sacred story psychologically, we often find ourselves astonished at the leaps of inclusiveness asked of us, particularly in consciously admitting our weaknesses.

When read mythologically, the story requires steps even more difficult to take. Mythologically, the Awesome Lady of Vast Appetite and the Bear King belong to a wild side of the universe. The rituals around Dionysus always spoke of a wilderness beyond the human, which could easily tear and destroy the human. The Bear King is related to the Wild Man, who is a god, not a man. Clarissa Pinkola Estés calls this being a "wild god." It's possible that in some preindustrial, preagricultural time, a woman and a man might have been able to sustain a long, or longer, union with the "wild force." But the more emphasis we put on morality, intellect and light, that is, the more civilized we become, the more we are separated from the Bear King, who represents our instincts. Deconstruction and logical analysis are just two more steps in the long series of intellectual maneuvers that separate us from the animal and the divine. The trouble with them is that they provide no way by which the soul can reconcile with the wild god.

Mythological themes often concentrate on ways in which the animal soul and the spiritual soul become rejoined. The fear that the wild god is within days of marrying All the Appetite in the World is a mythological theme. The glass mountain is a mythological theme. That we may not find the mysterious source of abundance inside us until we meet the wild god is a mythological theme. That there is a god or goddess of astounding appetite that we can distract with our abundance is a mythological theme.

This abundance, suggested at the earliest moment of the story by the golden wreath, shows how high the stakes are in a mythological reading; far higher than in a psychological reading. The golden wreath asks how much "gold" or greatness we allow ourselves to see in our own souls. Beyond "infantile grandiosity," which we make fun of in psychology, there is true grandness, the fragrance of greatness in us, the true gold of grandiosity.

What is amazing to me in this story is the amount of genuine grandness it allows and even encourages in us. Heinz Kohut, the Austrian-born psychoanalyst, believes that without genuine grandiosity, personalities fragment. In many contemporary personalities, there just isn't enough gold to hold the pieces together.

The sacred story tries to protect our grandness from belittlers, whether those belittlers are fathers who want to manufacture a golden wreath so we will remain domestic, or "stepsisters" inside us jealous of our association with a wild god. Secular stories talk of who you are; sacred stories playfully explore who you aren't. Antonio Machado, speaking to both men and women, says:

> Don't trace out your profile,
> forget your side view—
> all that is outer stuff.
>
> Look for your other half
> who walks always next to you
> and tends to be who you aren't.

▼▼▼

Chapter 9

Fairy Tales and the Psychology of Men and Women at Mid-Life

Allan B. Chinen

Allan B. Chinen is a psychiatrist in private practice in San Francisco and a member of the faculty of the University of California, San Francisco. His interest in fairy tales began nearly a decade ago, when vivid, archetypal images began coming to him while he was jogging or meditating. Although he did not understand the origins of these images, Chinen recognized them as the endings of fairy tales. But these fairy tales were different from the ones that most of us grew up with in that all of the protagonists were middle-aged or older.

Inspired by these snippets, he began writing his own mid-life stories and searching the literature of other cultures for stories with older heroes and heroines. Ten years later, Chinen has read more than five thousand fairy tales, unearthing hundreds that take as their protagonists characters in their middle or later years. Just as the more familiar fairy tales of childhood not only delight but instruct, these tales contain important information about the problems, decisions, and joys of mid-life. Chinen's books on this subject include In the Ever-After: Fairy Tales and the Second Half of Life, Once Upon a Mid-Life: Classic Stories and Mythic Tales for the Middle Years, *and most recently,* Dancing on the King's Grave: Emerging Archetypes Beyond the Patriarch and Hero.

Most of us became acquainted with fairy tales when we were children. The fairy tales we read then, such as *Cinderella* and *Snow White and the Seven Dwarfs*, have similar plot lines. A young hero and a young heroine meet and fall in love. They fight terrible enemies like witches or dragons. They marry and live happily ever after.

Because the most well-known fairy tales end as the hero and heroine's adult lives just begin, we tend to think of fairy tales as "kid's stuff." But historically, this was not the case. Before newspapers, radio, or television, fairy tales and folk tales were the only mass media, providing news, commentary, humor, and entertainment. Storytellers put insights about their lives and the human condition into their stories. Many dealt specifically with characters in the middle third of life.

Fairy tales that focus on the problems of mid-life talk about what happens in the "ever after." These stories contain the wisdom of men and women who survived the mid-life crisis and who tell us how they did it.

No matter where they originate, mid-life tales share common themes and structures. Unlike fairy tales about youth, mid-life stories are not necessarily heart-warming. In fact, middle tales are often disturbingly realistic; they portray marital conflicts, struggles with illness, and a coming to terms with death and tragedy. These stories emphasize the importance of dealing with life as we find it, not as we imagine or hope it to be.

Fairy tales about mid-life characters do not portray problems from childhood, such as the difficulties that result from a dysfunctional family background. This omission does not mean that individuals finally resolve childhood issues at mid-life. Rather, the stories focus their attention on the issues of the middle years. Fairy tales are short and cannot address everything. In emphasizing the problems and potentials of mid-life, these tales highlight an important point: that growth is possible in the middle years, no matter what kind of childhood one has had.

Often in mid-life tales, dramatic role reversals take place. For example, characters may have to take on the behavior or actions of another gender in order to make positive changes. A story from Persia called *Stubborn Husband, Stubborn Wife* deals cleverly with this theme.

ONCE UPON A time there lived a husband and wife in a far-away country. Every morning the husband would wake up, get dressed, eat breakfast, and sit on a bench outside his house. Then he would watch the world go by all day long.

Meanwhile, his wife would wake up, fetch water, chop wood, light the fire, cook breakfast, sweep the floor, and wash their clothes. As you can imagine, the two quarreled constantly about this.

"Why do you sit there like a bump on a log doing nothing?" the wife would ask.

The husband would say, "I am thinking deep thoughts."

"As deep as a pig's tail is long!" she would cry out.

The two would argue back and forth. One day their calf broke out of the barn as the husband was sitting on the bench and the wife was rushing around doing chores. The wife turned to the husband and asked, "Why don't you water the calf? You should at least do that. That's man's work."

The husband replied, "I inherited a flock of sheep from my father. A shepherd takes care of them and gives us cheese, milk, and wool. That's enough for us to live on. So that's enough work for me. Besides, the ancient prophets say that when a man speaks, a woman should obey. I say you should take care of the calf."

"A woman will obey when a real man speaks," she exclaimed. "Not donkey droppings like you."

They argued all morning and all afternoon. Then they both had the same idea. They turned to each other and said, "I know. The first one who speaks will have to take care of the calf from now on." They nodded in agreement and went to bed without speaking.

The next morning the husband woke up. He went out and sat on his bench as usual. His wife arose, chopped wood, lit the fire, and washed the clothes. She realized that if she stayed home any longer, watching her husband doing nothing, she would have to speak. So she quickly finished all her chores, put on her veil, and went to visit a friend.

"This is strange," the husband thought to himself. "My wife never leaves home this early. She must be up to something."

A little later, a beggar came by, saw the husband, and asked for food and money. The husband was about to say something when he caught himself. "Ah ha," he thought, "my wife has sent this man to make me talk. But I'm too smart for her tricks. No matter what happens, I won't speak."

The beggar asked several times, then decided that the man must be a deaf-mute. He went into the house and saw that it was full of cheese and bread. He ate everything and left. The husband was furious but would not allow himself to say a word.

While he was fuming, a barber came by and offered to trim his beard. The husband was about to say yes when he caught himself. "My wife is trying another trick," he thought. "But if heaven should fall to earth, I will not speak."

The barber asked again, then decided that the man must be a deaf-mute. But because the husband's beard really did need trimming, the barber went ahead and trimmed his beard. Then the barber motioned for money. The husband was silent. The barber became angry and said, "If you don't pay me, I'll shave off your beard and cut your hair so you look like a woman." The husband still did not speak or offer money. So the barber shaved off the husband's beard and cut his hair like a woman's. Then he left in a huff.

The husband was furious. He thought about all the different ways he would punish his wife. He vowed that he was going to win their bet no matter what.

A little while later, an old woman came up, selling cosmetics and beauty treatments. She was nearsighted and mistook the husband for a woman. So she hurried up and said, "Dear lady, what are you doing sitting outside without a veil? Have you no father or husband to take care of you?" The husband thought his wife must be very desperate to try all these tricks.

The old woman repeated her question, then decided that the woman must be a deaf-mute. "My goodness, how sad," she thought. "A deaf-mute and so ugly, too. Well, at least I know how to make women beautiful." She took out rouge, lipstick, and powder and put it on the husband's face. Then she motioned for money. But the husband still refused to say anything. So the old woman reached into his pockets, took all the money he had and left.

While the husband was sitting there, thinking of how he would punish his wife for these tricks, a thief came by. He thought it strange that a young woman should be sitting in public without a veil, especially an ugly young woman. So he went to her and said, "Dear lady, what are doing sitting out here without a veil? Have you no father or husband to take care of you?"

The husband refused to answer. "My wife still won't give up!" he thought. So the thief decided that the woman must be a deaf-mute. He went into the house and saw that it was full of costly carpets, vases, and clothes. He packed everything he could into a bag and left, waving to the husband.

The husband almost rolled over with laughter, thinking of how desperate his wife must be to win the wager. "No matter what my wife does," he thought, "I will not lose this bet."

By then it was midday. The poor calf had not had any food or water. So it broke out of the barn and ran around the village square, making a ruckus. The wife heard the noise from her friend's house and came running to see what was the matter. "How did the calf break loose?" she wondered. "My husband must be up to something."

She grabbed the calf and went back to her home, but stopped at the sight of a strange woman sitting in front of her house. "I've been gone only a few hours," she thought, "and my husband takes another wife!"

She went up to the husband and said, "Who are you, you shameless woman sitting in front of my house?" The husband sprang up and said, "Ha, you spoke first. You have to take care of the calf from now on."

The wife exclaimed, "You shaved off your beard and put on makeup just to win our wager?"

The husband replied, "I did no such thing. It was all those people you hired to get me to talk." "What are you talking about?" the wife said. "I did no such thing." She stormed into the house. A minute later she stormed out. "Where are all our belongings?"

The husband explained that the man she hired to act as a thief had stolen everything. "What are you talking about?" she demanded.

The husband said, "You cannot fool me. You lost the wager, so you have to take care of the calf from now on."

The wife cried out, "Foolish man! You lost your face and your fortune, all for the sake of a wager. I will take care of the calf from now on because I am leaving you and taking the calf with me. I do not want a husband as dumb and stubborn as you." With that she walked off with the calf.

She went to the village square and asked the children there if they had seen a man carrying a large bag. The children pointed to the desert. There in the distance she saw a man hurrying away, a big sack on his back.

The wife pulled her veil tight and went after the man, pulling her calf behind her. While she walked she came up with a plan.

When she caught up with the thief at an oasis, she sat a little ways away from him, sighed, and batted her eyelashes. The thief, who was not married, was flattered that an attractive woman would pay attention to him.

He said, "Dear lady, what are you doing in the middle of the desert with only a calf? Have you no father or husband to take care of you?" She said, "If I did, would I be in the middle of the desert with only my calf?"

The two of them started walking together and talking. The thief thought, "She seems like a strong, resourceful person. I should marry her." So he proposed to her. The wife said, "If we get married, how will you support us?"

The thief explained, "In this bag I have enough loot to last us a long while."

The wife said, "Let me see."

The thief replied, "No, you have to wait until we are married."

The two agreed to stop at the next village and have the chief marry them. The wife knew, however, that it was too late in the day to have a wedding. When they arrived at the village, the chief said as much. "Certainly," the chief told them, "I can marry you tomorrow. It's too late today for a wedding. You can stay in my house until tomorrow."

He put them up, the wife in one room and the thief in another. That night the wife waited until everyone was asleep. Then she crept into the thief's room, peeked into his bag, and found every-thing she owned—carpets, clothes, vases, and money. She closed the bag, loaded it quietly on her calf, and was about to walk away from the house when she stopped. She went to the kitchen, mixed flour and water together, and cooked the paste over a candle. She poured the dough into the thief's shoes and into the shoes of the village chief. Then she left with her calf.

The next morning the thief woke up to find that his bag and his bride-to-be were both gone. In the distance, he could see his fiancée hurrying away with his loot loaded on her calf. He ran to fetch his shoes but could not put them on because the dough had hardened like rock. So he grabbed the chief's shoes, but they were also ruined. Finally, he ran outside barefoot. By then the sun had risen and the desert sand was burning hot. In just a few steps, the thief's feet were burned and blistered. He had to give up the chase.

The woman started back to her village and while she was walking she thought about her husband. When she returned to her house, her husband's bench was empty. "Something must have happened," she thought. She rushed into the house, but nobody was there. Yet the wood had been chopped, the fire was going, and something was cooking on the stove.

She found her husband in the courtyard hanging the laundry. When the two of them saw each other, they ran together and embraced. The husband confessed, "While you were gone, I realized how foolish and stubborn I was. I lost my face, my fortune, and my wife!"

The woman said, "I realized how nagging I was and how awful I was to be around." The two of them came to an agreement. From then on, every day, they both woke up early and worked hard all day. Then, when evening came, they sat on the bench together, thinking deep thoughts.

THIS STORY HAS several themes that are common to mid-life fairy tales. First, the woman is courageous and resourceful. The story thus contrasts with most fairy tales about youth in which the woman is passive and saved by a gallant hero. Mid-life tales commonly show women in very strong roles; they do not need to be rescued by anyone!

The independence of the woman in this tale is striking because the story comes from a highly patriarchal culture that would not have allowed women very much freedom. The question arises, how did this story, which is so modern and even feminist, survive in a patriarchal culture? Similar tales can be found in other patriarchal societies.

Here we come to a second aspect of mid-life tales. Unlike myths, which usually conform to the prevailing ideology of their time, fairy tales, and especially middle tales, are often subversive. One reason for this is that fairy tales, like dreams, bring up material from the unconscious. Fairy tales as folk stories were usually told in an altered state of consciousness, at feasts after several gallons of wine, amid lots of festivity. In that altered state, unconscious, often radical symbolism will surface. Another reason for the subversive quality of mid-life tales is that women were often fairy tale storytellers. Myths, on the other hand, were often promulgated by patriarchs and priests. Finally, fairy tales allowed the storyteller to deal with controversial material in a socially acceptable way. If someone said, in response to a tale like *Stubborn Husband, Stubborn Wife*, "Why, this is heresy," the storyteller could say, "Oh, it's just a fairy tale. Why are you taking it so seriously?"

A third theme in *Stubborn Husband, Stubborn Wife* and other mid-life tales is one that Carl Jung pointed out: Women at mid-life often begin to reclaim the assertive, aggressive, and independent traits they repress during youth to fit with traditional stereotypes of the feminine. Conversely, men come to terms with their emotions, need for relationships, and vulnerability. In the story, the wife goes on a dangerous journey, outwits a thief, and returns with loot—the typical actions of a hero. Her husband, on the other hand, stays home, is painted with women's cosmetics, and does the housework. In portraying such a mid-life role reversal, this tale and others like it serve a very different function from fairy tales of youth. In the latter tales, the aim is to socialize children so they fit the prevailing social mores. Mid-life tales, by contrast, encourage us to break away from prevailing social mores in ways that will make our lives more satisfying.

The story presents this concept of role reversal in a hilarious way when the husband has makeup put on him and is mistaken for a woman. Such humor is a fourth theme common to mid-life tales. By contrast, fairy tales about young people are usually not funny. The predicaments of Cinderella or Snow White are very serious, even frightening to many children; ultimately, the triumph of hero and heroine in those stories is intended to be inspiring.

The humor of mid-life tales underscores a major task of maturity: learning to laugh at ourselves. At mid-life, we often feel stuck with responsibilities. We cannot run away from them, as we often believe young people can, and we cannot transcend difficult situations as we might in later life, when we are perhaps a bit more philosophical about our struggles. Sometimes the only healing that is available involves the ability to laugh at ourselves, which in turn helps us to grow psychologically by providing an element of detachment.

The story, like many mid-life tales, has a character who is reluctant to change. The husband is stubborn and refuses to speak, which leads to all sorts of disasters. That is a general theme in mid-life tales: If we refuse to change, something terrible will happen. The husband's unwillingness to be flexible costs him everything that is dear to him.

Some women have found it troublesome that in the tale the wife apologizes for her nagging. After all, she was simply asking her husband to do a fair share of the work. We might even question why she came back to the husband in the first place. One aspect of this is cultural. Realistically, in Islamic society she would not have had many options. But a deeper reason has to do with the issue of change. Her return home gives the husband an opportunity to demonstrate that he has changed. Fairy tales about young people show cruel, stubborn, or selfish people being destroyed in the end. They do not change, and they suffer for it. Mid-life tales, by contrast, stress the theme of self-reformation, embodied in characters who start out nasty and self-centered, like the husband, and then change their ways.

The self-reformation motif brings up another major task of mid-life: confronting the ugly side of ourselves. Characters in mid-life tales confront the shadow and change in response to it. This might seem surprising, because we tend to think of young people as the ones who grow and change. But in youth, many of us tend to blame others for our problems and refuse to change ourselves. It is part of mid-life maturity to realize that the source of our problems is very often ourselves.

It is significant, too, that reformation in this story has nothing to do with magic. We do not see, in tales of mid-life, evil witches or fairy godmothers. The real villain is the dark side of every person, and the real magic is the human transformation that is possible for each individual. The lesson is that in our middle years there is magic in flexibility and compromise.

Another lesson from the tale related to the need for flexibility is that in relationships, we often need to disentangle ourselves from our partners so that we can stop our projections and discover what is really going on. The husband in this tale assumes that the constant arguing between him and his wife is all her fault. Only after she leaves on her adventure does the husband discover his part in their problems. In many marriages, one spouse will put the blame for a particular problem entirely on the other, and only quiet reflection corrects the error. Of course, we cannot take the story literally as a script; spouses do not necessarily have to separate whenever there is a problem. But the emphasis on emotional disentanglement is valid.

Interpreting fairy tales in psychological terms can impose ideas and theories on the stories that may not be in them, so we must be cautious and even humble in approaching the tales. My feeling is that psychological interpretations of these tales might be replaced by a new approach in the next century, but the stories themselves will survive—as they have for centuries before. The tales always remain vital and alive in part because each succeeding generation finds something new in them. My intent in discussing the tales is not to give any "final" interpretation of the stories, but to use the tales to invoke reflection and reverie, which will hopefully lead to personal renewal, inspiration, and healing. Handed down over the centuries, the stories are a legacy from men and women who have gone before us, suffered with the age-old turmoil of mid-life and survived, leaving us the fruit of their experience—stories of magic, hope, and wisdom.

▼▼

Chapter 10

The Story the Child Keeps

RICHARD LEWIS

The author of several books for and about children, Richard Lewis is the founder and director of the Touchstone Center for Children in New York City. The center sponsors a variety of educational programs, including residencies at both public and private schools for artist-teachers who work to integrate arts into core curricula.

Touchstone was founded on the belief that all people have instinctual creative capacities and that any subject matter, from history to physics, can be taught by encouraging these capabilities. Lewis offers the example of watching his own preschool-age children playing with pebbles by a stream. Without any instruction from him, they began to sort the pebbles into different groups, adding and subtracting various amounts from each other. He saw that they had instinctually discovered mathematics at its most basic level. He realized that people are fascinated by the fact that they can make things smaller or larger. Therefore, one way to teach mathematics would be to devise exercises and activities that call upon and feed that fascination.

In the essay that follows, Lewis shows how encouraging children to find and tell their own stories helps them to learn about their own imaginative capacities and about the world in which they live.

Some children carry their stories so close to them that they can hardly stop talking; some carry their stories so close to them that they can hardly speak. Some become restless and impatient as they listen to another's story because their own stories are struggling to emerge. And some children, their stories still hidden from their view, do not always understand what a story is and does.

In a classroom in New York City not long ago, a child was frightened by a story I told to his class about a tree that could listen and, with its ever-changing leaves, talk to us. At first, Joel did not want to believe what I was saying—I was challenging a reality he had carefully fashioned. Then one day, when he realized how this story could open up his imagination without asking him to forfeit everything he knew of this world, he wrote:

> It's amazing how the wind moves the trees.
> It moves my mind also.
> When I look at a tree
> I feel brave and bold.
> When the wind blows through the trees,
> The trees whistle in tune
> for beautiful music.
> As I listen, I smile.

Another child, Michelle, in a classroom in a different part of the city, accepted a story I told her class about a magic flower that could become all the colors of the sky. She received my telling of the flower's story without any trace of doubt, her open face responding to every gesture of the story as it was being told. One day, she took one of us aside and confided her reaction to this kind of story. "When you imagine things . . . they start to grow," she said. "If you love them, they love you back. When you have an imaginary flower, it grows in your mind and you can dream it always. And no one can take that away from you."

In both instances, these children have begun to see the "mind" as more than a mechanical operation for correct answers. They sense that the mind is our inward ability to understand who we are as well as the nature of the world we inhabit. The "imaginary flower" Michelle speaks of has all the organic properties of a growing flower and we can, with the unique powers of our own imaginations, dream it into being. In other words, it is from the *inside of ourselves* that we are able to grasp and create the story of this flower or any flower. Because it is we who are dreaming this story, it becomes ours forever.

An adult who goes into a classroom needs to make it clear to each student that he or she has the tool with which to create meaning. That tool is the imagination. Once children recognize the imagination as something powerful within themselves, they are able, ultimately, to live more fully.

For many children, there is little opportunity to express realizations like those of Michelle and Joel. For these children, an entire childhood can pass without their ever realizing that they have an inward life. What is often experienced by these children is a one-dimensional self: eager to survive but ill-equipped to use the imagining self as part of that survival. How often we hear of children whose daily routine is made up of attending classes in which little attention is paid to the welfare of their inner lives. After school, they go home and sink despondently in front of television sets that whir away into the night. The television set has become a kind of myth-maker for children in our culture; the television set has become a substitute storyteller.

And what myths does television teach children? Much of what they see is advertising. Children, like the adults in our culture, often want the things that are advertised. An awareness of the kinds of pleasure that can be obtained by experiences or events like stories—which are not quite "things"—is absent from many children's lives.

Furthermore, much of what they see in between advertisements has to do with violence and death. Imagine the effect this has. One of the most subtle and difficult parts of childhood is the realization that to be alive, we also have to die. A culture such as ours, in which violent death has become a predominant fixture in our consciousness, instills in many children a kind of despair at the sense that maybe life isn't worth living. One might ask if any of these children were ever read to by a parent, teacher, or other caring adult, or if there was any effort made to help these children get closer to the stories they are telling themselves and would like to tell us, no matter how awkward or banal they may seem to our adult ears.

Over the years, I have been able to work with children who were often not aware of the richness of their own inner lives, and consequently, of the stories that lie within them. I am struck by certain similarities in the way these children perceive themselves and the world around them. Sometimes excessively "afraid," many of these children exhibit hostility to their peers and to adults. Their fear is, I suspect, an expression of a lack of connection to the inner self as well as to a sustained sense of outward community. This inability to move comfortably between different temporal and spatial experiences is often expressed by a dogged realism: Things can only be what they should be, not what they could become. In short, many of these children are caught in an arid rigidity where the imagination is suspect. This rigidity of thought tends to be reinforced by our societal distrust of the meaning and usefulness of the imagination. It is not until these children are given a chance to slow down and sink into themselves, by someone who takes the time to listen and to encourage listening in the child, that any kind of renewed response in the child is brought into being. I am often startled by what happens when we ask children to reflect on a simple object, to imagine what it feels like to be that object and to write a story from its standpoint. This small story—by a

nine-year-old boy imagining he was a typewriter—slowed the author down just enough for him to be amazed by how much he
could hear of himself inside the story of an object:

> Every now and then somebody sticks a piece of paper in
> Me. I don't get one thing that is I don't see why they keep
> clicking Me and turning My noise and changing My best
> color. Every time they are done with me they would
> always take the paper out of me. And there is one thing
> wrong with Me that I do not get. I keep on hitting Me.

By imagining himself as an object, this child was able to uncover
and share the sense that something very important had gone
wrong in his world. What he wrote was not a metaphor made by
an adult to try to explain his problem to him, but rather, a metaphor made from his sense of the problem. By creating that story, he
was able to express his own sense of his predicament.

I believe that most children really begin to listen to other stories
when they effectively become conscious of their own stories, when
they are made aware that what *they* have to tell us is equally perti-
nent to the world as the treasure-house of stories that have preceded them. Making children aware of their own stories can be as
easy as engaging them in conversations about how they feel, what
happened on the way to school, or what they talked about when
they last saw their grandparents. Because we tend, in our highly
accelerated culture, to distance ourselves from the details of everyday experience, many of our stories of daily events seem insignifi-
cant. And as we allow ourselves less and less time for simply
conversing, it isn't surprising that children often find it difficult to
savor stories passed from one person to another. Instead, children
and adults are captivated more by large-screen cinematic dramas,
underlined with music and fast-action editing.

To counter this, I once asked a group of children to look, for a
period of days, for the stories that lie just outside of their apartment

windows. Tony, who was then eleven years old, wrote a series of daily entries called *From My Window*, from which these two excerpts are taken:

> *Tuesday:* I see only two bags of garbage and about 20 pigeons. I see a boy looking out of a window. Then the mother comes and tells him to do something. I see that the sky is cloudy and it looks like it's going to rain. I see that a lot of smoke is coming out of our chimney. I see no lights are on and I see pigeons on our window. I see it is not maybe going to be a good day.

> *Friday:* I see pigeons flying around in circles around and around. I see people having a Birthday party and that the people are having a cake and taking pictures then they dance then they see as the person opens the presents. The person is a lady. She gets towels, perfume, powder, earrings. I think it is her husband who gives her the ring because they kiss then some go little by little.

When Tony read his "story" to the rest of the class, I remembered how, in my own childhood, I would spend hours staring out of my apartment window. Like Tony, I was able to see from this secret vantage point a world unfolding before me—a story, if you will, that was in large part constructed by my own imagination as I tried to fit the different elements of what I saw together. I will always remember the delight on Tony's face when I explained to him that the story he wrote was one that he had made. Unlike the stories that come from the television set, this story was coming from him—his observations and understanding. Though this may seem obvious to us, many children are not sure they actually have the ability to see and to construct from their seeing something uniquely their own. Added to this is their lack of faith in their own imagining. When children realize that they not only have the gift to see inwardly but also to take their inward vision, transpose it into a story, and then share that story with others, extraordinary growth can occur.

One child, when asked where his stories come from, said, "When I make up a story, it comes from the corner of my eye." Perhaps this is how we all find our stories—by extending our imagining self through the corners of our eyes. It is this play of imagination that inevitably leads to a sense of the "unknown," to those images and thoughts we have not yet fully envisioned.

Because of the premium we often put on pragmatic thought—on how much we "know" as opposed to what remains mysterious—children are sometimes afraid to imagine. The imagination itself, in fact, becomes another unknown. One child I worked with was able to confront this dilemma by making the unknown—which he identified as "the darkness"—a part of his story. When asked where stories come from, he responded:

> The earth got its stories from listening to other planets.
> And they got their stories from the stars. And they got their
> stories from the sun. The sun got its stories from the darkness, and the darkness got its stories from making them up.

What a pleasure it is for children to know that they, too, can be the source of this "making up," and to observe concurrently that throughout all of nature, including our human nature, things begin and can become something else. Perhaps a story is simply about *what happens*. If so, such stories are everywhere, both inside and outside of ourselves.

When Joel said, "It's amazing how the wind moves the trees. / It moves my mind also," he was, it seems to me, speaking to all of us about the story that each of us keeps. Within every one of us, whether child or adult, there is an elegant narrative of a story that exists between ourselves and the life around us.

That story is a place of possibility in which we take part in a world that enhances us, enlivens us, and offers us something with which we can identify. Through that identification, we grow. We become more than we are. We learn how to get from here to there. Though a story may challenge what we already believe about our world, ultimately, it is through stories that our spirit is nurtured.

In a time when children can so easily lose the birthright of their imaginations, we must find new ways to help children find the sources of the stories they so urgently wish to tell us. And each time they speak their stories, they establish once again the fertility and importance of their imagining selves.

▼▼▼

Chapter 11

Living Our Stories: Discovering and Replacing Limiting Family Myths

NANCY J. NAPIER

In every family, stories and family myths are told and retold. As children, we swallow them whole, and they become part of our unconscious map of the world. As we grow up, some of these maps can limit our growth.

In this chapter, marriage and family therapist Nancy J. Napier, M.A., M.F.C.C., the author of Recreating Yourself: Help for Adult Children of Dysfunctional Families, *and most recently,* Getting Through the Day: Strategies for Adults Hurt as Children, *summarizes a self-hypnotic process by which we can change these maps by consciously working with them via the imagination. In the vast freedom and flexibility of this realm, we can identify self-defeating beliefs and challenge old scripts to create a new tale to guide our lives.*

The family is our first map of the world. Family stories about life, the world, and ourselves are learned before we have words to explain them. Because we take in these stories without critical analysis, they live deeply, and often unquestioned, inside us. Unfortunately, these stories may contain negative information about ourselves or the world that limits our ability to live fully and effectively as adults.

Living with family myths can be like walking through a house of mirrors. Unfortunately, you cannot leave these internal mirrors behind. They create a distorted reflection of yourself and, if these distorted mirrors are all you have ever known, how would you know what you really look like? How could you possibly recognize your true reflection?

When we are children, adults are the mirrors that reflect who we are. When a child looks up into the face of a grown-up and sees an angry, disgusted, or depressed expression, the child does not say to herself, "Oh, Dad had a really rough day today. That's why he looks the way he does." Instead, the child learns from the reflection in her father's face, "I must really be a bad girl if this is what I look like in the face of someone else." If the adult uses a vicious tone of voice, or says ugly words, a child doesn't think, "What is going on with this person today?" Instead, he may think, "Look what I do to people. I must be a bad boy."

We can use self-hypnosis to correct the distorted reflections we received from childhood mirrors and to create new stories about ourselves and the world. The unconscious pays attention to whatever is experienced in the hypnotic state. If what you discover is useful and serves to heal you, the unconscious will keep working with it. This doesn't mean that we don't need the conscious mind to do important everyday tasks, like knowing that "two and two equal four," or figuring out the shopping list for that special dinner we may have planned. But the conscious mind doesn't have intuitive wisdom; it doesn't know where you need to go or how to get you there. The unconscious knows those things. In a self-hypnotic state, you are able to engage the unconscious part of you with useful information and experiences that promote healing.

I have seen powerful examples of how quickly the unconscious can work with the information you give it. For example, one client—a woman who suffered brutal physical abuse as a child—was exploring a major theme of the story of her childhood: Adults can't be trusted, *especially* those who pretend they care about you. Because the people who supposedly loved her were the very ones who hurt her—often without warning—she learned to distrust all grown-ups.

During a session where she was using hypnosis to explore her childhood wounds more deeply, she met an inner-child part of her who said, "I know about you grown-ups. You will hurt me. I'm not getting anywhere *near* you." In response, this client said, "Fine. You don't have to like me. I'll be here anyway." She made no demands, had no expectations of the inner child, even though this was, at first, difficult for her. Her response in this first, brief interaction began to weave a new theme into the child's story: Maybe some adults are different.

Although it took time to create a new story about what this inner child could expect from other people—a story that would, in turn, have an effect on how the grown-up self would feel in her present-day relationships—changes began within a relatively short time. During the next session, when the client went into another hypnotic experience, she was surprised to discover that the inner child seemed more approachable. Her unconscious mind had been doing work—creating a new story, a new possibility—that had been outside her conscious awareness.

In working with the unconscious, I maintain three premises. The first is that most of us have negative messages we took in from some of the stories and myths we learned as children. For just about everybody, there is some kind of negative programming left over from childhood. It needn't all be from the family, but there is bound to be some limiting reflection of ourselves from some experience growing up that needs to be brought to conscious attention and changed.

The second premise is that we have a need and a right to identify what holds us back from becoming all we are capable of being. Our primary relationship is with life itself. If we just live old family stories, we may deprive ourselves of the fullness of our capabilities. Not only do we have a *right* to be free from the family programming that has held us back, but we *need* to be free of it. Of all the human beings on the planet right now, there aren't two of us who are alike. If we are living someone else's story, we are not contributing our unique talents to our communities.

The third premise is that it *is* possible to change our programming. For example, a common family message I encounter in many clients is, "We really want you to succeed. Go out there and get 'em! But don't you dare exceed anything we know and find comfortable." With this kind of message buried in your unconscious, if your success happens in a completely different world from what your family knows, you may start to pull back. For example, a workshop participant talked about how he had always wanted to be an artist, even though the professions his family valued were in business and education. The family myth throughout much of his childhood was that professional pride could only be achieved if he held a "respectable" job—as a businessman or professor. He heard many stories of family members who had succeeded—and those who hadn't. The stories left no doubt about who was admired and loved more.

This man's boyhood was fraught with guilt and a basic sense of not measuring up. His natural creative ability kept pushing for expression, and yet he felt the inherent threat of disapproval and rejection implied in all the family stories about work. Because of this, he did his best to spark an interest in education as a field of endeavor. He went through school working hard to achieve an advanced degree in art history, something he hoped would make his parents proud. He didn't realize that his choice to teach art history was an unconscious compromise between his love of art and the family myth that pushed him to be a "respectable professional."

Finally, after years of internal conflict—as well as a chronic sense of dissatisfaction, of something missing from his life—he realized that he had to give his artistic talents a chance. It was a decision filled with conflict because of his family's stories. Eventually, though, this talented man became a successful artist. What continues to be hard for him is his parents' inability to share his deep satisfaction in his chosen career.

Using self-hypnosis to recognize and define the family myth that had caused him so much pain, this man was able to tell his inner child new stories. They were about people *he* respected who had the courage to express themselves in ways that honored their unique talents. He also told his inner child how much he appreciated his inborn creativity and artistic urges. Over time, he reported a lessening of his sadness at his family's inability to move beyond its old story. He also felt increasing courage to stretch his artistic talents and enjoy his mounting successes: He was creating a story that conveyed permission for him to give full expression to his creative urges.

Once you recognize that you are pulling back, perhaps because of a deep fear of being abandoned if you move away from the family's comfort zone, you have the power to choose to deal with the abandonment fears and change your response. In fact, the one thing you always maintain is your power to choose. Difficult experiences may take a lot away from you, but not your capacity to exercise *choice*. Someone I know said, "People go out and sometimes get dented." There are a lot of dents in life, but we can maintain the right to choose how we are going to deal with them. Self-hypnosis can help increase this ability. The more you know about how you got to be who you are, the greater your ability to decide which story you want to live: your own or a limiting one left over from childhood.

Family stories are learned in different ways. Let's say that you come from a social family, one that gives lots of parties. To outsiders, your family may seem warm and open. But when the guests go home, family members may talk about the visitors, criticizing their behavior, clothes, and other characteristics. If you are a child growing up in a family that does this, you learn that it isn't safe to reveal yourself to people. This is not something anyone actually tells you. It's what you take in without words, the reflections of the mirrors in your family. These reflections may sink into your unconscious mind quite deeply and build a conviction that people will be unkind to you when you aren't around. Thus, this family message can be limiting when, in adulthood, you move toward intimate relationships. For example, the stories you bring from the family may lead you to be suspicious of your mate, or worried that he or she talks about you behind your back. Or you may find yourself living out the family myth of talking critically about other people, the very thing that caused you so much discomfort as a child.

There are also more obvious family stories in which people tell you directly what the world is like and what you are supposed to do in it. A common example is when parents tell children, "No one will ever love you as we do," and then support it with tales of betrayal at the hands of outsiders. Or a family may have indirect stories about how precarious and unsafe success is by telling anecdotes about people who "got too big for their britches," then failed and were humiliated. All these stories become programmed, too, as reflections and expectations of yourself or the world. I think of these negative messages—whether they come to you directly or indirectly, as stories or myths—as hand-me-downs.

If you ever had to wear hand-me-down clothes, you know that the style, color, and fit may have been great for the person who had them originally, but not for you. You may have had to squeeze into them or convince yourself that you looked fine, when in fact they were all wrong for you. That is one way to characterize these family messages. They fit someone else. You did not decide that you were stupid, unsuccessful, or unattractive. Like hand-me-down clothes, those ideas are really about someone else: they reflect the stories and myths someone *else* learned to live by. It's a relief to know that you have the right to say, "No, this doesn't fit me. I'm going to return it to its owner."

When I talk about returning hand-me-downs, I am referring strictly to an *inner* experience. I'm not saying that you must race out and read your family the riot act. Instead, we can deal with the *internal* family. The internal family represents aspects of your own consciousness that reflect people who were important to you. For example, if you had a good and loving caretaker, some aspect of your own consciousness would reflect that goodness and love. In the same way, if someone important to you was abusive, frightened, or anxious and depressed, you would have internalized those characteristics as aspects of yourself. The internal family is the one that is with us twenty-four hours a day; it is the one we deal with in self-hypnosis. So, whenever I refer to giving such hand-me-downs back, I am talking about an inner experience: empowering yourself to say "no" to the internal family.

There are various forms of hand-me-downs. Some are verbal, as when someone tells you, "No one will ever marry you. You're too miserable." Some have to do with body language and facial expressions. Anyone who was abused sexually, physically, or emotionally will remember how the face of an abuser could change. That person, who a few minutes before was a reasonable human being, would suddenly wear a different, frightening face. One of the hand-me-downs from this kind of experience might be, "I can't trust the people I love. I never know when the monster inside them will come out and hurt me." Tone of voice can also create hand-me-downs, as when a parent yells about something you didn't do correctly. And of course, there is always shame, which is given out in huge doses through family hand-me-downs.

One way to use self-hypnosis to deal with disabling hand-me-downs is to construct a situation in which they may be given back, which is a way to begin rewriting your own stories. To do this, you might start by thinking of a theme or message you got from the family that you might truly be ready to give back. When it comes to mind, write it down and take a look at what you have written. See if you are ready to say, "Okay, I've had enough of this. I don't want this any more."

If you can, get a mental picture of the person who conveyed the message to you. You want to have as vivid a sense of this person as you can. If you know the person's first name, use it in your mind rather than, say, "Mom" or "Dad." When you allow yourself to focus on the person's first name, you define them for yourself as a human being, not a role or position of power. Ask yourself, "What kind of person says these things to a child? What goes on in a person who would say things like that?" Or you might ask yourself, "Who would wear his face that way?"

When you do this, you create some distance between yourself and that person's power to influence you. It is helpful to remember that when you wear your face a certain way, or use your voice or body a certain way, you reveal yourself. This is also true about the person who handed you the message. That hand-me-down says something about *them*, not you.

In the following exercise, it is helpful to have the hand-me-down represented as a symbol. You can give back a burlap sack, a stone, a piece of jewelry—anything at all. You may just want to give back a color that conveys the energy of the message or, if the message was spoken, the words themselves. With these things in mind—the image of the person who gave you the hand-me-down and the image of the hand-me-down itself—you can begin the following imaging process to give that old message back, to begin to say "no" to the limiting myths you were handed in childhood.

Begin by taking nice deep breaths. If you want, you can use a simple eye-roll technique to help you go inside. Looking straight ahead, roll your eyes up toward the ceiling as you inhale; then, as you exhale, keep your eyes rolled up as you close your eyelids. After a few seconds, allow your eyeballs to drop down, behind closed lids, to their comfortable resting place. Then, with your eyes closed, take two more deep, easy breaths.

Notice, as you continue to breathe gently, that your body seems to understand instinctively how to settle in quietly and easily, how it allows the chair to do the work of supporting you right now. With each breath, you may notice that your body continues to settle even more, that when you exhale, there is a deep wisdom that says it's all right to settle in. As you settle inside, you might become aware of the sensations your body has as you allow the chair to provide all the support you need right now.

There are many levels of support available to you. For example, the chair supports your body, the floor supports the chair, the building supports the floor, and the earth itself supports the building. There is support here upon which you can deeply depend, just as there are layers in your unconscious that are supporting your healing intent right now. In fact, for this exercise, allow your conscious mind to be a passenger that goes along, wonders or wanders, while your unconscious creates and brings into awareness what is really important.

Now, perhaps you could find yourself in a beautiful, safe place, indoors or outdoors. If you are walking, notice the surface underfoot. Is it hard or soft? Is it smooth or textured? And how does your body feel as the movement of your feet continues, as one foot follows the other?

You might ask yourself if there are any special smells or sounds that increase your feeling of safety or comfort, or some other feeling that is reassuring. Just take in the colors, shapes, and textures around you that increase your sense of safety. Remember, this is your inner world and you are safe here.

Bring to mind the hand-me-down you are ready to give back. And become aware, if you will, of the ways in which this hand-me-down has affected you in your life. Also notice what feelings come up when you connect with this hand-me-down. Allow yourself to discover that you can move back along a thread of awareness, taking your present-day adult consciousness back across time, across space, to the time and place where you received this hand-me-down. You may discover that you can observe a scene with a child who is having some kind of experience where this hand-me-down is being passed along. Just observe this. Remember to be the adult, focused in your present-day consciousness. You may even want to imagine that you're watching a movie, just observing.

Pay particular attention to the effect this has on the child's sense of self in the world, on how this impacts that child. Notice the learning that takes place and the feelings that the learning creates. Allow yourself to tune into the child's truth, to discover the child's experience of receiving this hand-me-down. Imagine the story the hand-me-down tells the child about himself or herself and the world.

Once the scene has run through to completion, see if—as the present-day adult—you are ready to step into that scene. Allow yourself to discover the symbol, object, or other representation of the hand-me-down, and see if you are ready to give it back to the person who gave it to you. Remember to allow yourself to do this in whatever way feels safe and powerful to you. Just hand it back. You have the right to do this. It is your right to choose to say, "No more." As you do this, be sure you keep the child safe; the child may hide behind you or stand somewhere else. You, the grown-up, take care of giving back the hand-me-down. A child is too small, too young, to do this.

As you give back the hand-me-down, you can carry a dual awareness—as your present-day self, and as the child you were. What do you feel within this dual awareness right now? Also, how does the other person respond as you give back the hand-me-down? Do they get angry? Do they get sad? Do they not care? Do they walk away? They cannot hurt you. This is your world. They have no real power except what you give them, what you were told they have.

Now, take a moment and review the whole experience, how the message was conveyed to you and your ability to give it back safely as the grown-up you are today. Then allow yourself to tell this other person whatever you need to say. You have all the inner time you could possibly need to speak your mind, to speak your truth.

Now, please bring the child with you into the present, where you are sitting in your safe place. Remember, the reality is that this child lives within you in the present. In fact, you are the most important person in this child's life. No one will be with this child every single day of his or her life as you will, and you have a right to bring the child to the safety of your adult world any time you choose. Now, if for some reason the child doesn't want to leave, that's fine too. Allow part of your adult self to stay there in the past, taking care of the child. Most often, you will find that the child is willing to come back with you to the present.

When you get back to your safe place, take a moment to be there with the child comfortably, safely. The process of giving back the hand-me-down has been set in motion and continues to develop, as does your capacity to construct a new, more empowering story to guide you. Each and every time you give back the hand-me-down that you have just relinquished—because you'll probably want to do it again, to get greater and greater strength in saying no—you will get stronger and the child will be safer. You have a right to choose to say "no" every time you need to. And now, when you are ready, reorient yourself to an alert state of mind until the next time you choose to take a healing inner journey.

WE HAVE ALL spent too much time alone in our childhood pain—living out rules and expectations laid down by limiting stories and myths from childhood. This process gives you the opportunity to step in as your present-day self, to watch what happened when that pain was handed over, and to give it back as the grown-up you are today. If you find yourself tempted to have the child give it back, *notice* the urge instead of acting on it. It may be telling you that you grew up in a family where you had to take care of the adults; they made you grow up too fast and do things you were too young to do. Now, you can change that learning by taking over as the adult and protecting the child as you give back the hand-me-down.

In giving back hand-me-downs, feel free to call on any guides, helpers, or whatever support you find in your inner world that strengthens your ability to heal. You don't have to do this alone; you can have any help you need because it's your inner world. Things don't have to be like they were when you were young and didn't have any power. Now, today, it is your choice. Now, today, you can construct new myths that build an expectation of having support, of being accepted, of living in a world where you have the right and the capacity to be *yourself.*

If the idea of hypnosis intimidates you, remember that we have all used self-hypnosis at one time or another. How many times have you been about to take a significant step and inside you said to yourself, "Oh no. I'm not going to be able to do this!" This is an example of negative self-hypnosis. Many of these negative messages come from family stories about failure, and it is empowering when you can say, "Wait a minute. This is *not* the message I choose to repeat to myself."

When you give yourself permission to do this, you can substitute a self-hypnotic message that says something like, "I'm surprised to discover that I am much more competent than I ever realized." And then you might actually discover that you are, indeed, more competent than you ever realized. That's a possibility. And the unconscious tends to take hold of healing possibilities.

The potential for healing through this kind of inner work is tremendous. One metaphor I often think of for this process is the Antelope Valley area in California. In the dry season, the land appears to be an endless brown dusty terrain. It's hard to imagine anything growing there. But when the spring rains come, the land becomes blanketed with fields of wildflowers. It's stunning to see an environment that looked, a few months before, as if it could not support life suddenly blossom with color.

I've always liked this metaphor because it speaks to the seeds of potential that are under the surface in the unconscious of each of us. No matter how harsh and unforgiving the environment in which you grew up, the seeds of your potential are still there, waiting for the "rainwater" of your healing process. As you create an internal environment that supports healing, your potential can blossom. Life might have given you dents, you might even be scarred, you probably have some limitations, but your potential is never really lost.

Every time you go inside and make connections with parts of yourself, you set things in motion that develop naturally and in a healing way over time; you give yourself permission to create healing myths. Whatever has come to mind can be the seed of a developing new awareness. You are the point of power in the present. It is in your open heart that change happens and that you manifest your unfolding optimal self. Reaching into the past means nothing if it does not change the present. Even when it is painful, you need to remind yourself that you can go forward on a healing journey that promotes change. It is a gift to your future self.

You need to allow yourself these gifts. Our society is not developing people who are likely to be open-hearted without some help. When I conduct workshops, I see more and more wounded people coming for help. There is a desperate need for those of us who are healing to be centered enough and safe enough in ourselves to open our hearts and say to those who are just beginning, "It's all right. I've been there. I know it's okay to explore the stories of your childhood, even when it is frightening or upsetting." As we heal, we demonstrate that the stories we have lived since childhood can be changed. We have the right and the capacity to choose how we want to live our lives today. By uncovering our limiting childhood stories, we create an opportunity to write new ones, to say "No thank-you" to those that were handed down to us when we were too young to know what we were being given.

▼▼

Chapter 12

Drug Rehabilitation Through Storytelling

John L. Johnson

John L. Johnson teaches at the University of the District of Columbia and maintains a private practice in Washington, D.C., specializing in addiction recovery and Jungian process-oriented counseling. He is also a staff counselor for RAP, a therapeutic residential community that works with drug addicts. RAP, which celebrated its twenty-second anniversary in 1993, is the oldest drug treatment center in Washington, D.C.

Johnson began working with addiction because of an interest in Jung's concept that alcoholism has its roots in a spiritual malaise. He believes that a rehabilitation program must provide the means and the encouragement to help residents examine the spiritual issues that brought them there. Storytelling provides one way to examine those issues. Many rehabilitation programs use the sharing of stories in community sessions as an aid to long-term sobriety, but Johnson's approach has an original component: He focuses on those storytelling traditions that are particular to African-Americans, exploring what he has named the African unconscious as a way to nurture the spirit of RAP residents.

•

In the community, there are two important processes that are served by the various forms of storytelling. First, a resident in the program may tell his or her story as a form of confessional to achieve catharsis. Second, telling a story increases self-discovery and self-insight. Sharing stories with a group benefits both the teller and the listeners.

The idea that stories work on both the teller and the listener is a part of the African tradition. This tradition is the basis of much of what is done in a therapeutic community for drug rehabilitation. We see storytelling as a way of bringing our own experiences to bear on our lives.

For the African-American, storytelling is the root of survival in this country. It is the way in which the values that we cherish, the behavior that we wish to censor, the fears that we can barely confess in ordinary language, and the aspirations and goals that we most dearly prize are encoded and preserved for the next generation. Stories are what we live by and through.

For the African-American deprived by law of the tools of literacy, the narration of our stories in black vernacular forms brings together the colorful fragments of lost African cultures in a spectacular weave. One aspect of that weave is what W. E. B. Du Bois, in his great work *The Souls of Black Folk,* called the double consciousness. For every story that's told, there is a story that's not being told. There is always a story of the "I" and a story of "we," the double consciousness of living in two worlds that we have inherited.

In Africa, in the Dogon culture, stories have no end. When one person has no more to tell, another one takes the story up. This is like the running of the world, whose end no one knows. If you have any experience with Twelve-Step programs, you can see that they took some of their inspiration from the Dogon culture in the emphasis on how stories continue.

Another aspect of Dogon culture is the idea that speech employs the whole body. As you listen to stories, your body position influences the words; the position of the storyteller's body influences the spoken word. For the Dogon, the true word is spoken sitting down. That is why the participants in encounter groups sit down. When one is sitting down, there is a balance of all faculties. The spirit is calm. The word spoken sitting down is thoughtful speech. The word spoken while walking is speech without position and therefore forgotten. Words spoken in bed are confidences.

How the individual creates words within her or his own body and psyche, and how by externalizing speech, that person acts upon others and so establishes an uninterrupted cycle of verbal exchange, is the root of all communication. The story is communication. We tell stories for ourselves, yes, but also to influence others.

The first thing we must do to encourage storytelling—both in addiction work and in our culture—is to get to know the storyteller. No one is going to tell us their story unless we know them, unless there is trust.

Then, when we listen to stories, we need to maintain the mindful awareness of how the story works on us. What experiences—visual, auditory, and bodily—occur in us? What movements do we make or not make when we are listening to the story? If as I am listening, I find that my body wants to move, I am mindful of why I want to move at that instant. I ask myself, "What might it be in the story at this point that is affecting me?" For instance, a story told about sniffing cocaine had the potential of causing members of the group, especially those with only a few days in the program, to have nasal sensations or begin to sniff. A story told about using crack can cause a range of physiological and mental symptoms known as "geeking" or "craving." A phrase that I use for this awareness is "catching the edge." The edge is the place in the story where the listener's awareness fades in and out, where dream or fantasy can step in. If we try to catch that edge as we sit listening to a story, it will give us information about the story and about ourselves.

There are some specific things we have to remember in listening to stories from substance abusers. First, we must be patient. Folks tend to be wordy and to work their way through lengthy introductions. Also, we cannot expect a person to use years for chronology. Experience and events are markers most of the time. So if we ask, "In what year did this happen?" we are going to get less information than if we pick up a thread in the story and say, "When you were doing this, what things happened?" Often, an event or a "happening" such as being arrested on the street for possession or distribution is recalled in the context of other life events: "It was right after my baby's second birthday" or "I had just moved to the southeast." In the stories, time moves backward and people are involved, not calendars or clocks.

Drugs impair memory and judgment, so we have to be prepared to accept gaps and inconsistencies on the first telling in the storyteller's memory. On the first telling it might be one story; the next time a little more will be added. People grow and develop as memory comes back, as judgment comes back.

Finally, we must expect outbursts of emotions. Stories can be very cathartic, so we have to allow for that element and encourage it. If we ask questions of the storyteller, we must be prepared for some very blunt answers.

For many members of the program, the first story they might tell to a group is the story of their first experience with drugs. Here is my story:

I grew up in a very stable family, and our social life was organized around the church. My father was a deacon in the church and sang in the choir. My grandfather was choir director. Everyone I knew went to church, and our whole social life was about that experience.

The church members used to have parties. There was always a summer party, and on the back porch there would be a big tin tub with beer in it, Stroh's Bohemian Beer, a Detroit beer. There were five kids in my family who used to go—myself, my two brothers, and my sisters, Marie and Shirley Ann—and the kids of the other church members. We just went; we never had baby-sitters.

So by the time I was maybe nine-and-a-half or ten, I had an image of these deacons, these men who were so officious, so strong, so powerful—they led choirs, they took up the collection, they ran everything—sitting in our kitchen and deciding when they would buy a church, how were they going to borrow the money, and things like that. While they did these important things, sometimes they were drinking beer at parties and picnics.

So I wanted to have a beer. For a while, my friends and I were at the age where you say, "You go first." "No, you go first." So that lasted for about a year. Then the next year it was, "I'll go if you go." And that lasted for about a year. Then we got a little tougher: "No, I don't feel like it right now." So maybe another year went by. Possibly about the third year of this, we decided—me, my friend James, and some other boys—that this was the year we were going to get us a beer. So we went out on the back porch and got a bottle of Stroh's beer, got the opener, opened it up, and took a drink.

It was the nastiest thing I have ever tasted in my life. None of us liked it. We were just at the point of admitting this and deciding what we were going to do with this beer when Mr. Bell, James's father, came out on the back porch. He stood there with his beer in his hand and he looked at us. My heart said, "Oh, shoot. Deep, deep, deep trouble!" And Mr. Bell said, "Well, fellows, let's drink our beer. Drink up." And we had to drink this terrible stuff. After a couple of swigs, he had mercy on us, and said, "Well, just put it down and go back to play," and we did.

Mr. Bell never said a word about that to anybody. He never said a word to our parents or anyone else in the church about how he had caught us out there with that beer. I remember talking to him at my father's wake, and I told him about that story. He had forgotten about it completely. But it was indelibly impressed in my mind. I can see Mr. Bell standing right there—Mr. Ernest Bell, who was a deacon officer—standing there, holding that Stroh's beer, saying, "Well, fellows, just drink up." That is my story, my first encounter with drugs.

There are a couple of things that you might have found out about me from reading that story. One, of course, has to do with my involvement with the church. That involvement has everything to do with my being where I am now.

As an adult working with addictions, I became very interested in group process. Then I realized that the whole time I was growing up, I lived in a system that was based on group process. One of the central tenets of our church, the Disciples of Christ, was that everything was taken to the table, every Sunday. Everyone came together. I knew, from watching my grandfather and how he could get a choir of sixty people to sing when he raised his hand, that you can get people to do things in a group, to face things, to try things, that they would never face or try alone. I mean, all of those people in the choir didn't have good voices.

I saw men who were chauffeurs, who had nothing jobs during the week, become transformed and make big decisions on Sunday. They knew how to run an organization. So watching them prepared me for the work that I do today. There was nothing that anybody could teach me about group process and group dynamics in graduate school, except perhaps a few new words. I already knew what you could get by working with a group.

In the therapeutic community, we have found that the group process can free people up to tell their stories. We have developed some interesting, specific techniques to help people say what they need to say within the safety of the group.

One exercise is called "the road to addiction." I have the group members each draw his or her own road to addiction. They draw it in terms of how hilly it is, and what kind of road it is: a two-lane highway, an alley, a dirt road. I make some suggestions about imagery choices and they simply make a drawing.

After they draw the road, I ask them to put in seven stop signs. Where were the places they could have stopped? Through the process of drawing those possible turning points, they find something to talk about, one way to tell their stories. Then the group shares their drawings and their stories about the road to addiction.

Another way to get people to begin to tell their stories is to give them a chance to describe their best friend to the group. When did they meet them? How did they get along? What did the friend do for the speaker? People will really open up with that one, talking about the loneliness and pain that friend shared. I am always amazed by the creativity that people tap into telling these stories.

We also use an autobiographical exercise. Everyone has to write an autobiography twice: once early in the program, and a second time near the end of the program. Both times, the residents take these into their groups. People read them and discuss them with each other.

There is an aspect of storytelling at RAP that is similar to the Alcoholics Anonymous (AA) model. It has to do with the idea of sponsorship. One of the first stories a resident is likely to hear in our program is from an older member, who will talk about his or her life before and after RAP. That story is offered both as a comfort and as a model for how to work the program. In a sense, the speaker represents the program to the audience.

In the AA model, three things are usually talked about. First, the speaker talks about when she or he hit bottom. Second, the speaker identifies the problem—alcohol, cocaine, whatever. Third, the speaker describes the conversion of that problem: I have turned my life around and I am in the program. If you listen to a skillful speaker at an AA meeting, you will hear each of those three stages.

These can be very useful ways to tell stories. There are some members who, once out in the community, go to AA. Sometimes we refer people to Twelve-Step programs, which use stories as tools for rehabilitation, but there are two ways in which a therapeutic community is very different from a Twelve-Step program.

First, we feel that any time you have an organization that says, "We don't stand for anything except our own sobriety," you lose track of your responsibility to the community. What can happen is that while all the members are sitting in a room the mayor of their city is taking taxpayer's money for drugs, and none of them are saying or doing anything about it. We believe we have the responsibility to be socially conscious and politically aware. We have always been in the vanguard of rehabilitation programs in that way. We encourage our residents to go out into the community, without anonymity, to tell their stories, to talk on the radio or TV programs, and to present sociodramas about personal experiences with drugs and the law. Sharing the type of life-styles they were living as addicts is an important aspect of storytelling in a therapeutic community. Each person goes out on speaking engagements, which are seen as a way to help learn the importance of one's personal story in one's self-reclamation and also learn the skill of storytelling as a way of informing others about the devastating effects of drug addiction.

The other difference has to do with the first of the Twelve Steps, which is an admission of powerlessness. Powerlessness is a troublesome idea for African-Americans, particularly because we were brought to this country with our power stripped from us. So we do not require a confession of powerlessness. We just require that a new person be on time, be where they are supposed to be, learn our philosophies, work on the service crew, and do a good job. We do not require any kind of large-scale confession. It is enough that they are able to learn the philosophies and converse with their big brothers or sisters, begin to share their stories.

All participants are assigned a big brother or sister—a peer—right from the beginning. While the peers are very loving people, they are also tough. They expect a lot from the residents, and the residents come to expect a lot from themselves. For example, we have what we call Ten Points of Liberalism, which is based on Mao Zedong's concept of liberalism as outlined in his Five Articles. Being liberal is being too easy on yourself or someone else. It is not a positive attribute.

For example, the first point of Ten Points of Liberalism is: "to let things slide for the sake of peace and friendship when a person has clearly gone wrong, and refrain from principled argument because he is an old acquaintance, fellow citizen, schoolmate, close friend, loved one, old colleague, or old jail-mate; or to touch on the matter lightly instead of going into it thoroughly so as to keep on good terms. The result is that both the family and the individual are harmed."

When a resident is liberal—whether with the self or with another person—the whole group is affected. The techniques we use to confront that are also forms of storytelling.

For example, if someone in the group needs to be reprimanded for being too liberal in one way or another, the group will give that person what we call a "haircut." Like most stories, a haircut has a very specific form. The group sits in a circle; the person who is getting the haircut sits in the middle. The members of the group each get to tell their stories about when or what that person has done that has been detrimental to their rehabilitation and the group.

It is important that these stories be uninterrupted. The person getting the haircut simply listens to what is being said. At the end, the person has a chance to respond but usually will just say something like, "Thanks for the information. I'll have to think about this."

In *The Tunnel Back* by Lewis Yablonsky (Macmillan, 1965, chapter 11, pages 233—259), there is a vivid example of this kind of storytelling. In the haircut, the more experienced "deliverers," those further into treatment, tell the story to the person with a problem, providing examples of behavior and encouragement to change as part of the process. It is often a direct, strongly worded attack on behavior, which is designed to pull the rug out from under the person. A central theme delivered to the person receiving the haircut is drawn from the experience of the person giving the haircut—"I know people like you because I used to be one of them, so you aren't pulling anything over on me."

Another example of an uninterrupted story is something called "cleaning your gut." This is a kind of reverse haircut. Sometimes, a member of the group does something they know is against the rules, such as getting high or making unauthorized trips or phone calls. They may get away with it, but they will feel it inside, like their gut was dirty. The person who has broken the rules can talk to the group about it, let everybody know what happened. It is a chance to let out the guilt and the tension that come from being liberal with yourself.

Both the haircut and cleaning your gut are about being able to be honest with the members of the group. Honesty is a very important part of treatment. People with substance abuse problems may have done a number of things that they are ashamed of and reluctant to share with others. It is essential that the group provide a place where honesty is possible.

We acknowledge and protect the difference between female stories and male stories. In addition to mixed rap groups, we have single-sex groups, because women and men might not want to talk about some things in front of each other. For example, some of the women in the program might have resorted to prostitution to get drugs or money for drugs. Some of them might have had their children taken away from them. It is very important that the women in the program feel protected, that they have a safe place—a container—in which to tell those stories. It is not a matter of sex discrimination, but a matter of recognizing that the therapeutic community, like many other communities, has traditionally been a very masculine place and that the concerns of women really do need to be protected.

A similar issue is true for men. For instance, many of our male residents have been in jail and have been subjected to various kinds of abuse there. They tend to be much more reluctant to tell those stories in a mixed group. Residents who have been subjected to various forms of abuse throughout their lives—and there are examples from both sexes—do not go into that in joint sessions.

The work I do now is more with the staff members than with the residents themselves. The stories that staff members have to tell are important too; people who work in this field really need someone to listen to them. This is the area that I have come to specialize in. Some people would call it supervision, but I call it just what it is: providing a safe place for people to tell their stories.

▼▼▼

Chapter 13

Letting Pictures Tell Their Stories

Shaun McNiff

Shaun McNiff is professor of expressive therapy and dean of the Institute for the Arts and Human Development at Lesley College in Cambridge, Massachusetts. A pioneer in the field of creative arts therapies, McNiff has done ground-breaking work in the education, theory, and practice of art therapy and has authored many books on the subject, including most recently, Art as Medicine: Creating a Therapy of the Imagination (1992). He also teaches in Switzerland and Israel.

In the essay that follows, McNiff discusses the theoretical basis for his approach to art therapy, which involves having clients create a drawing or painting and then tell stories from the point of view of the artwork itself. While McNiff's work has, in the past, found its audience primarily among other therapists, his insights extend well beyond that community, to anyone interested in examining the potential for positive change that comes from exploring the creative instinct, both in paintings and in stories.

The art therapy profession generally views the fruits of expression as fossilized substances from the subterranean id, which are used as resources to fuel therapy's advances. In this approach, the red color appearing in a painting that I make becomes a symbol of "my" aggression. The belly button in the figure I draw represents my dependency needs. In each case, the images of artistic expression are transformed into explanatory labels for the artist's pathology.

In other words, what we call psychological interpretations of art are often the viewer's projections disguised as fact. As Georgia O'Keeffe said to the critics analyzing her images, "You are talking about yourselves—not me."

Not only do such analyses degrade artists but also there is the issue of what they do to artistic expression. The root of the problem is that many of us are taught to believe in a theory that can, from its own perspective, explain experience. Rather than seeing an individual frame of reference as one of several possible biases, we project our own framework onto the world, believing it to be certain and accurate.

But life is an interactive process, an ongoing dialogue between perspectives that is, in its totality, a kind of ecology. In a healthy ecology, all participants are respected and allowed to speak. Rather than interpreting an image or gesture in a work of art as revealing only the artist's personal story, we need to open up to the image or gesture, as David Linge suggests, "By listening to it and allowing it to assert its viewpoint." We have to allow the image to tell its own story.

This means that we must temper the tendency to see the image as a part of the artist who made it. Artists, too, must step out of the center of artistic activity and see themselves as coparticipants in creation. This decentering of the ego is not an attack on its existence, but an attempted opening to an ecological interplay of expression.

When we allow images their autonomy, we depart from gestalt therapy as it is commonly practiced. Gestalt therapy, which works to unify a fragmented personality, interprets each separate individual response to a given situation as part of that whole personality. Although this approach has helped to liberate psychotherapy from one-sided analytical reductions, its belief that everything in personal psychic experience is part of the self has contributed to our era's monomania and our lack of respect for the imagination's autonomy. This in turn creates a kind of *me first* orientation that has turned many sensible people against therapy.

I recognize gestalt therapy's relevance and appeal. But I am concerned about its limited view of what constitutes the whole as well as its emphasis on the ego's centrality. Symbols, the vast treasury of cultural memories, and the autonomous existence of archetypal figures are consumed by this egocentric fantasy that sees the world as part of itself. If we return to our definition of healthy existence as a kind of ecology, then gestalt therapy's emphasis on the self as the center of meaning can result in a kind of ecological disease.

Jung urged people to become aware of the myths they are living. Our culture generally lives the myth of the heroic and self-sufficient ego rather than the collaborative community. We unconsciously act out the heroic story in our dealings with the world by conquering adversaries, actualizing personal potential, and practicing self-reliance. Creative collaboration is decentered rather than heroic, imaginal rather than literal, and spontaneous rather than planned.

A therapy of the imagination can emphasize the collaborative nature of art. One way to approach this is to create relationships with the imaginal other through dialogue. In this approach, the artist interacts with figures of the imagination rather than denying their presence. This therapeutic dramaturgy achieves depth and meaning by staying with the characters of the imagination, letting them speak, reveal themselves, and tell their stories.

Nothing creative exists in complete isolation. Therefore, the basis of creation and health is collaboration with others within our physical and psychic environments. Many artists find that in their work they return to the same figures, themes, and even materials, which we might call *familiars*. The artist returns to these familiars for medicine and inspiration, and these familiars interact with the artist throughout the creative process. But while we may cooperate with these familiars, we do not own them. They are not ours.

We have reached a point in psychotherapeutic and human history where it is imperative to liberate images from ourselves and restore the reality of imagination as a procreative and life-enhancing function. If we can step out of our self-referential thinking and imagine our dreams, pictures, poems, dramas, music, and movements as living things, with their own stories to tell, we can establish a new basis for approaching art both in and out of the therapeutic context. Respect for the autonomy of images neither replaces the art therapist's moral responsibilities to the patient nor denies the importance of the artist's role. Instead, it simply adds another dimension.

Jung established the psychological basis for viewing artistic expressions as independent entities and necessary contributors to psychic life:

> Archetypes are not whimsical inventions, but autonomous elements of the unconscious psyche which were there before any invention was thought of. They represent the unalterable structure of the psychic world whose "reality" is attested by the determining effects it has upon the conscious mind.

When we personify images, gestures, and other artistic expressions, allowing them full autonomous identity, we make it possible for them to act as agents of transformation. For example, people participating in my art therapy groups for the first time frequently make disparaging comments about their pictures: "It's a mess. Those are just childish scribbles." Rather than give validity to these expressions of insecurity or try to explain how the picture has value, I have found it more effective to ask the artist how the picture might feel about the remark. This simple personification immediately gives the picture dignity; the person who made it invariably begins to respond with compassion to the image. Reframing the situation in this way casts the person into an emotional relationship with the image. Speaking to the picture, the artist might say, "Yes, I see how my comment is offensive to you. Here I am, trying to get in touch with my inner child, and I dismiss you as childish." Then, responding from the perspective of the picture, the artist might say, "Yes, the child that stopped painting in kindergarten is still intact inside you."

Rather than simply functioning as illustrations of the psyches of their makers, the figures in our drawings and paintings can instruct and comfort us with their stories. We, in turn, may become concerned for their well-being and protection; we may feel gratitude for their assistance and delight in their presence. Some of us may even establish patterns or create environments that welcome their visitations.

While some may argue, "These persons you are talking about are all parts of your imagination," I maintain that yes, they are imaginal figures—that is, products of the imagination—but the imagination is not "mine." I do not possess the imagination or its personages. Imagination does not exist outside of reality, but is, in fact, another reality with which we interact.

Careful sensitivity to an object or movement of which we were previously unconscious becomes a basis for becoming more aware of otherness. Therefore, personifying images helps us to be more sensitive to other persons.

Simone Weil said that the most difficult and important thing is to truly listen to another person. Imaginal psychology extends that to include the others who live within us. Rather than being defined by boundaries between the self and the other, reality seems to be a continuous process of interaction. Therefore, our therapeutic purpose should be to further the sensitivity and scope of the interplay.

This task is not an easy one. Most of us find it very difficult to speak imaginatively from a perspective outside of the habitual ego position. We have to relearn the child's unconscious and instinctual ability to dramatize the figures of the imagination. Very little in our educational systems encourages us to keep that ability alive. Rather, our self-inflicted diseases of personal and cultural egocentrism amount to what James Hillman has described as an "education in psychopathy."

Hillman, who has inspired my image dialogue, urges us to "doctor" our outmoded and sick stories rather than exclusively focusing on changing the complex and elusive being we call the self. In *Healing Fiction*, he encourages us to revise and improve the stories by which we organize our lives. Hillman's method is based on the conviction that "no psychic phenomena can be truly dislodged from its fixity unless we first move the imagination into its heart."

If we change the particulars of our expression, we will change along with them. We benefit from the imaginal treatment of the world, especially because it liberates us from tedious literalism. Art therapy then becomes a creative collaboration with the imagination and the world from which it comes. The process requires that we relax the self and move it out of the way so that imagination can express itself according to its own wisdom.

This orientation to therapy is grounded in what I call "theory indigenous to art." When the methods and concepts of creative arts therapy are based in psychological theories unsympathetic to art, creative expressions lose their primacy: They literally serve another master. But therapeutic methods that respect the

expressions of art and enter *their* worlds demonstrate how everyone benefits from encouraging the full presence of imaginal figures.
We engage in creative collaboration with the imaginal other,
rather than reducing psychic reality to ourselves.

In my training studios for professional art therapists, I consistently see how simple exercises, such as speaking as a figure or gesture in a painting, meet with considerable feelings of resistance,
fear, and ineptitude. Some people project their inability to speak
imaginatively onto the method itself. But if we call imaginal
speech or dialogue worthless, what we really express is our inability to enter those realms. We tend to judge the relevance of a phenomenon based on our personal comfort with it, which is another
symptom of our culture's overidentification with the ego.

An art therapist who participated in one of my workshops revealed the nature of the difficulty of personifying paintings when
she smiled and said to me, "You are shaking my cosmology." Although this art therapist was keenly interested in seeing the colors,
gestures, and figures in her paintings as autonomous entities and
dialoguing with them, her notion of herself and of the art therapy
profession was based on the view that the image is always an expression of the artist who made it. She was accustomed to looking
at everything in her pictures, dreams, and imagination as parts of
herself. Rather than having the picture speak to her, she explained
what the picture was. The difficulty she had in approaching images as autonomous beings separate from her ego was connected to
attitudes and orientations so deeply rooted in all of us that she saw
them as a cosmology.

Our language structure reinforces our tendency to approach
the self as the center of consciousness. Objects and things are labeled "inanimate"; the painting I make is designated as "it." In
English, as contrasted to other European languages, nonhuman
forms of life and objects are neuter—without gender—and thoroughly depersonified.

When we shake the foundations of ego, the illusory nature of self-centered fixations is revealed. Then we can revise our preconceptions and engage the world from the perspective of the imaginal other. Our reluctance to personify is often based on the inability to relinquish control and act as agent for something outside our established concept of who we are.

Personifying images need not be an upsetting experience. There are times, of course, when spontaneous and unexpected expressions can shake up the existing order. But for many people, personifying involves a subtle shift of consciousness rather than a shattering of worldviews. I do not deny that dreams and pictures are closely associated with the inner life of their dreamer or maker. They carry messages, entertain, guide, and sometimes caution. But this relatedness is furthered rather than restricted by viewing expressions as autonomous forms of life.

I imagine artistic expressions as offspring: Like children, they are related to but separate from their makers. Artistic offspring flourish when we view them as individuated forms of life, coparticipants with us in life, whose beings are to be carefully protected. Neither children nor artistic expressions are statements about the psyches of their creators.

Imagining expressions as offspring actually increases their intimacy and psychological significance. The word *offspring* suggests how one thing springs from another in a kinesis of eternal emanations. When we label and analyze expressions as descriptive of the persons through which they emanate, we deny creation's movement. Labeling according to established categories is a defense against creative uncertainty, life's mystery, and the original stories that the imagination has to offer us. Nature will always shatter attempts to enclose and restrict her primal movements.

The "related but separate" basis of the connection between creator and image can be reversed with artists imagining themselves as expressions of archetypal processes. For example, a friend recently looked at a dreamlike painting I had made of two flying figures and asked if I was imitating Marc Chagall. Chagall's work was never particularly appealing to me until I began to make figures flying in space and many people drew my attention to the similarity. Then I began to feel that the archetypal process of flying figures was moving through me as it had through him. This sense is reconfirmed by my observation of similar themes constantly recurring in the images made by people in my studios.

Art history, then, can be re-imagined as an archetypal and constantly shifting process rather than a tidy chain of individual human inventions. Images of labyrinths, flight, dark openings, mystical spaces, crowded patterns, simple symmetries, embracing figures, and aggressive movements are eternal, recurring, and constantly rediscovered through an artist's journey into expression. There, images present themselves and pass into individuated forms as a result of the meeting.

If we ask the flying figures in my painting what they think about this issue, they say, "We do not belong to Chagall. We engaged him as we are now engaging you, others in the past, and those to come in the future." Archetypal movements cannot be exclusively identified with one person. Their very nature and purpose is to encourage us to look at art, history, and existence outside the framework of a single person or tradition.

Because images spring from our inner lives, personifying them enables us to dialogue with feelings and concerns that are not easily accessible to the ego consciousness and its existence in the external world. In keeping with the assumption that expressions want to speak to us, I often ask participants in my therapy studios to work in pairs after completing a painting. The painter's partner looks at the picture, not the artist, and encourages it to speak, asking it questions such as, "How do you feel?" and "What do you need?" These simple questions personify the image and acknowledge its independence.

The artist responds as the picture's "speaker," a term we take from shamanic cultures where masks and objects are considered to be alive but incapable of speaking alone. They require the presence of humans to function as their speakers and to tell their stories. Humans enter the imagination of the image or event and speak for it, rather than for themselves. Animistic cultures can teach us how it is possible to discipline, educate, and sensitize ourselves to become agents of another's expression.

Many artists participating in my art therapy studio for the first time are unable to speak for their paintings. They are stuck in their preconception that paintings do not talk; they are further hampered by the demands that they place on themselves to be "imaginative," "profound," and "psychologically clever." They are afraid to dialogue, in part because they fear ineptitude.

The painting may come to the speaker's assistance when asked what it needs:

> I need to be looked at for what I am. Let go of yourself so that you can see me. . . . If you can experience my unique nature, you will begin to feel emotion within yourself. Articulating my feelings will help you experience yours. You get confused when you try to find something within yourself and use me to present that to another person. I need you to experience me in order for me to enter the world. I need you for this. I come to life through you and maybe I can do the same for you.

An artist in my most recent studio found that her picture expressed a desire for autonomy when asked what it needed, saying "Let me go! Don't worry, I will be fine."

These dialogues may be similar to the life experiences of the artists. But the comparison is distinctly different from the reduction of one to another: Analogy implies separateness as well as relationship, and therefore fits the connection that I am suggesting between artist and image. I say that my red painting can be likened to my aggressive nature, but I cannot say that because I paint red I am aggressive. Red is not aggression; red is red. If I make comparisons between the color and my emotions, one should not be narrowly defined as expressing the other.

Creative arts therapy is a complex discipline with vast, unexplored depths, all of which can function simultaneously. Dialoguing with the image does not replace visual contemplation; it is not a more advanced state of experience. It simply engages another aspect of art and imagination, and, in the therapeutic context, enhances the therapeutic drama. Psychotherapy is an essentially dramatic process, involving rituals of storytelling.

The therapeutic meeting of persons and psychic figures is the basis of creative arts therapy. But this meeting cannot be separated from the ongoing drama of life, the multiplicity of stories that surround us. As we learn to pay attention to the imaginal other—to grant it respect, cooperation, and the room to tell its own story—we can begin to establish the basis for a new vision of art and therapy—not mine or yours alone, but a vision of the imagination that engages us all.

▼▼

Chapter 14

Drawing Your Own Story

MEINRAD CRAIGHEAD

Meinrad Craighead is an artist and writer who lives in Albuquerque, New Mexico. Craighead's life and her artistic expression were profoundly shaped by her religious heritage. Educated in Catholic institutions from grammar school through college, she spent fourteen years as a nun in a Benedictine monastery in England. But her Catholicism is decidedly not about dogma or theology; it is an emotional, intuitive experience of the divine as transmitted by the Church and her female ancestors.

Craighead identifies the church as feminine—Holy Mother the Church—and expresses beautifully her deep connections to God the Mother. Of the five books she has published, her two most recent volumes, The Mother's Songs and Litany of the Great River, exquisitely present her rich inner experience of the Feminine. In the following essay, she shows how that experience not only influenced her childhood but also continues to shape her work as an artist. She also encourages the reader to tell his or her own stories through visual, rather than verbal, means.

When we speak of the Great Spirit working in our world, within landscapes physical and metaphysical, we are telling the stories collected in world mythologies, world literature, and the history of art. But the greatest sacred stories are our own stories. This is because the Spirit tells our stories to us in the unfolding of our life journeys.

I was born in Little Rock, Arkansas, and spent my early years there. My mother tells me that I began working artistically in mud; shortly after that, I began drawing. I cannot remember not drawing almost daily after about the age of five, so I guess I was born to it. At a certain point, my family—my parents, two sisters, and I—moved to Chicago. I had never been that far from my maternal grandparents, and it was a grievous shock to me. Although I had drawn before, it was the separation from my grandmother that turned me to drawing in an intense, daily way.

She was not a literate woman, so I needed to draw to communicate with her. I also think that writing letters at that point in my life would have been too intellectual an exercise for the visceral, emotional bond I had with her. My original understanding of drawing was simply gift-giving, so I drew to have gifts to send to her.

Each painting I make still begins from some deep source where my mother, grandmother, and all my foremothers live. For me it is as if the line moving from my pen or brush coils back to the original matrix, back to the creative womb of the Great Mother. The artist, too, is a creative womb, a cauldron of transformation. What gestates in that cauldron are memories waiting for transformation into pictures. Like any artist, I animate what I remember, what has been given to me. I draw and paint from my own myth of personal origin, from my own remembering.

Obviously, we do not remember everything. We cannot. But some portion of memory—some portion of the faculty of the imagination—sorts out what we remember. I imagine it as a kind of centrifugal force that throws the memories that should stick with us against the walls of our creative soul. Those memories impressed within our very being are ours; we are never without memories.

One of my favorite stories about memory comes from Germanic mythology. Odin is the great Teutonic father God, not unlike Yahweh in the Old Testament, who lives as a thundering presence in the great World Ash Yggdrasill. Its roots spread out deep within the Earth to support it; its branches rise into the seven highest levels of heaven. Odin lives in those branches. Though he created the world, he is now out of contact with what is happening on Earth.

But Odin has two pet ravens called Thought and Memory. Each morning at dawn he sends forth his ravens to go down, circle the Earth, and find out what has been going on. Each evening, they come back to roost, and all through the night, they tell Odin all that they've seen and heard. In this way Odin stays in touch with his universe. One dawn, having sent forth his ravens, he begins to think, "What would happen if one of the ravens should fail to return? What would I do? How could I live without both ravens?" He ponders this. In his pondering, he comes to understand that he can live without thought but he cannot live without memory.

Remembering binds us together. Indeed, one of the meanings of *religion* is "to bind back to the origin." At this point of origin in God's being, we are all bound together at the same source. Stories begin in silence waiting for a word. In stories we rely on remembering, and remembering implies celebrating the word you have heard, that you must now speak, that is the visitation of the Spirit in your life.

From the very beginning of time, human beings have celebrated divine visitations by speaking, writing, singing, drawing, and dancing them. We cannot *not* tell of God's presence in our souls. We create, we build, we choreograph; we play music, paint paintings, or write poetry to communicate this divine presence. For the essential place, the point within us penetrated by the Spirit, is our creative soul. The Creator Spirit seeks out our own creativity; fire begets fire.

For my own paintings, imagery comes to me in three different ways: in night dreams, in daydreams, and in the act of painting itself. In night dreams, as we know, the imagery is like a running film. When I awake from certain dreams, often there is something about the imagery that makes it very clear to me that I'm supposed to paint it. Because night dreams are usually a sequence of events, I have to do a certain amount of choosing, organizing, and selecting to make the dream coherent as a two-dimensional painting.

The belief that God communicates with an individual through spontaneous imagery in dreams is ageless. In Wagner's opera, *Gotterdammerung*, which means "going into the shadow of the gods," the Great Earth Mother Erda sings, "My sleeping is my dreaming. My dreaming is my thinking. My thinking is my wisdom." In other words, sleep brings wisdom.

In sleep, fragmented memories rooted in our deepest seedbed grow into stories connected in a picture language. We see our stories illuminated in the Mother's dim dream light. In dreams She awakens us to ourselves. The Great Mother is the bed we are born in. In Her we sleep and dream. In Her we are healed. In Her we love. In Her we die.

In dreams we go down as if pushed into our depths by the hands of God. In my own dreams, I am often led down into the world of the unconscious by a turtle, a creature of both land and water. My paintings are very often about the union of the above and the below. Even in their composition, my paintings are often divided into halves or nearly equal halves. We might say that a dream is the union of the above and the below within our souls.

In daydreams, I see imagery as I gaze out into the landscape. My studio is built so that, from my work table, I can look out through a wall of glass to my cottonwood grove. As I'm looking out with what I call "loose eyes"—that is, not looking at anything specifically, but just looking out in an unfocused way—I receive images that come whole and complete. My kind of art—two-dimensional graphic statements—works differently in this respect than some other arts that work in a cumulative way.

In a cumulative creative experience, you build the work up piece by piece until you arrive at the whole; this happens, for instance, with music. In visual art, however, the process is just the opposite. In a museum or gallery, one sees a painting first as a whole; then you begin to see the pieces that make up that whole. When I receive imagery through daydreams, it is like seeing a painting in a gallery: I see the whole. Then I take what I have in that split second of seeing and make an image from it.

Imagery also comes to me as I paint. I begin just as a writer might put a piece of white paper into the typewriter; I just start painting. If you were to come into my studio in the first few weeks of a painting, you would think that I work abstractly, because in the beginning a landscape must be built up in which things will appear—animals, spirits, angels, human beings, suns, moons, trees, and so on. Those things appear as they want to and only gradually do I see what the story is becoming.

When I'm working, everything is in a state of flux. I apply paint with my hands, with wads of tissue, or with tiny brushes. Because I work on scratchboard, which has a surface layer of refined plaster, I use anything that will scratch the surface—razor blades, steel wool, sandpaper. I don't think about it in any logical order; it all happens at the same time. I move around shapes, forms, and color, and I watch to see what's coming out. Is this going to be a rock? Is this going to be a tree? Is this going to be an animal's face?

In this long period of being with each image, the images shift. For instance, an animal will appear and I think, "Oh wonderful, there's a badger in this painting." But that doesn't mean the badger is going to stay; the next week the badger might disappear, be over-laid by a tree. Everything is in flux. Only toward the very end do the images settle down and become secure with where they are and what they are saying.

You cannot force the images to settle before they are ready. I had, for example, "finished" a painting called *Throne*, which was published in my book *The Mother's Songs*, but I knew it didn't work. I brought it back to the workbench. For days I looked at it; then I opened it up again and began moving things around. Suddenly a wonderful mountain lion appeared, pushing into the painting sideways. It needed to be there. I had to allow that. I couldn't arbitrarily say, "I'm tired of working on this; therefore, it's finished."

The important thing is to trust the image that comes out. If that image doesn't seem to be telling you anything specifically, that doesn't mean it has no value. It is what it is; it has all of the fullness of its existence. An image is not based on your judgment of it but has value apart from your judgment.

In this way, images are like children. Children come out of our bodies as distinct creatures with their own life force. We can't really judge them; our children have independent lives. To "not like" our drawings or paintings doesn't have any meaning. It isn't a question of liking or not liking them. They have come out of us, but they have their own energy separate from us.

Women create—we all create—out of our bodies. I cannot speak of creating out of a man's body; no woman can. But the creativity in women's bodies, the potential in our bodies for making children from our many eggs is, I think, no different from the potential for making imagery from our many eggs. For many years, I have had a deep understanding that each egg within me had a face. But the face wasn't potentially a human face; it was the potential for a new painting. It is very important for we women to understand that whether we are creating biologically or metaphysically from those eggs, it is all the fruit of our body, the fruit of our creativity. It doesn't *need* to tell us anything. Of course, our creativity *will* tell us things, if we have the patience to see its slowly unfolding truth.

Whether or not a woman actually conceives, she carries the power and potential within her. Spirituality is like this. It is fertility. It is fullness and potential within, awaiting the catalyst of the Spirit to bear fruit. As a woman artist, I create out of my body, fertilized by the power of my imagination. One recurring image in my work, connected to this sense of fertility, is the sacred cave.

At the time of the winter solstice, during the sun's weakest period, natural forces draw in, go under, rest and gestate. For instance, when a bear enters a cave to hibernate for the winter, she is pregnant. The hibernation and the gestation period is one time, one movement. The cave/temple houses the bear, hiding and protecting her during this important period of withdrawal. She is enclosed within the mysterious sanctuary of her innermost being. This is where she creates.

St. John of the Cross, the great Catholic mystic, says that "contemplating is receiving." What we receive in prayer is the Spirit, who makes all creation new, moment by moment. It is the Spirit who rebirths us within the caves of our hearts. The cave is a metaphor for this silent withdrawal, this going away to be alone, to listen, to gestate the Spirit, to rebirth ourselves. The reborn self is the child of wisdom born in solitude.

When we begin to learn anything, the task is filled with structure, with discipline. When we are learning to pray, there is a long, structured, very specific learning period. But what no one tells us about prayer is that it is liberating. In fact, it is so liberating that all structures fall away. The theology we once thought was so important—that was going to lead us into the divine—falls away. It is prayer that leads us into the divine.

Praying is like any relationship. We have deep relationships because we spend time with someone. We can read a book about relationships, but what have those books got to do with real relationships? Reading books about prayer is not praying. When we have the Spirit in us, energy comes into our center, into our creativity. When we are filled with that energy we cannot *not* pray, paint, dance, sing, or compose; we can't be full of that divine energy without communicating it. Otherwise we would truly explode.

Someone once told me that mental institutions are filled with people who have seen too much of God. She implied that they had been filled with God, but because they hadn't had the means to express it, to give it back out again, their bodies couldn't deal with it. Art is a way to ground creative energy from God.

For fourteen years, I was in a Benedictine monastery. I entered the monastery when I was thirty years old. It was the last thing in the world I ever thought about doing, but it was an intuition that came to me with clarity and absolute understanding. I knew through prayer that this was what I was being asked to do, and I did it. Nearly fourteen years later, I knew the reverse: I knew it was time to leave. My decision was not preceded by a long period of soul searching, anger, or pain. Just as I knew so clearly and with such force that I was supposed to enter a monastery, fourteen years later the same voice came back and said, "You're out of here!"

I left with great joy and fear. I was in a foreign country. I was forty-four years old; I had no money and no place to go. I had nothing but a few books and the clothes on my back. But as frightening as it was, I did it. I did it because I felt a very deep understanding that there was something I had to do that couldn't be done in a monastery. I just didn't know yet what that was.

A number of months later, I was visiting a friend in London who used to visit me when I was in the monastery. She sat me down one day and said, "Well, now that you're out of the monastery, you've got to do it." "Do what?" I asked. She said, "You've got to tell your own story." I said, "What do you mean? What story?" She said, "Start from the beginning and tell your story. Whether you do it by writing or painting, I think what will come out is going to be very important to other women." I replied, "I cannot do that, so much of my story is my soul." She said, "That's what has to be told." I prayed about this. Soon after this meeting, new paintings of the Great Mother started pouring out. These paintings were published five years later as *The Mother's Songs: Images of God the Mother.*

When I paint the Great Mother, I feel I'm still painting within the Christian mysteries, for the central mystery of Christianity is the incarnation: The Spirit takes flesh so that flesh becomes Spirit. To recognize that mystery, we must go down deep into ourselves, into that place where the walls of our being are layered with our own memories. Remember that, as in any pool, when we cast one pebble we will see many, many concentric circles. One memory begets another and then another, building into stories.

To uncover your own stories, you might remember, for instance, the first place you lived as a child. Do you remember particular rooms and windows? What about the pieces of furniture, or pictures on the wall? Do you have concrete memories of vases of flowers on particular tables? Can you remember stories that were read to you as a child? What were your earliest memories of water? Of night and starlight? Of animals? Memories of your mother, your grandmother, of being in their laps? Of your father, your grandfather, of their arms around you? Of their smells? Do you remember playing hide-and-seek on summer evenings?

What about your fears of a place or a person? Do you remember recurring dreams? Which animals did you find most terrifying, or most mysterious? And what about your memories of losses? The loss of friends or animals, or deaths in the family? Who did you run to as a child? Who did you pray to?

These are just some of the universal memories that you might uncover. To remember is to *see* your own story. Remember that to take visual experience—the experience of dream and memory—and describe it in words is a translation. It would be just as easy to form the habit of drawing your dreams instead of writing them down. Take some of those memories which are already yours and put them on paper. Draw your story.

▼▼

Chapter 15

The Zen Koan: Lancet of Self-Inquiry

John Daido Loori

John Daido Loori is abbot of Zen Mountain Monastery in Mount Trem-per, New York, and the founder and spiritual director of the Mountains and Rivers Order, an international association of Zen Buddhist sitting groups, cen-ters, and temples. His published works on Buddhism include Mountain Record of Zen Talks and The Way of Everyday Life. A painter, pho-tographer, and former research scientist, Loori is committed to making Zen Buddhist instruction available to as wide an audience as possible. That commit-ment has led to the formation of Dharma Communications, Inc., which pro-duces not only books but also audiotapes and videotapes designed for Zen students of all levels.

In the following essay, Loori discusses the history and traditions of the koan in Zen Buddhist teachings. According to Loori, koans have no parallels in the literature of other religions. They are "unique narratives, culled from the life and teachings of enlightened masters. They contain a message, but it is not ex-pressed as direct exhortation or instruction. Rather, koans work like a lancet to cut away the masks that obscure our true nature. They are dark to the mind but radiant to the heart."

The history of the Zen koan begins with the birth of the Buddha. According to Buddhist legend, he walked out of his mother's side, took seven steps, pointed up, pointed down, and said, "Between heaven and earth, I alone am the honored one." This statement was probably Zen's first koan.

Like all koans, the Buddha's statement contains a seeming paradox. Amid all the diversity of life, how can the speaker be the only one between heaven and earth? Ultimately, the Zen truth contained in this koan is, "I can only nod to myself." There is nothing outside. We contain, each of us, the entire universe. In other words, the "I" in the Buddha's statement includes everything.

Again, when Buddha was enlightened, he said, "Isn't it marvelous? All sentient beings are already enlightened. All sentient beings have the Buddha nature." But if everyone is enlightened, how can we explain the suffering, pain, confusion, and delusion of this life? This statement, too, is a koan.

Koans, seemingly paradoxical statements or questions designed to further the spiritual evolution of the student of Buddhism, are often derived from historical tales or folk stories. Most religions use some form of story, such as the parable, to teach their doctrine. But there are two important ways in which koans differ from other religious stories.

First, koans are not parables or allegories; their significance is not explainable through symbols or moral lessons. Second, although most religions use stories at all levels, the student of Buddhism does not begin to work with koans until a certain amount of preparation has been made. To understand the function of the koan in Buddhist training, one must first understand the process of self-study that leads to the introduction of koans.

Zen study begins with the search. The search happens at that point in life where you begin to say to yourself, "Is this it? Is this what it's all about? There must be something more." That can happen to anyone at any age. You begin to question, not how things work, but the absolute basis of reality. That is what we call raising the bodhi mind, or the aspiration for realization.

In Zen, that aspiration must begin with self-study, and self-study begins with *zazen*, or sitting zen. For the beginner, zazen functions as meditation, a very still introspection. The point is for the student to cut off his or her internal dialogue and to focus on the present moment. Internal dialogue separates us from the moment by keeping us occupied with things that don't exist. We are preoccupied with the past, which doesn't exist any more. Or we are preoccupied with the future, which doesn't exist because it has not yet happened.

While we are preoccupied life slips by and we barely notice its passing. We look but do not see, listen but do not hear, eat but do not taste, love but do not feel. The senses are receiving information, but cognition does not occur because of our preoccupation with the past or with the future. Zazen gives the student an opportunity to end that preoccupation.

What zazen does, particularly in the beginning, is constantly bring the student back to the moment. Beginning students focus on their breath. Little by little, their internal dialogues quiet down. All of the input that constantly gives each of us the ability to say, "I'm here"—in a sense, to re-create the self—ultimately falls away.

At some point, the student reaches a point called *samadhi*, the falling away of body and mind. We describe that experience as "no eye, ear, nose, tongue, body or mind; no color, sound, smell, taste or touch phenomena; no world of sight, no world of consciousness." This is the absolute basis of reality. Needless to say, a person in that state of consciousness could not get across the street without getting hit by a car, because they have no sense of differentiation. No distinction is being made between things and oneself. The student needs to be able to leave that state when she has to walk across the street. But the fundamental experience of the unity of everything must begin to happen before the study of koans can begin.

As they go deep into meditation, students are also building *joriki*, the power of concentration. Each time they let go of a distracting thought and bring their attention back to the breath, they empower themselves with the ability to put their mind where they want it, when they want it there. This begins as mental power but becomes, as the students move deeper into Zen study, real spiritual power. When a teacher recognizes that a student has begun to perceive the fundamental unity of all things and to develop joriki, the koans are introduced.

This is a difficult time for the student. Koans are lancets of self-inquiry because they function like knives; they cut away all the extraneous ideas and concepts the student is immersed in. This is a very painful process, particularly because students tend to attach themselves to some definite ideas about the role of the teacher. In the first stage of Zen training, the teacher is supportive and nurturing because the student is often struggling just to find his or her footing. But once the koan work starts, the teacher pulls back and becomes adversarial. The function of the teacher at this point is to pull the rug out from under the student. The student gets back up and the teacher pulls the rug out again. That process is repeated again and again through the dynamic of face-to-face teaching, or *dokusan*, until the rug is pulled out and the student doesn't fall. Then the process is complete.

Koan work is also difficult because it completely frustrates the intellectual process. Most of you are probably familiar with this koan: You know the sound of two hands clapping. What is the sound of one hand clapping? This koan is often the first one that a student will work on. The teacher presents it and says, "Don't tell me, show me." The study of koans is not a matter of explanation or understanding. It is a matter of seeing the koan with the whole body and mind.

In this process, a whole other aspect of human consciousness is functioning, an intuitive aspect that is direct and immediate. This is why the students must start with zazen: They need to have some experience with breaking away from logical thought. While we do not spend much time developing intuition in our educational system, we must remember that many great scientific discoveries were made by intuitive leaps. Einstein's insight wasn't logical. The logic came later, when he had to justify what he had imagined: riding a beam of light into outer space. But his insight was immediate and intuitive. The same is true for the insights we receive in most aspects of our lives, particularly in spiritual work.

So it is the intuitive aspect of consciousness that is called on with the introduction of the koan, "You know the sound of two hands clapping. Show me the sound of one hand clapping." Another early koan is, "What is your original face, the face you had before your parents were born?" Again, the teacher will say, "Don't tell me, show me."

In the process of working with these apparently paradoxical questions, the student begins to realize that they are only apparently paradoxical. Paradox only exists in language. In reality, there is no paradox. When we start *talking* about things, paradox begins to emerge. The only way to see a koan is to be it, and the only way to be it is to forget the self.

But to grasp the koan in that way is initially very difficult. The teacher will assign a koan to the student, and the student will sit zazen with that koan, trying to become it. Imagine the context this happens in. About sixty students are gathered in a hall doing zazen from 4:30 in the morning until 9:00 in the evening. Every thirty-five minutes they get up and walk and there are breaks to eat and so on, but basically they just sit with themselves. There is no place to hide. It is an environment that forcibly turns you inward. After a while the mind becomes very, very quiet. The internal dialogue begins to stop and the student begins to open up.

Suddenly a bell rings for dokusan. The student, who has been working on the koan for several hours, goes into a little room where just the teacher and the student sit facing each other, only a couple of feet apart. The teacher says, "What is it?" and if the student starts to give a logical explanation, the teacher interrupts, cuts it off by ringing a bell. That ends the session. Usually the encounter lasts fifteen or twenty seconds, at the most a minute. There are all kinds of logical responses to a given koan, and inevitably a student will bring them to dokusan one after another.

Yet as soon as the student begins to engage the intellect, the teacher will cut off the encounter. "Don't tell me, show me," becomes the watchword. Little by little, the student frustrates or exhausts all the intellectual approaches. Sometimes the teacher will even allow a lengthy intellectual presentation and then say, "That's not it. Let go of the words, go deeper." This can go on for weeks or months.

Students may work on their first koan for as little as eight months or as much as several years. It is not a rapid process. It has to do with how much work the students have already done on themselves. You cannot forget the self until you have taken care of all the business of the self. Otherwise, your unresolved issues will constantly re-create the idea of separateness, the illusion of self.

For seventeen years, I was a scientist. My work was fundamental research, not practical research. That is, I wasn't making products; I was trying to find out how molecules interact with each other in space. Much of that process was intuitive. For example, sometimes I would come across a problem or a mathematical equation that I just could not solve. Out of frustration, I would put it aside. Suddenly, a week or two later, the solution would pop into my mind; I would see the entire problem with great clarity. Most of us have experienced that kind of intuitive process. Because that process is also the way to approach koans, I was perhaps a bit over-confident about my ability to work with them.

On the other hand, I had a great deal invested in being success-ful in the world. I went to school, I studied hard, I was bright, I was faster than some people, I was more aggressive than some people. This approach got me the things I thought I needed and wanted in life. I had achieved certain things that I thought were valuable, and I had achieved them with this intellect.

Suddenly, in entering Zen training, I was in an environment where I had to shut up and sit still. Every time I tried to say some-thing, I was told to just sit. I would go into dokusan with an ap-proach to a particular koan already worked out. I had done research, spent time in the library, used the approach that once brought me success. My teacher would say, "Stop reading books," and ring his bell. I went away thinking, "He doesn't mean it. He's just trying to be inscrutable." I would go back with the same ap-proach and he would ring his bell again.

After a while, the poor man would stick his fingers in his ears when I started talking. Then I began to take him seriously, to be-lieve that there was a whole other reality that I knew nothing about. The only way I was going to get there was not with the in-tellect and that linear, sequential aspect of my consciousness that had worked so well before. To get this, I was going to have to throw everything else away, to make myself empty. That was a very hard thing to do.

There was one particular koan that drove me to the edge. My teacher gave me these words: All things are equal, not some things big and other things small. He said, "How do you see it?" I said, "Well, that just refers to a way of talking. I mean, all things are re-ally the same. We just say big things, small things." He said, "But Rocky Mountains are big, Catskill Mountains are small." I said,

"Well, not really; they're really the same." He said, "But Rocky Mountains are big, Catskill Mountains are small." I said, "No, they're the same." He said, "You are big, I am small." He was a little guy. And I said, "No, we're the same." He rang his bell and chased me out.

So I stayed stuck there for a long time. Is bigger and smaller the same or different?

One of the functions of introducing a koan is to create what we call a "rhinoceros horn" of doubt. Doubt is absolutely critical to Zen study. Students working on a koan must have great faith in themselves and their own ability to see it. And coupled with that great faith is equally great doubt: Who am I? What is truth? What is reality? What is life? What is death? Great doubt and great faith are in dynamic tension with each other.

Along with faith and doubt is great determination. We call it "seven times knocked down, eight times get up." When faith, doubt, and determination are functioning together, sooner or later the student will begin to see the truth of a given koan.

One koan that is particularly challenging to many students is called "Senjo and Her Soul." Like many koans, this one is drawn from a folk tale. According to the story, there was once a man in China who had two daughters. The elder of the two daughters died very young, and, as a result, he ended up paying a lot of attention to the surviving daughter and making very much of her. During that time—and even to this day in Japan—marriages were often arranged by the parents, usually the father. Senjo had many suitors, and her father chose a young man from among those suitors. But Senjo also had a secret lover who had been her playmate since they were both children. Their parents had often kidded them, saying, "Oh, what a wonderful couple you'll make when you get married," and the children grew up believing that this would happen.

So, Senjo was shocked when her father announced that she was going to marry a stranger. Her lover was so distressed that he decided to leave the village; he could not bear to live in the same town if she was going to be married to someone else.

One evening he left secretly by boat and started paddling down the river. When he was a few hours away from the village, he noticed a figure running along the shoreline, following the boat. He went ashore to see who it was, and to his great joy it was Senjo. She was running away from home to avoid the arranged marriage. So Senjo and her lover continued the journey together and traveled to a remote country where they married.

Five years passed and Senjo became the mother of two children. She and her husband were very happy together, but they both missed their parents and wanted to return to their hometown. One day they decided that it was so important to see their parents, they would return and face the consequences of what they had done. When they got to the port of their hometown, the husband said, "Let me go and see how it is for us. You wait here with the children."

So he went to Senjo's old house and knocked at the door. Her father came out. The husband began to apologize for how he and Senjo had run away together but the father looked at him strangely and said, "What are you talking about? Senjo is here. She has always been here. She is in a state of deep depression, sick in bed, not responding to anything. She hasn't communicated with anyone for five years." Her husband said, "No, Senjo is with me. We have two children. You are a grandfather now."

The husband went to get Senjo for proof. In the meantime, her father went in to see if she was still in bed, and there she was. He told her the husband's story. Senjo sat up in bed and smiled for the first time in five years. She got out of bed and walked outside. And as the two Senjos came toward each other, they merged and became one.

The koan drawn from this story is "Senjo and her soul are separated. Which is the true one?"

Many intellectual interpretations are possible here. The Buddhist philosophy is that we should transcend the dualistic oppositions of true and false and look at absolute oneness. From this standpoint, a new vista will open up where we can live in true freedom and make use of dualistic phenomena. But these are just words and ideas, mere descriptions. They don't reach the koan. These words are simply an explanation—what is the truth of the koan?

We can say that this koan talks about many dualities—good and bad, up and down, one Senjo and the other Senjo, secular and sacred, holy and mundane, and so on. The koan points to the unity of all of that. But again the phrase "Don't tell me, show me" comes up. And again, the only way to see it is to be it. That is the critical importance of this koan, and of koans in general: They differ from other kinds of stories that are intended to enlighten or instruct, in that you must change the way you think to be able to grasp them.

Through working with koans, students realize that the double binds that seem to appear in this life are the products of the way the conscious mind works. You have to experience for yourself the falling away of body and mind. Then you come back into the world of differentiation with an understanding of its absolute basis.

When you understand that, you understand the dynamic of all dualities in a very intimate way, and your way of functioning in the world changes. Zen is, finally, about a person's life and nothing else. It is about eating, loving, laughing, crying, dancing, raising children, driving a car. It is doing that with the whole body and mind. It is doing that and being totally present.

It is said in Zen training that the first part is ascending the mountain. Eventually you get to the peak: realization. It is very easy to get stuck there, and there are many schools of Buddhism that do, in fact, end there. But in Zen, the practice continues after realization. It is tempting to stay in that quiet place where the view is clear and boundless, but in Zen you must proceed. When you're on top of the mountain, the question is, "Where do you go? How do you proceed?" The answer is, "Straight ahead," and straight ahead means down the other side, back into the world. Until that which has been realized has been actualized in everything we do—in the way we drive a car, have a relationship, or raise a child—formal Zen training is not considered complete.

The thing that binds, restricts, and defines the limits of your life is your mind and the way you use it. It has nothing to do with other things. Once you realize that, you begin to empower yourself, you begin to take responsibility. You realize that what you do and what happens to you are the same thing. Realizing that responsibility means that you can no longer make the statement, "He made me angry." Only you can make you angry. When you realize that, you empower yourself to do something about anger. But so long as "he" made you angry, you're a victim who depends on someone else.

All sentient beings are perfect and complete, lacking nothing. All sentient beings are enlightened. That's the truth of the matter. Each one of us is perfect and complete, lacking nothing. There is nothing to be added, there is nothing that we lack; each and every sentient being has all of the equipment, spiritual or otherwise, that a Buddha or an enlightened being has.

So what is the point of Zen practice and Zen teachers? We say that there are no Zen teachers, nor is there anything to teach, because we already have what we need. But the point of practice and teaching is to realize that. We call it "raising waves where there is no wind." The fact is that perfection is already there. The complications arise when you do what I, in fact, am doing now: try to explain the nature of the universe in words.

There is a difference between looking and seeing. In looking, you stand aside from what you are looking at and there is a relationship between the looker and the thing being looked at. Seeing is about intimacy. There is no seer. The same difference exists between knowledge and wisdom. Knowledge involves a knower and a thing the knower knows. In wisdom, there is no knower, so wisdom has nothing to do with knowledge. Knowledge has to do with accumulation of information. Wisdom has to do with intimacy.

Through meditation or contemplation of the koan, you experience intimacy with the koan. A student who has made some progress in zazen makes the point of concentration not the breath, but the koan, and sees the koan from the perspective of the koan, which means to forget the self. If you forget the self and become the koan, the koan fills the whole universe.

Initially, the koan is like a barrier. From a Zen perspective, the only way through a barrier is to be the barrier. When you become the barrier, there is no barrier. It fills the whole universe. When my students are angry, I say, "Be the anger." Sometimes they think I mean, "Punch somebody," but that is not what I mean at all.

"Be the anger" means become intimate with the anger, don't separate yourself from it; allow it, don't suppress it; let it manifest itself and see where it is coming from. Anger is only a thought. It is nothing more than the mind getting away from the present moment. Anger usually has to do with what has already happened, or what is going to happen next. That is the mind moving. When the mind doesn't move, there is no anger. When the mind doesn't move, there is no universe. When the mind doesn't move, the self is forgotten.

I realize that there is something contradictory in even writing about this. When I came into Zen practice, I had an intuitive feeling that I wanted to sit and be quiet. I would find myself going to sesshins where we would sit all day long, and I would leave frustrated and swearing that I would never come back again. Two months later, I would find myself going back.

I was keeping a journal at the time. I remember apologizing in the journal: "I'm going back again and I'm doing all this ritual. I don't know what it's all about, but it feels like I want to do it." The intellectual justification became so hopeless that after a while I stopped keeping the journal. I didn't want to talk about it any more. I just wanted to do it.

It is that same duality that the koan of "Senjo and Her Soul" and all koans approach. Finally, you can't talk about it. You have to have faith in your ability to be it.

Faith—not just in Zen or the process in general—is faith in oneself. I have found that concept to be a big barrier in working with beginning students. I don't know what we do to people in this culture, but the lack of trust in ourselves is absolutely dominant. I find myself constantly saying the same thing, knowing how hard it is for students to hear it: Really trust yourself. Really be yourself.

When I say trust, that does not mean that you have to fulfill your expectations. Trust has nothing to do with expectation. Trust means to give yourself permission to be yourself, however it is. No expectations. If you succeed, wonderful; if you fail, wonderful. Either way is okay, if you are just being true to yourself. That is where Zen starts. If you trust yourself—with no expectations— you can do the same thing with anything. If something interests you, you explore it, with no expectations as to how it's going to turn out. That is how you work on a koan.

You never. work on a koan while you are doing other things. That, too, is a basic aspect of Zen. You always do what you are doing while you are doing it. When you drive a car, that is what you should be doing: driving a car, not working on a koan. When you chop carrots, you chop carrots. When you talk or listen, you are totally there. That is what zazen teaches you to do: be in the moment. Life takes place in the moment. If you miss the moment, you miss your life.

It is your life, and not the life of some higher being, to which Buddhism directs you. Buddhism is nontheistic. Buddha is not a god, and Buddhism does not take up the question of whether or not a god exists as being relevant to religion. From a Buddhist point of view, that is a philosophical question, not a religious one. This brings up one of the most common questions people ask about Buddhism: "If it's nontheistic, what is the basis of the moral and ethical teachings?"

One of the primary elements of Buddhism's moral and ethical teachings is *karma,* or cause and effect. What you do and what happens to you are the same thing. Every action has a reaction. It sounds like one of the laws of thermodynamics, but it goes much further than that. Once you recognize that what you do and what happens to you are the same thing, you have the basis of taking responsibility, not just for what happens to you but for the whole universe. What we call good and bad are the consequences of those things we experience in this life and how we process them.

One way to understand karma is through the Buddhist concept of the Diamond Net of Indra. According to this concept, the universe consists of a vast net that contains all time and all space. At every nexus point in the net, there is a multifaceted diamond. Each of the facets of that diamond reflects every other diamond; in a sense, each diamond contains every other diamond.

If you look at one diamond, you see the entire net throughout space and throughout time, into the past and into the future. If you shake one piece of the net, the entire net reverberates from it. What you do to any one part, you do to the totality. So each diamond represents every single thing in the universe: every particle, every speck of dust, every atom. They are codependent and mutually arising. They co-originate: When one comes alive, they all come alive.

That image of the Diamond Net was considered for many centuries to be a Buddhist folk tale, a quaint, primitive way of looking at whatever it is that Buddhists believe. Then, in the twentieth century, science discovered the truth of the Diamond Net, when the discovery of laser light made it possible to make a hologram.

A hologram is a three-dimensional image that we can walk into. That in itself is extraordinary. But what is more extraordinary is that if you take the photographic plate used to produce that hologram, cut it in half, and project only half of it, you still see the whole image. And if you cut the half in half and project it, you still see the whole image. This can mean only one thing: that each particle of that photograph contains all of the information of the totality. That is the principle of the Diamond Net.

It is within the recognition of the Diamond Net that the whole study of koans comes to blossom. Koans are not simply formal devices drawn from the classic collections. At the monastery, training takes place in many areas. The most fundamental area is zazen, which functions as the digestive process for everything else. It is in zazen that the training is assimilated with every cell in your body. But in addition to zazen, there are academic studies, liturgy, study of the precepts, art practice, body practice, and the teacher-student relationship. In all of the different areas of training taking place each day at the monastery, koans of one kind or other come up.

For example, in academic study, students focus on the *sutras*, or discourses of the Buddha. If you open the sutras anywhere, there are seemingly preposterous statements being made. Those are koans. We chant lines from the Heart Sutra together every day that say, "Form is emptiness, emptiness is form." That doesn't make sense. How can that statement be made? So, again, we are confronted with a koan.

Koans all point to the same questions: What is truth? What is reality? What is life? What is death? Who am I? All of those questions address the fundamental nature of reality, which is the ultimate question for all religions, not just Buddhism. And so the "answer" to a koan is a state of consciousness. That is what needs to be present and communicated, student to teacher, in whatever way is appropriate to those people and that moment. It can be a look, it can be a touch, it can be a word, it can be anything, but it has to do with a student-teacher relationship that most of us have never had before.

After studying for years with my teacher, I realized that the man never gave me approval. In all the years I studied the koans, whenever I made a presentation, he would either grunt and say I should go on to the next one or say, "Not good enough; go deeper," and ring his bell. But he never said, "That was great. You are really sharp." Toward the end of my training, when we were going over the koans and talking about all the possible ways of working them with students, I realized that he never built me up in any way. There was never an affirmation. Did I really know what I hoped to know or did he just begrudgingly let me go on? I finally realized that I had seen things as clearly as he had seen them, but he never confirmed that fact. I had to confirm it for myself.

You see, empowerment always comes from the student. If the teacher approves, that becomes another leash. You find yourself performing for the teacher. You figure out what he or she wants and you deliver it. That is the way many of us go through life, and it is a problem, especially in relationships. We start marriages thinking, "I'll give them what they want and then they'll take care of me." But nobody can take care of us; nobody can give us what we want. We all need to empower ourselves. When a relationship starts from that place of empowerment, it is a totally different kind of relationship than the dependence that most people have. Self-empowerment is the only kind of empowerment there is.

I referred earlier to the koan as a lancet of self-inquiry because it constantly cuts away all of the ideas and concepts we hold onto. The lancet cuts away ideas, opinions, positions, material things, even our concepts of Buddhism and enlightenment. That is the only way you can make yourself empty. Whatever thought you hold onto separates heaven and earth. A single thought, and the world of differentiation appears. The absolute basis of things is missed.

It is no small thing to be born human because of the incredible potential of our human consciousness. Most of us go from cradle to grave never realizing that, never understanding the possibility of going beyond what is generally accepted as true. Yes, this world is dualistic. It is also unified in ways so incredibly profound that we have not even begun to get a glimpse of that profundity. It could be a very different world. And if we are ever going to survive the twenty-first century—if this planet is ever going to survive us— we must keep in mind that all of the problems we face today are self-inflicted wounds. They are human created and can only be healed by humans. This is a major koan for each one of us, and the only way to resolve a koan is to be intimate with it. In doing so, you are intimate with the whole universe and with yourself. No one else can do it.

▼▼▼

Chapter 16

Our Stories, Cosmic Stories, and the Biblical Story

WALTER WINK

Theology professor Walter Wink is interested in the context of stories, in the philosophies and values—the worldviews—that underlie our informing myths. While acknowledging that many biblical stories imply worldviews detrimental to human life—sexism, patriarchy, violence—Wink looks to Bible stories that contain humanistic values and builds a bridge between those tales and the stories that stem from new, more holistic trends in human thought, such as feminism, ecology, and the new physics. He believes that by naming the values that underlie all our stories—whether religious or secular, traditional or contemporary—we can be freer, not only to recognize the connections between seemingly different modes of thought, but also to make conscious choices about what we believe in and how we live.

Wink is a professor of biblical interpretation at Auburn Theological Seminary in New York City. From 1989 to 1990 he was a Peace Fellow at the United States Institute of Peace. He is the author of many books, including Transforming Bible Study, The Bible in Human Transformation, *and a trilogy,* Naming the Powers, Unmasking the Powers, *and* Engaging the Powers. *The following essay develops and expands on material that Wink has discussed in the introduction to* Engaging the Powers.

The word "worldview" has only recently made its way into public discourse. It is listed without definition in *Webster's Ninth New Collegiate Dictionary* (1985), and the reader is referred to "Weltanschauung," a German loan-word defined as "a comprehensive conception or apprehension of the world especially from a specific point of view." A worldview is thus a cosmology, an implicit or explicit philosophy of the nature of reality. Broader than myth, it provides the mental structure within which myths are fashioned. One's worldview limits the kind of myths that can be developed. We might liken a worldview to a house, and myth to the furnishings and decor. The worldview limits the myth, just as a homemaker is constrained by the given structure. A variety of myths can be constructed within a single worldview, just as a variety of rooms can be created within the constraints of a house.

Generally, worldviews are invisible. Their "picture" fits the reality they depict sufficiently well that no one notices the inevitable discrepancies. One's worldview appears to *be* reality. Our time is unusual in that we have become aware that there are a variety of worldviews competing for our allegiance.

Perhaps the most common of these is the *ancient* worldview, which is reflected in the Bible. In this conception, everything earthly has its heavenly counterpart, and everything heavenly has its earthly counterpart. If war begins on earth, then there must be, at the same time, war in heaven between the angels of the nations involved on earth. Likewise, events initiated in heaven are mirrored on earth.

There is nothing intrinsically biblical about this imagery. It was shared by the Greeks, Romans, Egyptians, Babylonians, Assyrians, Sumerians, and indeed everyone in the ancient world; it is still held by large numbers of people in Africa, Asia, and Latin America. It is a profoundly true picture of reality.

Another worldview, the *spiritualistic* worldview, is distinguished from all other worldviews in that it divides human beings into "soul" and "body." One is the same as one's soul and other than one's body. In this account, the created order is false and corrupted. Creation itself was the fall; matter is either indifferent or evil. When the soul leaves its heavenly bliss and is entrapped in a body as a result of sexual intercourse, it forgets its divine origins and falls into lust and ignorance. The body is a place of exile and punishment, but also of temptation and contamination. Salvation comes through knowledge of one's lost heavenly origins and the secret of the way back. Soul and body are irreparably split.

The *materialistic* worldview is in many ways the antithesis of the world rejection of spiritualism. In this view, there is no heaven, no spiritual world, no God, no soul; there is nothing but material existence and what can be known through the five senses and reason. We are merely complexes of matter, and when we die we cease to exist except as the chemicals and atoms that once constituted us. The materialistic worldview, which has penetrated deeply into our culture, causes many to ignore the spiritual dimensions of life and the spiritual resources of faith.

Christian theologians created the *theological* worldview in reaction to materialism. Acknowledging that the supernatural realm could not be known by the senses, they conceded earthly reality to modern science and preserved a privileged "spiritual" realm immune to confirmation or refutation—at the cost of an integral view of reality and the simultaneity of heavenly and earthly aspects of existence. Science would discover the "how," theology would discern the "why."

According to the *Eastern* worldview, the world is not so much evil as illusion. Suffering results from attachment to earthly things. The phenomenal world is an everlasting deception; salvation comes through enlightenment. This view appears to be similar to the soul/body split but differs in that, unlike the latter, which concedes the reality of the created order but deplores it, the Eastern worldview stresses the illusory nature of physical reality.

All of these different worldviews determine our responses to the raw data of our experience. Take the question of "spiritual healing." I place it in quotation marks to indicate that its very existence is questionable from the point of view of materialism, and perhaps the spiritualistic and Eastern worldviews as well—why even attempt healing if the body is slime that one seeks to escape, or if our suffering is caused by our refusal to recognize that the physical world is all illusion? According to the ancient worldview, however, spiritual healing can occur when heavenly power penetrates the earthly realm. Perhaps the healer was a shaman who had control over certain local spirits that could affect the cure; perhaps the healer trusted directly in a more universally conceived God. But such events, though rare and wondrous, could happen because the worldview permitted them.

Materialism, on the other hand, cannot acknowledge the existence of spiritual healing because it denies the very existence of spirit. When such events are sufficiently credible, materialists will "explain" them as random remissions. Science itself comes to the materialists' aid, rejecting as "anecdotal" all such accounts, however well documented. No cause-and-effect relationship can be shown between the ministrations of the spiritual healer and the patient; therefore, no empirical grounds exist for regarding spiritual healing as real.

Worldviews are highly resistant to disconfirmation. Disconfirming data are usually either rejected or accommodated in a way that preserves the basic structure of the belief. An example of this accommodation can be found in interpretations of the healing stories in the gospels. In the early part of the century, biblical scholars who were influenced by the materialistic worldview tended to explain miracles as legends invented to magnify the greatness of Jesus. The materialistic worldview dictated that the world was ruled by iron physical laws that not even God could bend.

In the last decade, advances in the understanding of the placebo effect, the functioning of the immune system, empirical studies of the control yogis can exercise over their internal organs, and above all, the shift from Newtonian lawfulness to Heisenberg's uncertainty principle have changed the way many people look at the possibilities of healing. We simply no longer know for certain what is within the realm of possibility. Consequently, some scientists are beginning, *through* science, to jettison the materialistic worldview as reductionist.

Thus, we can no longer limit the possibility of Jesus' healing stories. These changes in attitude are based, not on the discovery of a single scrap of new evidence from the first century, but on shifting evaluations of the possible. The possible is always a function of one's worldview.

Take, for example, intercessory prayer, prayer intended to draw God's attention to a particular situation in the hope of affecting change. Whether one engages in such prayer is probably not a matter of one's theology as much as one's worldview. No biblically based theology can deny such prayer a central place; nevertheless, a great many Christians are dubious as to its value. This skepticism is often simply a consequence of the materialistic worldview and its symbiotic twin, the theological worldview. It is hard enough to believe in God; to believe that God actually intervenes in the physical world is either preposterous—the materialistic worldview—or a violation of the rules of the theological worldview, which leaves the physical universe to the scientists.

What happens, though, when one's child is dying? Most of us would pray, whatever our theologies and perhaps despite our worldviews. We may not be certain that such prayer can help; we may have grave doubts that it can. But still we pray. Soldiers in fox-holes often discover themselves praying, some for the first time in their lives.

Only extremely powerful experiences are able to disconfirm a worldview; after these experiences are over, most people will set the anomalous experience aside and rehabilitate their worldview. Changing worldviews is tantamount to a revolution in the presup-positions of thought.

Today, however, we are witnessing the birth of a new world-view, one that insists on the unity of science and religion, the spiri-tual and the physical, the body and soul. I call it the *integral* worldview. This new worldview is emerging from a confluence of sources, including the work of Carl Jung, Pierre Teilhard de Chardin, Morton Kelsey, Matthew Fox, the process philosophers and the new physics. This worldview attempts to take seriously the spiritual insights of the ancient or biblical worldview by af-firming an interiority of all things, what the ancients called "heaven." But it sees this inner spiritual reality as inextricably re-lated to a physical manifestation, the earthly. It is no more intrinsi-cally "Christian" than the ancient worldview, but I believe it makes biblical data more intelligible for people today than any other available worldview, including the ancient one.

This new worldview sees that not only do we humans have an outer and inner aspect, but social institutions and structures do as well. What people of the ancient worldview called gods, angels, demons, principalities, and powers were, according to their world-view, real. These powers were the spirituality at the center of the political, cultural, and economic institutions of their day.

In the ancient worldview, every church and nation was pre-sided over by a guardian angel. In the integral worldview, we might see these angels as real, but not as separate supernatural entities.

They are, rather, the totality, the collective ethos or corporate personality of a congregation or nation. Institutions have an actual spiritual ethos, and we neglect this aspect of institutional life to our peril. At the same time, institutions bear that entity's divine vocation. Therefore, to speak of a church's angel is to recognize that every congregation has its own destiny under God. This is not reductionist; that angel is real. But it has no identity separate from the church—it is its spirituality.

This is also true of other realities that the Bible refers to as *powers*. In the biblical view, they are both visible and invisible, earthly and heavenly, spiritual and institutional. The powers possess an outer, physical manifestation (buildings, portfolios, personnel, trucks, fax machines) and an inner, spiritual essence. The New Testament uses the language of power to refer at times to the outer aspect, at other times to the inner aspect, and at still other times to both together. It is the spiritual aspect, however, that is harder for people accustomed to materialism to grasp.

The integral worldview that is emerging in our time takes seriously all the aspects of the ancient worldview, but combines them in a different way. For example, the idea of heaven as "up" is a natural, almost unavoidable way of indicating transcendence. But few of us in the West who have been irremediably touched by modern science think that God, the angels, and the departed spirits are somewhere in the sky, as most ancients literally did.

According to the integral worldview, the spiritual still has a spatial dimension; that dimension, however, is not literally recognizable as "up." Instead, this view establishes spirituality as "withinness," an inner realm every bit as rich and extensive as the outer realm. Carl Jung spoke of this rich inner dimension as the collective unconscious—a realm of largely unexplored spiritual reality linking everyone to everything. The amazement of mystics at the discovery of this realm is matched only by the amazement of physicists upon discovering that the "final" building block of matter, the atom, has an interiority also, and that the electrons and protons that make up atoms are made up of smaller particles, and these of even smaller particles, apparently ad infinitum. It appears that everything, from subatomic particles to corporations to empires, has both an outer and an inner aspect.

The theological worldview permits two cosmologies: a scientific one, made up of pure facts that possess no theological interest, and a mythical cosmology, which reinterprets the creation stories as meaningful tales wholly lacking in truth at the literal level. According to this view, the religious realm is hermetically sealed and immune to challenge from the sciences. By contrast, in the integral worldview, what science currently says about the origin of reality is taken with utter seriousness, even though these views are highly speculative and subject to change or even rejection. Theological reflection on cosmology is as contingent and ephemeral as is the science that it tries to digest. Both science and religion are ongoing processes of approximation to the truth of the one spiritual-physical universe as we are able to perceive it. And the story that emerges is *literally*, as well as mythologically, true, as best we can grasp the truth at the moment. Therefore, scientists cannot avoid the question, "Why?" and theologians cannot avoid the question, "How?" An integral worldview seeks a unified theory of reality, however difficult to achieve. It tries to integrate every fact and every glimpse of truth into a single picture of the world.

The integral worldview is science's gift to the world. Having first depicted the world as a mechanism and people as things, physics went on to the discovery that matter as such does not exist. Even the tiniest particle of energy is now seen to possess a rudimentary "freedom" or indeterminacy; even gluons, hadrons, and quarks have an interiority. First science despiritualized the world; then it discovered spirit at the heart of matter.

When people speak to me about their experiences of evil in the world, they often use the language of the ancient worldview, treating demons and angels as separate beings residing in the sky somewhere, rather than as the spirituality of institutions and systems. When I suggest restating the same thought using the new integral worldview, they often respond, "Oh yes, that's what I meant." In fact, they have said something utterly different. This anomalous behavior indicates that the new, integral worldview has just come of age, and that the old concept is repeated for lack of a better vocabulary. When a more adequate language is suggested, it is instantly recognized, not as a *new* idea to which they capitulate, but as *what they wanted to say all along*. People are groping for a more adequate language to talk about spiritual realities than our tradition provides.

A worldview is quite different from ideas, beliefs, opinions, or even myths. It represents the largely unconscious assumptions and shared images sometimes held by participants on all sides of a debate. It is enshrined in their presuppositions and premises, not in their declared convictions. There were many myths in the ancient world, often in flagrant contradiction with each other. But they all presupposed the ancient worldview, whether they originated in Mesopotamia, Egypt, Palestine, India, or China.

Myths serve many functions, but one of the chief functions is to answer the perennial human question, "How did evil come into the world?" Philosopher Paul Ricoeur finds four basic mythic types; theologian Morton Kelsey finds seven. Drawing on them both, I have come up with seven mythic patterns.

The first is derived from the *goddess religions* of Paleolithic and Neolithic cultures. Written sources do not survive from those times, but surviving figurines and the presence of spiritual focal points in almost every woman's room indicate that goddess worship was noncentralized, nonhierarchical, and nonmilitaristic. The goddess was often associated with the dying and rising motif of nature and was seen as both creator and devourer, the sovereign of life and death. Therefore death, though still a melancholy fact, was explained as a natural feature in the cycle of nature.

According to the *combat* myth, good gods and evil gods vie in eternal warfare for supremacy. In one of its most influential forms, Marduk (male) kills Tiamat (female, probably representing the earlier goddess religion) and from her cadaver creates the universe. Violence is necessary to overcome chaos and establish order. Evil thus exists from the very beginning and has ontological priority over good. Human beings do not introduce sin into the world but find it already there. They are themselves created from the body of a murdered god. Therefore, human beings are constitutionally violent. Murder is in our blood, and conquest in our genes.

According to this myth, violence is redemptive. Cosmic order equals the violent suppression of the goddess and is mirrored in the social order through the subjection of women to men. Far from defunct, this mythic structure underlies the redemptive violence of popular culture—children's comic books, cartoon shows, westerns, cop and spy thrillers, horror movies, and the like—and the foreign policy of nations. It was the ideological substrate of the Cold War and the arms race and remains the most popular and pervasive of all myths in modern culture.

The *tragic vision of existence* is enshrined in drama rather than thought. Greek myth depicts the high god, Zeus, as wicked, unjust, and arbitrary. Human beings are the victims of a transcendent aggression. As Paul Ricoeur notes, the fall is not the fall of human beings; rather it is being that falls on humans. The gods ordain immutable fate. The hero struggles against fate, however, and seems at times to make it hesitate, as if the gods might reconsider. But the evil is predestined and it comes. There is no salvation, no forgiveness, no transformation; there is only catharsis, through dramatic identification with the hero.

According to *biblical* myth, on the other hand, a good god creates a good universe. Evil only enters the story after it has begun, and not as a result of divine creation. Evil is freely chosen by humanity and each individual continues to make that choice. Because evil enters a story already in progress, the myth takes the form of a narrative, with tension between beginning and end: Something must be done about evil. Redemption is required, a redemption that will deal with the evil without creating more violence. The biblical myth also creates a tension between the primordial and the historical. God is not primarily revealed through myths—as in Greece and elsewhere—but by prophetic interpretation of the meaning of actual events.

Thus every dimension of human experience—language, law, sexuality, institutions—is marked by human ambivalence: We are destined for good and inclined toward evil. Since we are all thus mixed, we must love our enemies, because that is what God does for us. And because God is only revealed in historical events, redemption must come in time, in a way that does not abridge our freedom to do evil. In a world structured for domination, in which contending powers seek advantage through violence, redemption must come in a way that ends domination without using dominating means.

All these Western mythic forms coexisted within the ancient worldview. The following mythic types, however, draw on different worldviews. For example, the idea of the *soul/body split*, which first appears in Plato, is no more Greek than Hebraic. Neither of the latter divided human beings into two realities. It was the Greek hero as a whole person who was stricken and condemned by the gods, just as the Hebraic individual was an indissoluble being, at once God's good creation and a sinner. But in Orphism—and its later forms, Neoplatonism, Gnosticism, Manicheanism, Albigensianism, and Catharism—the essential self is divine, fallen into the tomb of a body and longing for release from the flesh. According to many Gnostics, the created material order is evil, false and corrupted. Only the spiritual is true. Earthly life was a mistake, presided over by imperfect or evil powers. Salvation consists of escaping the realm of matter and ascending into the spiritual realm above, which alone is pure.

In a strange way, the *materialist* myth is a by-product of the soul/body split, but it so vehemently rejects the soul as to deny its existence altogether. As a consequence, it forms a unique worldview, one that exercises tremendous power in modern life but is able to coexist with other, more traditional myths. That coexistence is made possible because materialism separates the realms of experience into hermetically sealed units. Thus, 50 percent of the world's scientists—ostensibly rational people—are involved in military research. They are unwitting devotees, or at the very least grudging servants, of the myth of redemptive violence.

Finally, Eastern religions have presented us with a worldview that could be called *the world as illusion*. Eastern religions have been teaching us in the West a great deal over the past decades, and Christians and Jews are especially in their debt, having largely abandoned, because of the corrosive acids of materialism, their own mystical, meditative traditions. But most Westerners draw only on the more attractive elements of Eastern thought, integrating them into other Western traditions. Few go the whole way, denying the reality of phenomenal existence, and finding in the higher realm of the spirit the sole genuine existence.

Unlike the Gnostics and their allies, Eastern religions did not find it necessary to split body and soul. In many ways, their cosmology is still that of the ancient worldview. Christians could profit from their treatment of the world as illusion if they defined "world" as the New Testament does: the alienating social order or system that conditions us to acquiesce to injustice and dehumanizing policies. Since the Vietnam War, social activists both Buddhist and Christian have been reinterpreting their traditions and finding common cause in the struggle against socially induced illusions and delusions.

In considering all of the preceding, it is important to remember that our worldviews determine what we think is possible. "Unbelief" is not so much a theological problem as it is a matter of preconscious prohibition by a contrary worldview. We have not taken seriously the fact that virtually *everyone* in the ancient world, with the exception of a handful of philosophers, believed in the divine realm regardless of what their myths may have been. Atheism as a cultural phenomenon is quite a modern invention; it is, specifically, the child of materialism. It is not modern science that renders belief in God problematic; after all, many of the greatest scientists have believed in God, including Newton, Darwin, and Einstein. But science has been until recently allied with materialism, and it is the materialist *myth* and *worldview* that denies, in principle, that God can exist. Materialism also denies the existence of that inner reality that all other myths have acknowledged and named spirit, soul, or self. What has given added credibility to materialism is that it is both myth and worldview and produces values that power the unparalleled productivity and destructiveness of modern consumerism.

The crisis of unbelief in modern times is not, in short, a crisis of *unbelief* at all, but of *other-belief.* People have been unconsciously caught in a worldview that denies elements of their existence that they cannot wholly surrender to the materialist perspective, yet cannot quite affirm with one of the other myths or worldviews. There is no such thing as unbelief. Everyone has a functional cosmology, however confused or eclectic or unarticulated. That worldview—not intellectual reservations—determines what they are free to believe.

Our age is possibly unique in the opportunity it affords to *see* our worldviews and even to choose among them. This freedom delivers us from undergoing a worldview as a fate laid on us by the accident of our birth at a given time and locale. We can even combine elements of different worldviews and myths. For example, we might want to include in the Jewish or Christian traditions aspects of the goddess religion without reverting to it entirely. We can even bring in new elements made urgent by crises faced for the first time today: ecological reverence, a sense of unity with all that is, a new appreciation of Native American religions or other mystical traditions. We need not become religious junkies; the ecumenical spirit requires not the attempt to embrace all religions as one's own, but to stand deeply rooted in one's own tradition, receptive to learning all one can from others.

What we believe is not, however, merely a matter of preference. To a far greater degree than we have acknowledged, it is a function of what we are allowed to believe by our functional worldviews. Perhaps for the first time in history, we are now able to step outside the worldviews that shape us and choose which we will believe. As this happens, the Age of Doubt may be replaced by a new Age of Belief, dictated not by ecclesiastical authorities, but by individuals free to make conscious choices.

▼▼▼

Chapter 17

Exploring Your Personal Myth

JAMES P. CARSE

James P. Carse, Ph.D., has been director of religious studies and professor of the history of literature and religion at New York University since 1966. A repeated winner of the university's Distinguished Teaching Award, he is the author of five books, including The Silence of God: Meditation on Prayer *and* Finite and Infinite Games. *He recently completed a book on the mystical qualities of ordinary experience and is currently working on a book of sacred narrative. For eight years, he hosted the Sunday morning WCBS-TV program "The Way to Go."*

In his chapter, Carse shows us that we discover new insights about ourselves when we become aware of our personal "resonance" with the sacred stories and myths of the world's great religions. We can achieve this resonance, he says, by comparing and contrasting our personal stories—the stories of our birth, leaving home, and so on—with traditional myths and religious stories. Similar to views expressed in the chapter by Price and Simpkinson, Carse believes that by experiencing this resonance, we may grasp the wider meaning, or the sacred nature, of our personal stories.

Sitting in Washington Square Park one day, I remembered a story my college girlfriend had told me some twenty-five years earlier. "According to my mother," Gerry said, "the way I was born was that she went to the A&P and when she came home I jumped out from behind the kitchen door and surprised her." That's the whole story: one sentence.

I was about to pass this off as a merely accidental recollection when I realized that this was not the first time I had recalled Gerry's birth story. In fact, it had come up quite often, and always without my intention. The story is so spare that I could, at first, find nothing much in it to think about. But I decided to investigate the story, to try to discover why it persisted in calling for my attention.

Of course, stories have a way of emerging out of nowhere. Rather than making them up, we seem, instead, to find them; it may even be more accurate to say they find us. Ask storytellers where their ideas come from and they will never have an adequate answer, if they answer at all. Even the earliest writers already speak of the muse: the being who brings the story to you.

Similarly, myths—the stories that most persistently call themselves to our attention over the centuries and millennia—never have a known origin. The authors we sometimes associate with classical myths, such as Homer, Hesiod, Virgil, and Apuleius, make it clear that they are simply retelling what they have heard. The same can be said of the Christian gospels. It is not Mark's Gospel but the Gospel According to Mark—that is, the story was there first and then Mark undertook to tell it.

This connection between our own life stories and the stories of the great myths leads to another connection. When we come to know the stories of our lives, we come to know the *meaning* of our lives as well; stories shape the way we see ourselves. Because the active study of myth has the power to change the way we tell our life stories, it can also transform the very meaning of our lives.

What is the active study of myth? To answer this question, it is necessary first to recognize what might be called the *resonance* of myths. Great stories seem to resound with deeper, often hidden stories. We cannot get to the absolute origin of a given story, but we can often hear echoes of it in older and deeper tales. Shakespeare's *Hamlet*, for example, is a veritable cavern of mythic echoes: the love of Oedipus for his mother, Cain's betrayal of Abel, the orphan's quest for identity, the loss of innocence, Amor's search for Psyche, Echo's loss of voice in her love of Narcissus, the presence of the father as (holy) ghost. And there is more, much more.

Hearing what sounds and re-sounds in Hamlet is made easier because it is one of the most celebrated and studied literary works ever composed. But our stories don't need to be as brilliantly told as Shakespeare's. We can learn to hear the resonance in much more modest narratives, such as Gerry's birth story—an ordinary child's tale told with a perfect lack of artifice or self-consciousness.

The way I was born was that my mother went to the A&P and when she came home I jumped out from behind the kitchen door and surprised her.

This is, at the very least, a story of childhood prowess. A new-born leaps out from behind a door, a bold and calculated gesture of advanced skill and a grown-up sense of theater. The resonance here is enormous, for the myths of heroes' births are full of such amazing acts, like Heracles strangling deadly serpents in his cradle, or the Buddha dropping without warning from his mother's womb, radiantly dressed in princely armor, announcing his greatness to the universe, or the infant Jesus, threatening the earthly rule of a powerful Roman prince.

The element of surprise in the tale is also rich with mythic echoes. Surprise, of course, can mean either delight or menace. Sarah, astounding those around her by giving birth to Isaac when she was at an advanced age, was an object of laughter. Jesus' birth occasioned both joy and terror. The unexpected appearance of the child Krishna was an erotic delight to the milkmaids but brought only jealous grief to their husbands.

If birth can be a surprise, it can also be shocking and dangerous to those around it. Rival or prior children are displaced, as in the case of the illegitimate Arthur overshadowing his stepbrother Sir Kay, or Jacob tricking the firstborn Esau out of his inheritance. Gerry had older sisters but they were certainly crowded out of this myth.

This cautions us not to see the newborn as a helpless babe in arms, dependent on those around her, for in doing so we would overlook one of the central features of many birth narratives: A small being can be a terror. Even the possibility of a birth threatens existing orders of power; in many tales, this possibility causes the mighty to protect themselves by such desperate measures as locking wives and daughters away to prevent their conceiving an heir and competitor. Any number of tiny rivals have been abandoned to rivers and seas, locked into cells or caves, or left for dead in wastelands. The Pharaoh, King Herod, and even the legendarily gentle Arthur of Camelot went so far as to slaughter an entire generation of children to make sure no babe would undo them.

On a less grand scale, we can see that any birth affects the existing power structure in a family. On first hearing Gerry's story, we might think the mother's reaction would be one of happiness. But she appears unprepared for this surprise; therefore, her authority as parent is already in question. Despite her intentions, anything can happen. There wasn't a hint when Gerry's mother left for the store that there would be a surprise waiting for her, much less a child. The child is an angel of surprise but *what* she is surprising her mother with is not revealed. In fact, the mother may have told this story because she herself did not know the outcome.

Nonetheless, the mother's importance is clearly represented in Gerry's myth. She has come back from a journey to the A&P like Demeter with the seasonal fruits to greet Persephone at her emergence from the obscurity of Tartarus. In mythic record, providing food and consuming it often overlap. What the mother gives she can take away; the child is fed by her but can also be eaten by her. Gerry surprises an unprepared mother, but she is even less prepared for the surprises her mother has for her.

The mother finds Gerry, after all, in the kitchen. Children know the kitchen as the place where you not only can be burned and cut but also fed and mended; there are countless other interpretive approaches one might apply to this particular location. But one recurring mythic image is of the kitchen as a hag's workshop, where knife and fire are the chief media and where small animals and children are chopped up and brewed into magical potions.

And where in the kitchen did Gerry hide? Behind the door, a symbol of passage, a boundary between realms. It is a barrier at which one age meets another, and a threshold across which one age becomes another. Just as it can lock away the old it can open to the new, but what it opens onto we can never know before we knock.

Although both Gerry and her mother are at risk due to the story's many possible levels of surprise, the greater threat is to the father. His absence is far more conspicuous in this story than the absence of the sisters: This is a fatherless birth. It is typical of the great birth myths that the father's role is either ignored or played out of view, like the Holy Spirit secretly entering the Virgin's womb, or Zeus sneaking through the bars of Danae's cell disguised as a shower of gold. The father in Gerry's myth has been done away with as decisively as Oedipus's father, Laertes, leaving only her mother to love, hate, or fear.

PERHAPS THE PRECEDING is enough to show how the active study of a simple tale can resonate with an indefinite number of stories outside itself. To be sure, there is no precise list of connections to be made here, and interpretation could vary widely from reader to reader. The question remains: What is to be gained by developing the skill of listening to the resonance of myths?

Such a practice enlarges at least four areas of insight. First, it brings into clearer focus the fact that our life is indeed an unfolding story and therefore helps us to understand where we are in that story. Gerry and I had, of course, no awareness of the resonance of her birth story on the day she first told it to me; none of what I have traced out in the last few pages went through our heads on that gentle spring evening. Rather, we believed that we had been adequately prepared for life's surprises; we were unaware of the levels of risk and danger that lie beneath any unexpected occurrence. The story's deeper insights were unavailable to us.

Had we been more aware, we might have seen that we were about to leap out from behind the door of our relatively protected childhood and adolescence: We were in a birth process ourselves. The story was not only about Gerry as a child but also about both of us as emerging adults. By listening to the resonance of a myth, we hear our own lives resounding in it. The active study of myth is the active study of the narration of our own lives.

Second, it exposes the great range of possible paths lying ahead of us. Because mythic heroes and heroines acquire vision and self-understanding in so many different ways, we can free ourselves from the notion that our life is a failure if it strays from a chosen path. Indeed, disappointments in love, reversals of fortune, attacks of despair, and the appearance of terrifying and insurmountable obstacles are not interruptions of our journey but the very means by which we continue it. Mythically speaking, nothing happens to us that does not provide the possibility for deeper vision.

Gerry and I could never have realized this. We knew the world was a risky place, to be sure, but we also thought that if we were careful and disciplined we would elude heartbreak, disillusion, and misfortune. We certainly did not know that our life stories could be enriched by them.

Third, because there is no story with just one character, there is no way we can reach greater self-understanding without achieving greater intimacy with others. True heroes and heroines must, as a rule, undertake their journeys alone, but they also find many helpers and fellow travelers along the way. Notice how a family is transformed when its members stop seeing each other as obstacles and begin to understand that they are all seekers for something as yet unattainable. Suddenly, deadly competition and conflicts of authority vanish, and a new spirit of support and affection takes their place.

Although Gerry and I took separate paths when we left college, we still have an important place in each other's story. But there are many other people less obviously connected to me without whom my story would be very different indeed. The active study of myth can reveal how intimately connected we are to both the living and the dead. Indeed, not only our ancestors but also our descendants belong in the larger narratives of our lives. The lines of one person's story lead out in many directions. We are members of a great congregation of persons whose members have affected us by their actions in the past or who will be affected by our actions in the future.

Fourth, by exposing ourselves to the boundless power of myth to transform the meaning of our lives and to give us an intimate place in the larger human community, we open ourselves to the divine. There is, however, a paradoxical element here: It is not our incipient divinity that brings us close to the gods but our incorrigible humanity. One does not need to be a scholarly reader of myth to discover that heroes and heroines are often deeply flawed. Heroes like Gilgamesh, David, and Theseus may be unforgettable precisely because so much of their lives was nonheroic. Reading such stories, we become more aware of the stark limitations—physical, moral, psychic, and cultural—of human life.

Heroes and heroines of the great myths are profoundly mortal; unlike gods, they die. In fact, they must die or their journeys would become tales of endless wandering. In mythic terms, limitations are not grounds for despair; on the contrary, to be aware of limits is to enlarge our humanity. By acknowledging our imperfections, we enter into communion with others; by accepting all the limitations of our humanness, we enter into communion with the gods.

It is rare for mortals to become gods in mythology, but it is common for them to acquire vision and wisdom that have the quality of immortality. Indeed, the gods are rarely credited with wisdom. Carl Jung pointed out that after Job had gone through his suffering, he became far superior to the God who had caused it and who remained, in fact, a psychic and moral adolescent.

The active study of myth draws the chief narrative features of our own lives into relief. It shows us that a great variety of possible futures awaits us, awakening hope that what now appears as an impasse will prove to be an opening to a life yet unseen. It reveals the significant part we play in the larger human community. And it confronts us with the paradox that our very mortality can be the basis for immortal insight and wisdom. Ideally, the active study of mythology is practiced in small groups of people willing to risk the telling and retelling of their past and future lives. But it can be done individually with great effectiveness. The following are a few suggestions for individual study.

The first step is to read mythology. There is no systematic way to do this reading—myths are not easily organized by chronology, topic, or ethnic group. They seem to appear indiscriminately, where and when they will. Therefore, let your reading be wide and indiscriminate as well. Use the mythology sections of bookstores and libraries; let one book lead you to another; read in as many traditions as possible.

Read secondary literature in the same way. You will quickly see how differently scholars interpret various myths. Books such as Bruno Bettelheim's *The Uses of Enchantment* and James Hillman's *Dreams and the Underworld* offer suggestive and distinctive interpretations of famous myths. There is also a rich literature that uses myths for self-analysis or as the basis of a novel. Jean Bolen's *Goddesses in Every Woman* and T. H. White's *The Once and Future King* are examples of this kind of literature.

But it is not enough to be a reader. A more active exercise is required to hear and make use of the resonance of these stories. I suggest a simple one that can be used individually as well as in groups.

You might begin by examining a story that has caught your attention. Write down where you feel the resonance of it in your own life—episodes that reflect or repeat events in the myth. You might then try retelling the myth with yourself as its central character, letting other people in your life appear where appropriate in the story. Don't spend a lot of time at this; write as the thoughts come to you. When you come to a dead end, try another myth. As you practice this technique, you will discover that the same experiences in your life can appear radically different to you as you look at them through each new myth.

You might, for example, recall a conflict with your parents while you were still a child. Now look at the way in which Athena, Jesus, Gilgamesh, Oedipus, Persephone, Isaac, and Cassandra resolved or failed to resolve conflicts with their parents. Write down what parallels or differences you find in these stories and what they reveal to you about yourself.

As you acquire more skill at this exercise, you might try writing out whole periods of your life in the form of a myth. Tell the story of your birth, for example, or your flight from home. An especially revealing technique is to write out the final scene of your present life—the place toward which all of your actions are leading you. Do not describe the place you *hope* you will reach but the one that lies ahead of what you are actually doing. Then look around and list the persons from your life, dead or alive, who are there watching.

There are a few things to keep in mind while using this process. Much of what you discover can be dark and painful. For that reason, it is important to proceed slowly. Do not push your insights but wait for them to come. Remember that the most brilliant and hopeful myths often have the darkest episodes in them. Remember, too, to be honest. Read your life as a complicated text, but do not invent the text. Even when you are looking ahead, do not project your wishes but try to see, instead, what comes into view when you stand where you are.

Most important, pay attention to the stories that most frequently appear in your recollection or imagination. Their persistence means they have something to tell you. They may be as brief as Gerry's birth story; they may be so powerful that you are obsessed with them. Write them out and see where they lead you.

Myths, after all, are stories that we tell over and over again and cannot forget. They exercise great power over our lives and have, as well, rich and enduring lives of their own. When we listen to the resonance of these sacred stories, we find that they can lead us to greater self-awareness and even self-transformation.

▼▼

Chapter 18

Telling Our Stories of God: The Contributions of a Psychoanalytic Perspective

JOHN MCDARGH

John McDargh, Ph.D., is an associate professor in the department of theology at Boston College. He researches and writes about the psychology of religious development, with particular interest in the relationship between psychotherapy and spirituality.

In addressing the question, "What makes a story sacred?" McDargh begins by describing an alternative to the Freudian model. In Freud's own original "story" about human motivation, he explains that the human person is conceptualized as an enclosed system of hard-wired intellectual drives, which attempts to maintain itself in equilibration. By contrast, according to McDargh, contemporary psychoanalysis understands the psyche as inherently "relational" and interactive, organized by the experience of being a self in relationship to others. The quality and character of these relationships—particularly the earliest and most primary—profoundly shape the individual's conscious and unconscious self-narrative. Based on the latter model, which emphasizes connections, McDargh suggests that our stories of God are based, not in any official dogma, but in the history of our own relatedness to what is real in our lives.

In the minds of most modern people even vaguely aware of Freud's insights, religion appears antithetical to psychoanalysis. The suspicions that Freud and Marx held about religion have strongly shaped the way most educated persons have approached religious matters over the last hundred years. This antipathy between religion and the modes of critical analysis associated with Marx and Freud is illustrated in the autobiography of Dorothy Day, a Catholic social activist and founder of the Catholic Worker Movement.

In her book, *The Long Loneliness*, Day describes her inner dialogue when as a young woman she was pregnant and living with her anarchist common-law husband on the beach in Staten Island. She was, perhaps for the first time in her life, deeply happy. In this condition, she found herself spontaneously praying with gratitude and thanksgiving. Because Dorothy identified strongly with leftist politics and had given up any formal religious practice, she found this activity inexplicable and was immediately skeptical. She criticized herself, saying, "Here you are in a stupor of content. You are biological. Like a cow. Prayer for you is like the opiate of the people." The language of her critique is from Marx; had she taken a Freudian approach, she might well have said to herself, "This prayer is nothing but a projection of your desire for solace and protection in a threatening world." Religion, from these perspectives, is always understood in terms of some deeper, underlying motivation that has to do with unacknowledged need, deficiency, or wish. Psychological maturity, on the other hand, requires that we face our fears and learn to separate our projections from our desires. In the case of Dorothy Day, she was only able to sustain her new practice of prayer when she had questioned the critique of it that surfaced in her mind. She describes this internal debate:

> "But," I reasoned with myself, "I am praying because I am happy, not because I am unhappy. I did not turn to God in

> unhappiness, in grief, in despair—to get something from
> Him." And encouraged that I was praying because I wanted
> to thank Him, I went on praying.

Dorothy Day wrestled with the question of the psychological
and moral status of religion in the 1930s because of the dominance
of Freud's critique of religion. Even in our own time, educated
people do not typically think of Freud and his followers as likely
sources of help in appreciating and appropriating the practice of
sacred storytelling. These reservations are understandable but in-
complete. Psychoanalytic thinking itself has shifted over the last
twenty years, particularly with respect to interpreting religious
storytelling. I believe these developments form a basis for renewed
insight into the profoundly important function of "our stories of
God."

Two principles hold true across any psychoanalytic understanding of human behavior, including that which we call prayer or religious storytelling. First, such behavior has deep meanings and
motivations of which the individual may not be fully aware. Second, exploring such meanings will lead one back to examine earlier
or more primary patterns of desire. The latter is the characteristic
psychoanalytic assumption that the child is in some fashion the
"parent of the adult." While the two principles endure as corner-
stones of psychoanalytic thinking, what has undergone significant
development is how we understand fundamental, motivating
human desire. In other words, a shift has occurred in how psychoanalysis answers the question, "What does it mean to be fully
human?" This is a foundational change, and in understanding it, it
is useful to review Freud's approach.

Freud began his career as a neurologist under the reigning paradigms of physics. He wanted to render an account of the laws of
human mental life that would trace the pathways of "psychic energy," in its conservation and discharge, through the "psychic

system." Though the project was never realized, its influence lingered in the way in which Freudian psychoanalysis initially offered a "one person" psychological model. The primary unit of analysis was the individual psyche as it attempted to maintain equilibrium by negotiating the conflict between instinctual drives—primarily sex and aggression—and a social order that precluded the satisfaction or discharge of those drives. According to this paradigm, the human being at his or her happiest is the satiated post-feeding infant contentedly sleeping at the breast, an image Freud paralleled to the postcoital sleeping adult. Our needs satisfied for the moment, we rest in the lowest level of psychic excitation.

Therefore, classical psychoanalysis may be said to offer its own preferred story or narrative of the human condition. This story views a person's individual history as a never-ending conflict in which the embattled ego strives to maintain itself between the pressure of forbidden unconscious wishes and the expectations and gratifications of life in society. This narrative makes human history a dramatic struggle between the instinctual endowments of the species—which threaten at any moment to undo the fragile accomplishments of civilization—and the still, small voice of reason, Freud's *logos*.

But there is another story about human beings that takes with equal seriousness the evidence of unconscious conflict and social destructiveness, but accounts for it differently. Say that the paradigmatic human person in this narrative is not the solitary, sleeping infant but rather the infant at the breast who will interrupt feeding for the sheer delight of exchanging a look of recognition and response with the parent. This is a very different model of human motivation, one in which desire is not a matter of regulating a closed system but is always to be understood in the context of human relationship. The key motivating force in human living, in this story, is the inherent need for *recognition*—the experience of mutuality and relatedness whereby interacting human beings cocreate both selves and worlds. The pains human beings inflict on each other are, according to this narrative, not the explosive expressions of aggressive energies, but responses derived from profound self-deficits that are themselves the consequences of failures in recognition and lack of mutuality. In this story, human beings realize their human potentiality by the way in which they are given to themselves *by the other*. The psychologist Andras Angyal expressed it in these words:

> To be is to mean something to someone else. This existence we cannot directly create for ourselves; it can only be given to us by another. The true human problem is this: In a sense that matters to us above everything else, we are nothing in ourselves. All we have is a profound urge to exist and the dreadful experience of non-existence. A poem written in a language no one can read does not exist as a poem. Neither do we exist in a human sense until someone decodes us . . . Starting with the small child who urgently wants to be noticed, we all want to have a life in the thoughts and feelings of others, to have them reflect our individual existence, and reflect it in an understanding affectionate way.

But how does this new paradigm of human development shift the terms by which we understand and evaluate *religious* storytelling, or our stories of God?

The implications of that shift are slowly manifesting themselves. The first significant development was the publication, in 1979, of Ana Maria Rizzuto's ground-breaking study, *The Birth of the Living God*. In this book, Rizzuto presents clinical evidence of how individuals creatively elaborate conscious and unconscious mental representations associated with the word-symbol "God." These are not simply images of the protective but limited father, as Freud originally would have claimed; rather, they are compounds of a whole range of relational experiences with mothers, fathers,

available grandparents, or other caretakers. Nor do these representations remain static, frozen in the conditions of their origin.
Rather, they often undergo elaboration and change in a way that
keeps pace with an individual's ongoing intellectual, spiritual, and
psychological maturation. Representations outlive their usefulness
and must be set aside in favor of others that allow vital living to go
forward.

This point of view lends complexity and richness to what can
be heard in any discourse about "God." The variety of experiences that contributes to an individual's representations of God
ensure that the person's relationship with those representations is
as dynamic and complicated as any relationship in life. As Rizzuto
describes it:

> Ambivalent feelings mix with longings; wishes to avoid
> God intermingle with wishes for closeness. The search for
> love, approval and guidance alternates with noisy and re-
> bellious rejection, doubt and displays of independence. The
> pride of faithful service to God contrasts with painful doubts
> about being unworthy.

This revised perspective on the origins and function of psychic
representations of God carries with it important implications for
both religious professionals—ministers, spiritual directors, and
pastoral counselors—and secular health care workers. For the former group, including myself, this means that we cannot automati-
cally assume that we know what it means when someone says
"God." This was impressed upon me early in my graduate career
when I found myself conversing with a deeply disturbed Roman
Catholic man I will call "Joe."

Joe was eloquent about the fierce and relentless demands that
God made upon him. With all the naïveté of a new doctoral
student, I assumed that what would be most helpful to him would

be a bit of theological updating. In one particularly disastrous conversation, I made the mistake of challenging the adequacy of Joe's representation with the more merciful and benign images found in Jesus' discourses. I thought I was being tactful and helpful; I was wrong. Joe's visible anxiousness in the face of this representation warned me to back off and left me with the question of why a human being would *need* this kind of God so desperately that any threat to it, even from an apparently better alternative, would arouse unbearable anxiety.

The revised psychoanalytic paradigm that underlies the work of Rizzuto and others offers a possible answer. It suggests that we see in every person's formulation of "God" a richly layered history of internal relationships that, in some way, hold that individual's self together. It requires us to listen with deep respect and few assumptions to how that act of psychic creativity functions in an individual life. In Joe's case, this perspective led me to wonder about how his particular "God" representation might parallel the process one finds in abused children who, as adults, seek out abusive relationships because that has come to represent a kind of "love." Perhaps Joe's dilemma was that a God who punishes offers connection and a meaningful universe in the absence of any experiential alternative. Perhaps all my talk of a loving God could only be emotionally credible and psychologically safe to Joe if offered in the context of a real relationship that was genuinely loving and trustworthy enough to alter the internalizations that were the foundations of his sense of God.

In other words, our stories of God reflect, at their deepest levels, our most profound experiences of being met or overlooked, of being taken up and decoded or left unread. Providing life-giving stories, inside or outside of the Church, is not a matter of imposing doctrines or metaphors upon people, but is, rather, a delicate process of hearing people's stories as they present them and then translating those stories into the living terms of interpersonal relatedness.

For mental health professionals, this paradigm gives permission to listen with fresh, serious attention to material that previously was either dismissed as irrelevant or reduced to projection. Now, clinicians may find in any individual's stories of God another road to the understanding of the deeply private inner world of self and object relations. I witnessed a demonstration of this when attending an inpatient psychiatric case conference to which Dr. Rizzuto had been invited.

The patient was a child who had been hospitalized for severe, chronic self-beating. Dr. Rizzuto had been given very little prior information about the child's psychiatric or familial background. Her conversation with the child was a sensitive and respectful inquiry into what the child thought "God" was like, handled in the safer third-person discourse (e.g., "some children think that God is . . . ").

After the interview, with the child out of the room, Dr. Rizzuto presented a diagnosis and a formulation that were impressively congruent with what had been determined by professionals already familiar with the case. More memorable, however, was a comment she made on prognosis. If, she said, there was a way of determining that when the child is engaged in self-battering he is also able to pray or be in any way mindful of what he names "God," then the prognosis for recovery would be much more positive. Her point was that if this child, in the throes of annihilating rage and despair, is nevertheless able to maintain some sense of being connected to or accompanied by an "other," then there is some foothold for hope, some bridge across the sense of being totally abandoned and alone.

IF HUMAN BEINGS become who they are only by virtue of their being-in-relationship, we might ask if there is a fundamental

and primal "relatedness" for which all of our particular relationships, from parents outward, are necessary but still partial reflections. Another way of phrasing this might be to ask, "What
makes a story *sacred?*" The sacredness of anyone's story cannot be
tied to particular contents or given religious symbols. This is why
an inquiry into how a person uses the word-symbol "God," while
potentially enlightening, could also entirely miss the heart of the
matter. For example, if one interviewed Alan Strang, the troubled
adolescent in Peter Shaffer's brilliant play *Equus*, about God, one
would perhaps discover only pallid, conventionally correct answers. Such an inquiry might totally overlook the presence of
Equus, the great god of Alan's imagination. This example reminds
us that, as the great scholar of religion, Mircea Eliade, repeatedly
emphasizes, the "sacred" is the realm of the "really real"—where
human beings feel themselves to be in vital contact with the very
source of their existence in some reality that utterly exceeds them.

In other words, a personal story is *sacred* when it functions to
communicate an individual's sense of *being*. A story told sacredly
evokes the numinosity and transcendent mystery of our existence
as creatures oriented to relatedness from the beginnings of sentient
life. In *Contemporary Psychoanalysis and Religion: Transference
and Transcendence*, James Jones says that the psychoanalytic listening perspective should help us to tune our ears to those self-
stories in which we catch a glimpse of "that matrix out of which
the self originates." We will perhaps know those stories less by
their particular contents than by their impact upon us.

Thus we can return to Dorothy Day's interior monologue on
the beach in Staten island and argue that contemporary psychoanalytic discourse supports what she intuited: that what legitimates
her spontaneous prayer is not that it is an address to "God" but
that it proceeds from a place of thanksgiving. That is, her impulse

is to give expression, in whatever symbolic language is at hand, to a sense of primal gratefulness for the gift of her self-in-relation and the miracle of life growing within her. This prayer is not a response to something or someone extrinsic—over and beyond her—or a projection of her dependency. Rather, out of the recognition that her being participates in "being," she discovers her own authentic sacred story.

▼▼

Chapter 19

Stories That Need Telling Today

MATTHEW FOX

Matthew Fox, a former Dominican priest, internationally known author and lecturer, and founder of the Institute in Culture and Creation Spirituality, has been working for decades to change the stories the Catholic church tells. Ordained in 1967, Fox traces his liberal—some would say radical—theological roots to his studies in Paris under the tutelage of liberation theologian Father M. D. Chenu.

For the past fifteen years, Fox has been articulating a new creation story called "Creation Spirituality," which attempts to revision traditional Catholic dogma. Fox argues, for example, that original blessings is a more healthy way of viewing the essence of our existence than the Church's focus on original sin. Fox's Creation Spirituality emphasizes feminism, environmental awareness, Eastern and Native American spirituality, as well as Catholic mysticism.

Quoting Rabbi Heschel, he cites three ways human beings can respond to the world around them. "We can exploit it, we can enjoy it, or we can accept it with awe. To accept creation with awe," Fox continues, "is to work out of a mystical base instead of a duty base or an anthropocentric base." Stories are important ve-hicles in this process as Fox explains in the following essay.

Our culture is filled with storytelling. Every advertisement we read or see is really a story—cleverly, artistically, and expensively told. Consumerism is the primary tale of our civilization. It feeds on our unsated appetites; it feeds on the fact that we have not been nourished spiritually, that there is a gaping hole in us that cannot be filled, no matter how many goods and goodies we buy.

Consumerism is a dangerous and debilitating story, but we can take back—we need to take back—our storytelling powers. We can take back our addictions, on which we spend billions of dollars and hours. We can take this waste back and recycle it by creating more authentic stories. We can overcome the toxins of our pseudostories and replace them with fuller stories that satisfy the heart, the mind, the imagination, and the quest in every one of us for justice and peace, for the return of blessing to our daily lives.

Healthy people base their lives on healing, authentic stories. Empowerment comes through the process of telling those stories. The theological word for empowerment is "spirit." The spirit is fed and moved when people tell their true tales, with all their inherent grief but also with possibility and hope.

Storytelling is the basis of tribal survival all over the world; it is the way that we pass on wisdom to the young, the way we displace despair with hope and disempowerment with power. Meister Eckhart, the great German mystic, said, "Become aware of what is in you. Announce it, pronounce it, produce it and give birth to it." There is passion behind our yearning to tell stories. When we become aware of what is in us, it is altogether natural to announce it, pronounce it, produce it, and give birth to it.

Getting to know our own stories is the key. This requires that we work through our denial to discover what is really there. As we cut through the denial that is often born of abuse—whether religious, sexual, physical, emotional, or racial—we discover our true stories. We get back the energy to announce, pronounce, produce, and give birth. We are all endowed as storytellers; there is a mystic in every one of us.

The mystic in all of us is that part that refuses to take anything for granted. What we have to wake up to today as a species is that we can no longer take water, soil, or healthy air for granted. Taking the world for granted is what has caused our dysfunctional relationship to the wonders of the earth.

I believe that to change that dysfunctional relationship to a healthy and blessed one, we must begin to tell the stories that both the Earth and our species are yearning to hear. There are six kinds of stories that can help us at this apocalyptic time in human history.

The first can be called the story of the sky. The sky is the source of our home; we came from "out there." Our entire history is reflected, refracted, and rediscovered when we look out to the sky. Our most powerful sky story today is a new creation story—a new vision, discovered by contemporary physics, of how we got here.

This new story can help correct the dangerous worldview we have been carrying since the Enlightenment, which taught us to see our bodies, our minds, and even the universe as machines. This is an extremely anthropocentric view—only humans make machines—and one of the dangers of it is that it assumes the Earth is dead. The stories we inherited from the Enlightenment are, in fact, part of why we are killing the Earth: For many years, we thought it was dead already.

But in the new story we receive from today's physics, the cosmos is a continually expanding organism that came from a fireball 18 billion years ago. It is constantly growing and changing; it is truly alive. To rediscover our relationship to our universe, we need to recover the awesome stories of the living sky. Why is it that the moon is just the right distance from the Earth so that tides can happen, so that life can come from the ocean? Why is it that we had the perfect ozone layer—an original blessing—that we have now seriously endangered? Why is it that all the elements of our bodies were birthed in a supernova explosion that connects us to all the other bodies in this universe? All these creation stories have the capacity to move our species to new realms.

Another kind of story that needs to be told now is the Earth story. For we two-legged ones, this is the body story that helps us rediscover the awesomeness of our physical being. Thomas Aquinas said that revelation comes in two volumes: nature and the Bible. During the last few hundred years, theology has cut itself off from nature. If we can rediscover the mystery and inherent sacredness of all of nature, including our bodies, we can rediscover the revelatory nature of our bodily experiences. Our experience in our earthly bodies is connected to all the wildernesses we experience on the planet.

We all carry wilderness within us. Our passions—such as desire, anger, and grief—are all wildernesses and should be honored as such. The sacred experience of sexuality is a wilderness and it, too, needs to be rediscovered as revelatory of the divine. Part of why our culture has come to hate the Earth is because we hate our own bodies; we need to recover our Earth stories to recover the sense of our bodies and our planet as blessings.

The third kind of story we need to hear today is the story of the north. The north is a direction of great power, great storms, great wind, and great surprises. Stories of the north, therefore, are about developing the heart-power known as courage—courage to face the strong winds and the long winter nights. We need courage to face the beauty of the universe because part of beauty is terror. We need stories about ways to help the human heart grow; we need stories of magnanimity and great soulfulness.

We also need the story of the west. In the west, the sun sets; the west is the direction of darkness, of letting go, and of dying. It is what mystics call the *via negativa*, the negative way. It encompasses the dark night of the soul. As a species, we are today in a dark night of the soul. That is a frightening place, but it is also sacred and revelatory. It is in darkness that we can learn to be transformed in a deep way. When our hearts break, the cosmos opens up.

Stories of anger are also stories of the west. Thomas Aquinas says a trustworthy person is someone who is angry at the right people for the right reasons, expresses it in the right way and for the appropriate length of time. Permission to see anger as part of our power and to convert it into creative energy is part of the path of the west.

There is also a dimension of silence that comes when the sun goes down. Stories from the west teach us to honor the silence within us and within the universe. We have to return to the mystical naming of divinity as the Godhead, because the Godhead is where silence lives. Theologically speaking, God is the divinity who acts; the Godhead is that aspect of divinity that is pure being and awesome silence. The Godhead is the radically feminine side of God, and part of rediscovering women's energy is honoring the Godhead as well as God, allowing those stories of silence from the west to participate in our conception of the divine.

The east is another source of important stories. The sun rises in the east; this is where day begins and hope emerges. The east is about resurrection. Aquinas says that there are two resurrections. The first is waking up in this life; if we pay attention to that resurrection, the next one will take care of itself.

We are in desperate need right now of resurrection in this life. Despair is in the hearts of young people all over the world today; in a sense, our civilization teaches despair. This is why we need so many distractions. I believe that the best way to resurrect hope, the antidote to despair, is to resurrect worship itself.

Look, for example, at the native peoples who have suffered genocide, such as the Native Americans and the Native Africans. What has bonded those peoples and kept their cultures intact is their rituals, their forms of worship. We are bereft of worship in the white world, which is the world that still dictates the basic paradigms of our civilization.

We can resurrect worship using ancient archetypes from both Christian and Jewish traditions. But to do so, we have to recover the idea that every creature is a word of God and a book about God. When we bring that energy into worship, we can move into resurrection. We can move into the healing stories of the east.

Finally, we need to recover the story of the south. The south is the direction of the feminine; stories of the south remind us to honor Sophia, the embodiment of wisdom. Christian biblical scholars are rediscovering what was already known in the Middle Ages: The first name given to Jesus in the Christian Bible is Sophia, or Lady Wisdom.

Wisdom honors the whole, the cosmos. When Lady Wisdom sits happily on her throne, there is order and justice in the universe. We need to honor wisdom today. Instead of the knowledge factories we call schools, we need wisdom schools, which would honor the revelatory nature of the body, of art, and of storytelling.

The Druids required their teachers to also be poets. One obvious way to reinvent education in our culture would be to take the Druids as our example and bring artists back into the classroom. I am not referring to those artists who have absorbed the capitalistic idea that art is a product; I mean artists who can lead us in the six directions of our healing stories and into the depths of ourselves, and who therefore can help us to recover the wonder of our universe.

We are here to get drunk on the universe. If we believe that we live in a soulless and inert machine, there is no room for intoxication. We can fit or not fit into a machine, but there is no place to dance, to be spontaneous, to be overcome with awe. One reason for the tremendous addiction problem in our culture is that we have no sacred place to get intoxicated on the mysteries of the universe.

What is sacred is awesome; when we learn to accept creation with awe, we can bring about a whole new beginning for our civilization. We can create schools that work from a mystical base rather than an anthropocentric base. I have been running a wisdom school based on this model for fifteen years, and I have found that when we bring scientists, artists, creation mystics, and social activists together, a new cosmology gets born. We ignite one another; we go on deep journeys in all six directions. No one gets bored. There are surprises every day.

Alice Miller, the Swiss psychiatrist, says that the possibility of rebirth exists as long as the human body draws breath. We are all capable of being resurrected. No one is lost. Perhaps the most important place to begin wisdom schools would be in our prisons and ghettos, where our models of education have most clearly failed. The wisdom model puts creativity at the center of everything, which is the new law of the universe we have learned from physics: continual regeneration, continual creation. This is what leads us to authentic ritual—people keeping themselves together through the power of wisdom expressed as creativity and as story.

When we recover our sense of ritual, we can use it to create a more meaningful connection to each other and to our Earth. Take, for example, the issue of vegetarianism. We have to realize that our depletion of forests, soil, and water is related to our addiction to meat. It is morally and spiritually indefensible that every one of us would not critique our own consciousness, and with the help of our family and community, decide how much meat we can eliminate from our diets. What I propose is that we should then ritualize our decision and commitment.

We could gather in our town squares or campuses and create papier-mâché calves—in a sense, borrowing an icon from our past. We could dance around the calves; we could take vows to one another, promising to let go of 10 or 20 percent of our meat consumption. We could light a bonfire. In this way, we would relearn what ritual is and how it can help us to cement our common promises.

This is not about duty; it is not about the stewardship model that tells us that we are doing, in a sense, God's dirty work on Earth. It's about pleasure and delight. The Earth is a garden radiating a divine presence. Aquinas said, "You change people by delight. You change people by pleasure." Awe is pleasurable; awe is the beginning of wisdom. When we recapture our awe through ritual, we learn to live wisely.

We must remember that what Christians call the Paschal Mystery—the life, death, and resurrection of Christ in Jesus—is not restricted to Jesus or even to our species. We now know that the whole universe has been involved in great moments of life, death, and resurrection. When the supernova came to its death after flourishing for billions of years, it spit out the elements that make up our Earth and our bodies. We are the resurrection of the supernova. We are the resurrection of the original fireball. I believe that every authentic religious doctrine contains an authentic cosmic story. Resurrection, after all, is part of the story of the sun rising every day.

▼▼

Chapter 20

The Wisdom of Ancient Healers

RICHARD KATZ

Richard Katz is a clinical psychologist who over the past twenty-five years has worked with the healing systems among several indigenous peoples: the Kalahari !Kung, the Fijians, the Inupiat of Alaska, and the Lakota of Rosebud. He received his doctorate from Harvard and taught there for twenty years. Today he teaches at the Saskatchewan Indian Federated College in Saskatoon, Saskatchewan, Canada. He has also authored three books: Boiling Energy: Community Healing Among the Kalahari Kung, Nobody's Child *(coauthored with Marie Balter), and* The Straight Path: A Story of Healing and Transformation in Fiji.

Katz strives to promote a respectful exchange of healing wisdom, fulfilling the task given him by traditional elders and healers to serve as a bridge between them and contemporary Western therapists. Respecting those parts of the healing rituals that must remain in the oral tradition, he focuses on the principles of healing he has been taught, principles like love for all and humility. Katz takes great care in sharing only those stories which he has permission to tell, those stories he has lived, and those which he has been ceremonially given. As we in the West learn from indigenous stories of healing, we assume an obligation to exchange, supporting the struggle of indigenous peoples for the very life source of these stories, their land, and their culture.

When I first visited the Kalahari, I was told something by the *!Kung*-speaking *Zhu/twa* people there that has been repeated to me by other indigenous groups I've worked with: Tell our story to your people. At first, I was not sure that the *Zhu/twa* really knew what they were saying. They are hunter-gatherers with no written language; did they know what it meant to publish a book or give a lecture? I kept wrestling with that question and couldn't answer it. Finally, I realized that they were simply giving me permission to tell the story; it was up to me to decide the best form. I am grateful to all my teachers for what they have given me—and for their trust in my ways of telling their stories. This essay speaks their wisdom.

Learning from ancient healing wisdom—we hear that phrase often these days. But I've been taught that we must go beyond learning from. We must *exchange*—giving to our teachers as we learn, and in order to learn. And what we actually *can* learn is how to apply principles of healing, which are really ways of being; extracting specific healing rituals for our own use can deteriorate into a cultural kleptomania. The learning must be respectful, putting into practice *only* what we have been given specific permission to do by the traditional guardians of that knowledge, and then only to serve the people, not for personal gain. "This healing is a gift . . . it comes to us from the Creator of all things." Again and again I have been told that. And then it follows that whatever healing knowledge we have been given is to be offered to others as a gift.

One story that indicates what we can learn about healing from indigenous peoples involves my work with a *Zhu/twa* healer named Toma Zho in the Kalahari. As any good field researcher would, I had my tape recorder with me during our conversations; I didn't want to miss a word. We were talking about healing one day when suddenly he began to ask me questions about how the tape recorder worked. I said, "This little box is a microphone, which catches the voice, and this cord carries the voice to this bigger box which stores it on the tape." He said, "I can see that." I then retreated to popular physics, talking about energy waves and sound waves—things I'm not very familiar with. He said again, "We already know those things ... but what I *really* want to know is, how does it work?" I had to admit that while there were people back home who knew how it worked, I was not one of them. He looked at me with great sadness and said, "That's too bad. Whenever we are given a thing of power by our teachers or ancestors, we are always told how to use it and how it works."

This story suggests the kind of things the wisdom of ancient healers can teach us. For example, I was trained in the word world—the university—but I was never really taught how to use words. It was only after I participated in a Lakota (Sioux) ceremony, during which the spirits gave me a message, saying "Voice is a thing of power," that I began to realize what a powerful thing words really are. "Speak from the heart," Lakota elder Stanley Red Bird told me as he saw me struggle with preparing notes for a talk I had to give. "Then you'll never be at a loss for words." One way of showing respect for healing power and the power of words is to share what I have been taught by ancient healers—speaking from my heart.

The phrase *ancient healers* is something of a misnomer. The ancient systems of healing that I have worked with are intact, indigenous systems in use today. I have worked with several indigenous cultures with strong healing traditions: the Kalahari *Zhu/twasi*, the Fiji Islanders, the Inupiat (Eskimos) of Alaska, and the Lakota (Sioux) Indians of South Dakota. Despite their differences, there are certain elements common to the healing traditions in all of these cultures.

One of those elements is an emphasis on exchange: To learn anything, one must give something back, and that something must matter. In fact, the concept of exchange extends to all aspects of life in indigenous cultures. For example, I was married in a traditional Lakota ceremony; in part of the ceremony my wife and I were wrapped in a beautiful star quilt. We were told by Joe Eagle Elk, the medicine man who married us, that that quilt was our home, our hearth; it would keep us together and envelop us. That quilt meant everything to us. But when we later gave it to a very special person in our lives, my wife's sister, that act was considered within that culture to be entirely appropriate. Among indigenous peoples, it is understood that we give away the things we value most; whether or not we can see it at the time, we will get something we need in return.

One aspect of exchange is listening. When I first talked to Toma Zho, all I was interested in was healing. When he told stories about the gods, I tried to steer him back to the subject that interested me; he persisted, however, in talking about what he felt was important. I learned two things from that encounter. First, when we ask an elder or healer a question, it is disrespectful and shortsighted to put conditions on it; rather, we should come with our question, and then simply sit and listen. Also, we cannot understand the healing system of a particular culture without knowing something about the culture as a whole. Traditional healing is always part of the life story of the people who practice it.

For example, the hunting and gathering *Zhu/twa* people share all their resources; no one goes hungry when there is food in the camp. This communal approach is also reflected in the arrangement of their huts; each one faces onto a central circle of communal land. That communal land is where the healing dance occurs.

The *Zhu/twa* healing dance often begins informally, as the people feel the need for a dance—the need to be together, to share, to heal. The women, who will sing the medicine songs throughout the night, gather around the fire easily, gracefully. Very often, children will begin dancing, in a sense showing off for the adults, as children do everywhere. Then the dance becomes more serious—the healers arrive, the older men and women, always accompanied by the powerful singing. In the early morning hours, the dance rests, with just a few women singing very softly for those who are still quietly dancing. Then, as the sun begins to rise, the singing gets stronger and more people get up and dance. The dance is open to the entire community and to others as well; if you were to go to the Kalahari and happen upon a healing dance, you could enter it.

In Fiji, healing ceremonies are more complex and less informal than among the *Zhu/twa*. There are subtly elaborate rituals, specific prayers and chants. But what matters most to the Fijians is not the specific rituals, but the concept of the "straight path," which again is not just about healing but is a significant aspect of their entire culture.

According to this concept, what is "straight" is not the path but your attitude; you find the path by walking with honesty, respect, love for all, proper behavior, humility, and service. At first I thought, "This is easier than learning chants." But the further one goes along the path, the more difficult it becomes. The Fijians say that when anyone comes to our door seeking help, we must feel love for that person. But how can we do that consistently? They emphasize humility and service—these are words we know, but how very difficult they are to practice.

Another aspect of healing common to indigenous cultures is that healing itself is not based on rational, acquired knowledge but on shared, spiritual energy. Among the Inupiat people in Alaska, there is a strong tradition of healing through deep massage. But before the indigenous healers begin to work, they pray to God that their hands will help and not hurt. They do very technical work, but the basis of it is prayer.

We cannot hoard healing energy. In the Kalahari, everything of importance can be made easily. If the *Zhu/twasi* need to make a hut, they can find all the materials in the bush. As they move—which they do five or six times a year—they don't have to take much with them. Their healing reflects this circumstance. They don't accumulate healing energy, they use it. And there is no esoteric process to becoming a healer. How do you learn to become a *Zhu/twa* healer? Experience—from your earliest days, you go to dances wrapped onto your mother's back. Practice, experience, and an "open heart"—a willingness to risk the pain of becoming a healer.

Among the *Zhu/twasi*, the name for healing energy is *n/um*; when a healer is filled with *n/um*, he or she is in the state of *!kia*. In that state, very deep things happen. Here is what K"au/Dwa, a *Zhu/twa* healer who is totally blind, says about *!kia*:

> God keeps my eyeballs in a little cloth bag . . . On the nights that I dance and when the singing rises up, God comes down from heaven swinging the bag with the eyeballs above my head, and he lowers the eyeballs to my eye level, and as the singing gets strong, he puts the eyeballs into my sockets and they stay there and I heal. And when the women stop singing and separate out, he removes the eyeballs, puts them back in the cloth bag, and takes them up to heaven.

I was at one dance where K"au/Dwa was working, and he found everyone in the group he needed to find; it was as if he was able to see.

Healing energy is demanding. Though it leads to expanded states of consciousness, it is exhausting and painful for the healer. Becoming a healer is a long, slow, difficult process. No shortcuts. All of the cultures I've lived in share the knowledge that the healer must, in some way, suffer. Sometimes suffering is what leads healers to their calling. Most Fijian healers come to their work through an experience of having been very sick themselves and having been healed. Among Lakota medicine men, there is almost always a tremendous amount of suffering in their early lives that leads them to their work.

The healing act itself is often an occasion of suffering. For example, n/um burns; the healer filled with n/um experiences a boiling feeling in the body. This is something that everyone in the culture recognizes. I worked for a time with a young man who was one of the first Zhu/twasi to learn to read and write. I asked him once, was he interested in healing? Part of Zhu/twa healing is the idea that healers climb the threads of the gods. These threads go up into the sky, into the gods' village, where the healer can rescue the soul of the sick person. This young man said, "Sure, I would love to be a healer; I would love to climb the threads of the gods. But I don't want to go through the first part. I don't want to feel the boiling n/um."

There is no boundary between the healer and the one being healed; each is suffering, and each needs the healing ceremony. Perhaps because of that, people in these cultures are constantly aware of the vulnerability of the healer. How much we need to remind ourselves of that vulnerability in this country was made clear to me in an experience I had a few years ago.

I was asked to give a lecture on healing to a group of students and professors at the Harvard Medical School. They were part of a special Harvard-M.I.T. program in biomedical research. I assumed that my work would be something they couldn't believe in at all; I anticipated a humiliating experience.

At first, they listened rather passively but politely. Then I began to talk about the vulnerability of healers. People moved forward in their seats. "We are vulnerable," I said, "and that is part of the reason we heal: We are not in control. We hurt, we forget, we do things incorrectly." The students told me afterward that I was the first person who had talked to them about what they were, in fact, feeling in that program. They felt enormous pressure to be competent, to be "in charge," but they were often confused and vulnerable. Indigenous healers know the wisdom of admitting that.

Indigenous healers also place much less emphasis on goals and results than the methods we are accustomed to in this country. When I first became a therapist, I worked in a system that required me to account for all of my therapy hours. I was doing outreach work on the streets. There were informal, unpredictable encounters with clients—maybe five minutes here, a half-hour there, two hours over there. But still I had to fill out forms designed for the fifty-minute therapy hour. The forms also required a statement of goals and outcomes. It was tremendously frustrating, trying to accurately describe my work on those forms.

Much more recently, I worked with a group of six Native men who were labeled schizophrenic. My goal with them was simply to have a group, to work with them in creating a sense of family, of community. I had learned from my work with indigenous healing that that goal was enough. We don't need to emphasize outcome; all of the people I have talked to would gladly be rid of their sickness. But curing a particular illness is only one small part of healing.

At the end of a *Zhu/twa* healing dance, people say, "Our hearts are happy." The *Zhu/twa* healing journey is painful; it can be frightening. But healing occurs amid family and friends who stay together from dusk to dawn, dancing and resting, powered by the strong and beautiful medicine songs. Their journey has a home. Then the morning sun comes out, warming the skin, softening the soul. "Our hearts are happy," they say. "We are happy to have helped others." That is healing.

The *Zhu/twasi* say we are all sick; in some of us, that sickness is manifest. But everyone at a healing dance receives healing energy because everyone needs it.

Healing is a process, a movement; it is a transition toward balance, connectedness, meaning, and wholeness. When we see healing as movement rather than outcome, we discover a beautiful truth: Healing is not a once-and-for-all process. We can return to our healers again and again. A car doesn't run forever on only one tank of gas, so why should we? If we create healing communities—people who get together, work with each other, and warmly support each other—healing becomes a part of everyday life.

Healing is one of the most ancient and important services that human beings can give each other. One of the reasons, I think, that more and more of us are looking to ancient healing techniques is that the health-care system in this country lacks certain very important elements. If we look at indigenous healing systems, we see that the very things we miss—exchange, service, humility, availability—are essential characteristics of those systems and those cultures. The question is, how can we learn respectfully from indigenous healers?

I think the necessary first step has to be an awareness that almost all indigenous cultures are at risk in terms of their survival. We cannot talk about indigenous peoples without recognizing that they face the possibility of cultural genocide. If we want to learn from these peoples, our first obligation is to give back to them—and not what we think they need, but what they say they need.

The second step is to work toward collaboration, not appropriation. In many parts of North America, there are indigenous healers who can share their knowledge and skills with us. Unfortunately, what very often happens is that traditional healers get invited into our own hospitals and healing centers; we ask them to work in an unfamiliar context, without respect for their needs or traditions. But we need to try to understand their worlds—to see into the wholeness of their cultures—rather than selecting out those aspects that we think might be useful. Then we can begin to collaborate from a basis of mutual respect, acknowledging each other's areas of competence.

Good indigenous healers are not imperialistic. They will say, "This is not mine," when confronted with an illness they cannot treat. They respect the contributions Western medicine can make to curing certain illnesses. We need this kind of generous and respectful attitude. Indigenous and Western healing systems each have their unique and valued contribution to make. I don't believe integration is the answer. Respectful collaboration, with informed and appropriate referrals—in both directions—can bring more healing to all.

The third, very concrete step, is to know how to make a referral, to know how to collaborate. If we go to an indigenous healer, we must know how to present ourselves in a respectful manner. We don't just ask for something as if we were entitled to it. If there is a sacred exchange ritual that should be performed, we must learn it and perform it. If we follow these three principles, I believe that we can begin to expand our concept of healing so that it can be enriched with the wisdom of many traditions and many approaches.

If we do not learn to collaborate with indigenous healers, we will all be less. Traditional healing systems suffer from the racism of scientific materialism. There is nothing in the way the dominant world moves now that supports the preservation of these systems. They take time, they're not "efficient"—so many things work against them. I believe that through collaboration and respect, we can support indigenous healers in their own processes of revitalization.

The question of how to bridge the gap between indigenous approaches and Western approaches is one that we need to continue to examine. The gap is often unbridgeable. The differences are real. We need to respect them. I'd like to conclude with a story that addresses this subject. This story was told to me by Emile Piapot, my adopted Cree grandfather. It takes place in Saskatchewan at the time when white people had just arrived as missionaries; it concerns my grandfather's father, who at that time was very old.

The missionaries were very eager, aggressively so, particularly about the requirement of baptism. One priest used to come often to the house, always asking the old man about coming to church. He'd say, "Your family is involved with the church. You should also come. And when are you going to be baptized?"

The old man did not want to go to church, but he also didn't want to offend the priest. The priest kept coming, getting more and more persistent. "Your wife and children are strong church members," he'd say. "Why aren't you one of us? You should be baptized."

Finally the old man said, "I've already been baptized." The priest said, "I don't know. I looked through all of our records and you aren't there. How could you be baptized?" My grandfather's father said, "One day when I was in the tipi, I saw a storm coming up. The rain began to fall and the thunderclouds began to make their sounds. I went outside, took off all of my clothes except for my breech cloth and I stood and stood in the rain. And I was baptized."

▼▼▼

Chapter 21

The Story of the Earth and Us

ALBERT GORE, JR.

Vice-President Albert Gore, Jr., graduated with honors from Harvard University, attended Vanderbilt University's Graduate School of Religion and earned a law degree from Vanderbilt Law School. He was a journalist for seven years before winning a seat in the United States House of Representatives in 1976. Elected to the Senate in 1984 and to the vice-presidency in 1992, he has won great respect for his commitment to protecting the environment. Additionally, his environmental concerns have been informed by a consistent psychological and spiritual awareness.

For example, in 1992, he authored the best-selling Earth in the Balance, *a comprehensive overview of the current ecological state of the planet. In it, he explains the concept of a dysfunctional family system and then applies it to Western civilization's relationship to the environment. Behaving according to unwritten and harmful rules passed down from previous generations, a dysfunctional family often experiences a succession of increasingly serious crises. So too our global civilization's dysfunctional relationship to the earth, says Gore, is responsible for the current series of worsening environmental crises. In the essay that follows, Gore shows that by developing a clear understanding of the unwritten rules woven into the fabric of modern industrial culture, we can begin to create a new relationship between humankind and the natural world that honors the sacredness of each.*

In my religious tradition, there is a story that tells us something about the dangers of the way we treat our planet. It is the parable of the unfaithful servant, and it's a very simple story. A master goes on a journey and leaves his servant in charge of the house. He says, "While I'm gone, if vandals ransack this house or steal my belongings, it will not be a good enough excuse for you to say, 'I was asleep.'"

In our relationship with this planet, we have become like the unfaithful servant—even as we witness environmental vandalism on a global scale, we are implicitly preparing to say we were asleep. The effects of rapidly increasing population, the emergence of many powerful new technologies, and our own dysfunctional attitudes toward the Earth are manifesting themselves at a rapidly escalating rate. Human civilization and the natural world are on a collision course, and the only way to change that is to wake up from our unhealthy attitudes toward the planet and find a new model—a new story—for the way we treat the Earth.

One of the reasons we have been so slow to react to this impending collision is that the damage we have caused to our environment seems to be happening slowly when considered within the context of our individual lifetimes. If we consider it within the lifetime of the Earth, however, it is happening with incredible speed. There is a science experiment that illustrates the point I'm trying to make. When a frog is placed in a pot of boiling water, it jumps right out. But when the same frog is put in a pot of lukewarm water that is slowly brought to a boil, the frog just stays there; its nervous system is so primitive, it needs a sudden jolt to realize that it is in danger. Otherwise, it will just sit there until it is rescued. But no one, of course, can rescue us except us.

Another reason that it is difficult to see and feel this impending collision is because information about it is coming from so many different sources. A large mosaic of destruction is being assembled, but it's hard for us to see the pattern. The single most prominent manifestation of the crisis is, perhaps, global warming; other aspects include the destruction of the rainforests, the energy crisis, the deterioration of the ozone layer, all of the oil spills around the world, the garbage crisis in every community, and the starvation of tens of millions of people. The scale of this mosaic challenges our ability to recognize its content not only intellectually, but emotionally. The image of 37,000 children under the age of five starving to death every single day on this planet is not one that we are emotionally prepared to grasp.

Starvation, of course, is linked to our ever-increasing population. For many centuries, the population on this planet increased at a slow, steady rate. When Christ was born, there were 250 million people on the Earth. By the time Christopher Columbus sailed in 1492, there were half a billion. By the time Thomas Jefferson wrote the Declaration of Independence, there were one billion people on Earth, and by the end of World War II, there were two billion people.

But the rate of population growth in the years since has greatly increased. In my lifetime of forty-four years, we have gone from a little over two billion to five-and-a-half billion people on Earth. And in the next forty-four years, we will go from five-and-a-half billion to ten billion people. We're adding the equivalent of the population of China every ten years.

The effect that this has on our consumption of natural resources is easy to track. The loss of topsoil has followed this same pattern of acceleration, as has the accumulation of poisons in water and air. The loss of stratospheric ozone is also increasing rapidly. And this pattern can be seen particularly clearly in the loss of other living species.

Sixty-five million years ago, all the dinosaurs and many other species disappeared. But since that time, the background rate of extinction of species stayed almost exactly the same until our century; now it is shooting up at a rate one thousand times faster than at any point in the last 65 million years. If extinction continues at its current rate, our children may live to see the disappearance of more than half of all the living creatures God put on Earth. Loss of species is, of course, linked to deforestation. Currently, we are losing our forests at the rate of one-and-a-half acres per second. Every year, we destroy an amount of forest equal to the size of Belgium, Switzerland, and Iceland combined. This also affects the air we breathe. For example, we harm the Earth's ability to absorb carbon dioxide by cutting down the trees that take it in.

Meanwhile, our accelerating levels of technology are pouring more carbon dioxide and other chemicals into the atmosphere than ever before. The air we breathe contains 600 percent more chlorine atoms than it did forty years ago—not enough to make it look green, but enough to destroy part of the ozone layer, which, of course, shields us from ultraviolet radiation. Part of the problem is that we put technological developments into use before we know what their effects will be. We didn't know about the effects of chlorofluorocarbons until long after we started using them, and now we've changed the composition of the entire Earth's atmosphere and put holes in the ozone layer.

Underlying all these individual crises is a set of assumptions about our relationship to this planet that have to be changed. We have operated for many centuries with an underlying story that says the Earth is so vast and nature is so powerful, we cannot possibly have any meaningful impact on it. The cost of these assumptions has become so great that it cannot be ignored anymore. I believe that we are involved in a dysfunctional relationship with our planet, and that that relationship is destroying the ecological balance between ourselves and the Earth.

A dysfunctional family is one that operates according to unwritten rules that are unhealthy and destructive. These rules—these stories about what a family should be and how its members should interact—are passed on unwittingly from one generation to the next; they operate on a largely unconscious level even though they often lead toward a crisis or successive crises. It is important to understand what these stories are and how they are passed on so that we can then set about healing our dysfunctional relationships by creating healthier stories.

Children absorb everything like sponges; they take in the bad with the good. That's why, in a dysfunctional family, it can be so hard to heal a dysfunctional pattern: It's imprinted in the stories, behaviors, and ways of being that generations pass down to each other. Our civilization does the same thing writ large: We imprint each generation with destructive stories about our relationship to the Earth.

If we examine Western philosophical and religious traditions, we can see something of how this occurred. Three hundred years before Christ was born, Greek philosophy spread throughout the known world. One of the primary tensions in Greek philosophy is in the difference between Plato's and Aristotle's views of the relationship between humankind and nature. Plato believed in a realm apart from the body where the soul exists; he felt that the thinker is essentially separate from the world that he or she thinks about. But Aristotle believed that everything in the intellect comes to us through our senses. In this view, human beings are deeply and profoundly connected to the world.

Within the Judeo-Christian tradition, there was also a struggle between these two worldviews, and for centuries, the Platonic view won. This was probably due in part to the struggle with paganism, a way of believing that found animating spirits in nature. Please don't misunderstand; I believe very deeply in a single Spirit, a single God. But the zealous pursuit of eradicating all of paganism's accompanying ideology inadvertently eclipsed the acknowledgment, by early Christians, of revelations that come directly from God's creation. In the process of winning that struggle, the sense that there was holiness in physical reality and sacredness in the earth itself was wiped out.

Aristotle's ideas were kept alive principally in the Arabic-speaking world, particularly through the work of Maimonedes, the great Jewish scholar who reinterpreted Judaism through Aristotelian thought. His work inspired Thomas Aquinas to reinterpret Christianity with an emphasis on the connection between the soul and physical reality. Though his books were banned and burned, a rediscovery of Aquinas and his approach to Aristotle occurred with the Renaissance. You can see this in the Raphael painting *The School of Athens*. In this painting, we see Plato pointing his finger upward, as if to indicate where knowledge comes from. Next to him, Aristotle is gesturing toward the earth.

In 1619, however, the philosopher René Descartes dealt the resurgence of Aristotelian thought a severe blow. Descartes had a startling vision on the banks of the Danube: Observing how dead, inanimate matter floated on the surface of the water in predictable patterns, he envisioned a mechanistic world whose patterns could be discerned and mastered by analytical minds engaged in sustained inquiry and detached observation. He said, "I think, therefore I am."

Descartes's influence on contemporary thought was and is profound; ever since the philosophical movement of which he was the exemplar, we have believed that a detached human intellect could enable us to understand nature and control it. But we need to feel as well as think; we need to understand the context, not just the individual. We need to recognize that we are part of each other and of the planet, and that the scientific revolution seduced us with false promises, with the idea that if we concentrated on the realm of the intellect, we could solve all our problems. That is a dysfunctional story; that is the story we have to replace.

Because it can be so painful to confront and replace a dysfunctional story, we often look for diversions. Members of dysfunctional families often manifest this in addictions, which are, in essence, distractions from the confrontation with what's real. Our civilization now contains massive engines of distraction; in this time of global crisis, we are holding ever more tightly to our habits of consuming larger and larger quantities of oil, air, water, and trees. Just as a child in the pattern of a dysfunctional family can build an artificial, false self to play out the role that has been carved for him or her, we create an artificial world in which advertising tells us what we want, and the rituals of production and consumption tell us who we are. In the meantime, we lose contact with what is real in our relationship to the natural world.

So where can we look for a real story, a story that heals our relationship to this planet? One way to look for a healing story is to reexamine those stories in our various religious traditions that might have been misinterpreted before. For example, in the Judeo-Christian tradition, we can reexamine what was taught about humankind's dominion over the Earth and its creatures. We can look at the Old Testament story of Noah's Ark and recognize that God made a covenant with Noah to preserve biodiversity, to care for and ensure the reproduction of all His creatures. Whatever traditions we may come from, we need to find healing stories.

We have to heal the lack of connection between the mind and the body, which is emblematic of the lack of connection between us and our larger physical context, the earth itself. We haven't yet accepted the truth that despite whatever divides us—gender, race, nationality, and ethnicity—we are a single global civilization. We need a new awareness of that connection, a new personal commitment, and new leadership.

That leadership must be fed by each of us as individuals. If we all believed in the importance of creating a healing relationship with the planet and acted on that belief not only in our personal lives but also in the larger context of our communities and our nation, our political leaders would be forced to support that conviction. Leadership can accelerate the healing process, but we have to bring it up from the grassroots, not wait for it to come from the top down.

There is one final obstacle, however, and that is the loss of our ability to find hope for the future. Perhaps this happened, in part, when we realized that nuclear weaponry had given us the power to end civilization. Because so many of us lost the ability to care about the future, we acquiesce in borrowing a billion dollars a day. We keep creating pollution. We don't give a moment's thought to our grandchildren, much less their grandchildren. That attitude must be replaced with new hope based on a new faith in the future.

Not long ago, I had a long conversation with a scientist in which I listed many specific solutions for the crisis of our relationship to the planet. He said, "I agree with you, but I know enough about politics to believe that it is very unlikely that these solutions will ever be enacted." And I said, "What if I had suggested two years ago that the Soviet Union would tear down its statues of Lenin; that all over Eastern Europe, people would gather in their city squares singing "We Shall Overcome"; that the Berlin Wall would come down?" He replied, "I would have said you were wrong."

Change is very difficult, but not impossible. I believe in a God of miracles, and I believe that we are capable of experiencing miracles in our own lives. Become involved in the life of your community, in the life of your nation, and in the life of the planet. Together, we can transform the story of our presence here and heal our relationship with this world. Together, we shall overcome.

▼▼▼

Chapter 22

Human Family

MAYA ANGELOU

The popularity of Joseph Campbell has brought widespread attention to the great stories of classical mythology and to the ageless wisdom they offer in terms of understanding our current dilemmas. However, as Robert Bly once remarked, we must not let our current fascination with myth obscure the importance of our own family stories as sources of knowledge and inspiration.

No one is a better family storyteller than poet, educator, historian, author, actress, playwright, civil rights activist, producer, and director Maya Angelou. Ms. Angelou is rightly hailed as one of the great voices of contemporary literature. She is also living evidence of the power of sharing stories. Raped at the age of seven, she stopped talking for five years. In her book I Know Why the Caged Bird Sings, she tells the story of her long silence—which she says served as a kind of meditation—and of her need to share her stories as a way of illustrating how both silence and communication can heal and nurture the life-affirming spirit.

In the poem that follows, Ms. Angelou offers her view of the human family from the book I Shall Not Be Moved.

Human Family*

I note the obvious differences
in the human family.
Some of us are serious,
some thrive on comedy.

Some declare their lives are lived
as true profundity,
and others claim they really live
the real reality.

The variety of our skin tones
can confuse, bemuse, delight,
brown and pink and beige and purple,
tan and blue and white.

I've sailed upon the seven seas
and stopped in every land,
I've seen the wonders of the world,
not yet one common man.

I know ten thousand women
called Jane and Mary Jane,
but I've not seen any two
who really were the same.

Mirror twins are different
although their features jibe, and lovers think
    quite different thoughts
while lying side by side.

We love and lose in China,
we weep on England's moors,
we laugh and moan in Guinea,
and thrive on Spanish shores.

We seek success in Finland,
are born and die in Maine.
In minor ways we differ,
in major we're the same.

I note the obvious differences
between each sort and type,
but we are more alike, my friends,
than we are unalike.

We are more alike, my friends,
than we are unalike.

We are more alike, my friends,
than we are unalike.

▼▼▼

Afterword: What Is Common Boundary?

Common Boundary is a private, nonprofit 501(c)(3) organization founded in 1980 to foster communication among and support for mental health professionals and others in the helping and healing professions who are interested in exploring the relationship of psychotherapy, spirituality and creativity.

In order to do this, Common Boundary publishes a bimonthly magazine, holds a conference each November in Washington, D.C., and organizes seminars and invitational think tanks on important issues in the field. An annual award of $500 is made to the author of the outstanding M.A. thesis or Ph.D. dissertation on a psychospiritual topic. Common Boundary also publishes a Graduate Education Guide which lists training and educational resources in the holistic education field. Through the magazine, Common Boundary also encourages the formation of support groups, known as the Kindred Spirits Network.

For more information, contact: Common Boundary, Inc., 4304 East-West Highway, Bethesda, MD 20814. (301) 652-9495.